PRAISE FOR LILY AND THE DUKE

This book was fantastic. It was steamy, funny, romantic, and just about any other emotion you can think of...
~Steamy Book Mama

The writing was fast paced, and HOT for an historical romance...with lots of chemistry between Daniel and Lily, and lots of fun on Lily's part! There was the requisite drama, well played out. The characters were full of fun, laughter, mischief and of course some hot sexy!
~Bound by Books

It's a very heartfelt story between Lily and Daniel and the intense love and passion they come to feel for each other.
~All is Read

LILY

AND THE DUKE

A Sex and the Season Novel

HELEN HARDT

WATERHOUSE PRESS

LILY

AND THE DUKE

A SEX AND THE SEASON NOVEL

HELEN HARDT

For Dean, Eric, and Grant

CHAPTER ONE

Laurel Ridge, the Lybrook Estate, Wiltshire, England, 1845
Lady Lily Jameson set down her portable easel and palette of watercolors to smooth her mussed sable curls. The September day was sweltering, and beads of sweat trickled down her face. She gazed around the small alcove that appeared to be the remains of an old stone chapel. The long grass tickled her ankles under her skirt. White and yellow daisies poked cheerful heads through the lush green foliage, and yellow and magenta blooms dotted the abundant vegetation like confetti. A tiny brook babbled nearby.

Lily sighed, hoping she could capture the beauty of the alcove in watercolor before her mother and father noticed she was missing from the afternoon lawn party.

She tied on her painting smock, set a piece of thick cotton paper on the easel, and coated it with water. She started with the bright cerulean of the sky, and then the brook and the rich greenery behind it.

"That's quite good."

Lily jumped up, knocking over the small tin of water sitting in her lap. She turned and stared up into a golden face and striking green eyes. Her breath caught.

"I'm sorry," the young man said. "I didn't mean to frighten you."

"No, I'm fine." Lily, trembling, wiped her stained fingers on her apron.

His hair was the color of ripe wheat, and it fell to his shoulders in gleaming layers that brushed the collar of his brown jacket. He was tall—taller than her father or her brother—and his broad shoulders led down to slim hips and legs clad in tight tan trousers and brown riding boots. He wore no cravat, and a few tawny hairs peeked out of his crisp linen shirt. His face was handsome, with a strong jaw, full lips, and a Grecian nose. Long mahogany lashes adorned his arresting eyes.

Lily swallowed. Something new and uncomfortable churned in her stomach. Like butterflies. Or rolling water.

"How did you come to be here?" the man asked.

"I-I wanted to paint."

He smiled, revealing straight white teeth. "My mother likes to paint. I find her here often."

Lily clenched her clammy fists in her stained smock. "Your mother?"

"Yes. My mother. Your hostess. The duchess."

"Oh." Lily widened her eyes and willed herself not to stammer. "You're the marquess, then?"

"No. The marquess is my older brother, Morgan. I'm Lord Daniel Farnsworth." He smiled again. "And who might you be?"

"Lily, my lord." She offered a quick curtsy.

"Lily who?"

"Lady Lily Jameson."

"You're Ashford's daughter?"

"Yes, one of them."

"Is the other as pretty as you are?" he asked, winking.

Warmth crept into Lily's cheeks, and she hoped the young lord didn't notice. Imagining her blond-haired, blue-eyed sister, she said, "More so, I think."

"That, I doubt." He cleared his throat. "You have quite an eye for painting. I shall leave you to your work. I'd love to see it when you're finished."

"Yes, my lord."

He turned to leave, but looked over his shoulder. "How old are you, Lily?"

"Thirteen, my lord."

"Be sure to come back in five or six years," he said, and walked lazily out of the alcove.

★ ★ ★ ★

Eight years later

"Now we'll never catch up with Mummy and Papa." Lady Rose Jameson tucked herself into her carriage seat. "Why you had to go searching for some old painting is beyond me."

"Because I want to take it back to the little alcove at Laurel Ridge and paint the scene again." Lily smoothed her sage green skirt. She remembered fondly the beauty of the Lybrook estate and planned to paint to her heart's content during the upcoming two-week house party. "Besides, we'll catch up. Won't we, Thomas?"

Her older brother, Viscount Jameson, nodded. "My team can outrun those antiques of Papa's any day. We may even get there first."

"Thank goodness," Rose said, smiling. "I'm filled with excitement about spending the next few weeks at Laurel Ridge."

"I'm looking forward to it myself," Lily said.

Rose's sapphire eyes widened. "You want to meet the

duke?"

"You know me better than that." Lily laughed. "I couldn't give two figs about His Grace. It's his art collection that intrigues me. It's rumored that he has a Vermeer!"

"Good God, Lily," her brother said, winking. "The most eligible men in England will be at Laurel Ridge, and you want to see a painting?"

"Thomas, darling, we all know that you have about as much appreciation for art as a tree toad." Lily smirked. "No doubt there will be plenty of beautiful women at Laurel Ridge who couldn't care less about Vermeer, and I'm sure His Grace will send hoards of castoffs your way. I, on the other hand, have better things to do than pant after the Duke of Lybrook like a bitch in heat."

Thomas laughed. "God help the duke if he crosses your path."

"Lily," Rose said, admonishing, "it's a good thing Mummy isn't around to hear you talk like that."

"Have you forgotten that he's only the duke by virtue of the untimely deaths of his father and brother? He's still a renowned rake. No self-respecting father would have dared allow his daughter to so much as blink in his presence." Lily rolled her eyes. "But now he's a duke, and all is forgotten and forgiven? The hypocrisy makes me want to cast my crumpets."

"Of course you're right, but—"

"He spent his entire mourning period touring the continent, no doubt visiting every whorehouse he came upon."

"I wish you wouldn't use such language."

"Brothel, then. House of ill repute. Is that better?"

"Lily..."

"He left his poor mother here alone to deal with her grief.

He's nothing but a scoundrel."

"The duchess was in good hands, Lily," Thomas said.

"I suppose so. She was no doubt better off with her spinster sister than with that son of hers." Lily inhaled and fidgeted with her dress. "The duke does have a beautiful estate, though. I intend to spend a great deal of time admiring the artwork, strolling in the vineyards, and painting and writing."

"Don't you want to take part in any of the festivities?" Rose asked.

"Maybe some. But don't worry. Sophie and Alexandra will be there for you. We'll all spend time together. I'm sure Mummy won't hear of me going off alone as much as I wish to."

"I'm quite thankful for that."

"I'm not. What I wouldn't give for two weeks of freedom before I'm thrust into that barbaric meat market of a ritual that London calls a season."

"Lily," Rose said. "I'm not sure why Mummy and Papa made you wait until this year for your season. You could have started last year, and you would be happily married by now."

"Me, happily married?" Lily scoffed. "Of course I had to wait for you. Mummy and Papa know that you'll attract the right type of suitor, and they're hoping I can follow along on your tail."

"That's ridiculous and you know it."

"Ridiculous, maybe, since I have no desire to bind myself to some stuffy aristocrat for eternity, but true nonetheless."

"But you're just as beautiful as I. Perhaps more so."

"You know beauty has nothing to do with it." Lily turned to her brother, who was watching her intently. "I see you have that overprotective look in your eye, Thomas."

Lily adored her brother, but lately he had become a

hindrance to her preferred way of life. Pretty soon he was likely to insist she have a chaperone to use the convenience!

He needed a hobby. Better yet, he needed a woman. If she could interest him in someone at Laurel Ridge... Yes, and then he would be occupied. She might as well find a man for Rose, as well. The Duke of Lybrook was out of the question, of course, but there would be no shortage of decent men at the estate. With both her brother and her sister out of the way, she would be free to paint and write to her heart's content.

A match for Thomas and a match for Rose. It would be startlingly easy. There wasn't a more beautiful woman alive than Rose, with her honey blond locks and vivid blue eyes, and she came with a generous dowry and the Ashford name. And Thomas was a wonderful catch, with handsome chiseled features and sleek sable hair, not to mention he was a viscount and heir to one of the most respected earldoms in England.

Lily smiled.

"What on earth have you got up your sleeve?" Rose asked.

"What makes you think I've anything up my sleeve?"

"I know that look, Lily. You're up to no good. I can tell."

"You're up to something, for sure," Thomas said. "Sometimes you forget you're a lady."

"I'm no more a lady than you are."

Thomas smiled lazily. "Most of my friends would beg to differ. Wentworth asks about you frequently."

"That balding fool? You only keep company with him because you have your eye on his sister. You can do much better, you know."

"I could do a lot worse than Lady Regina Wentworth. I find her quite engaging."

"Thomas, she has all the intelligence of a blood pudding.

Whatever do you find to talk about?"

"I suppose she's not much of a conversationalist. But she has her charms."

"Dear God, if you're not exactly like every other man in England. Taken in by a pretty face and a pair of big... I suppose I expected more of you, Thomas. I've idolized you since I was a babe. How you can stand that phony is beyond me. If you're so taken with her, why didn't you offer for her last season?"

"I'm still young, Lily. No need to rush things."

"You're twenty-eight! I'm barely twenty-one, and Papa can't wait to marry me off."

"It's just the way it is. Do yourself a favor and accept it."

"Never! I want more than that, Thomas. I will not shackle myself to some peer and become his breeder."

"I won't let anyone make you his breeder. Papa and I will see that both you and Rose are treated kindly by any interested gentlemen."

"But I don't want to be courted. There are too many other things I want to do first." She sighed. "I absolutely must see that Vermeer."

"Sorry, Lily," Thomas said. "The Lybrook collection can only be viewed by private invitation."

"Perhaps the duke will invite me to see it. Surely he would appreciate my interest."

"I'm sure he'll appreciate many things about you," her brother said, "the least of which is your commitment to the arts."

Lily rolled her eyes at her brother and then closed them, remembering her previous visit to Laurel Ridge. When she had uncovered her painting, she had been surprised at how ghastly her technique had been a mere eight years earlier. But it had a cheerful innocence to it. She had never shown it to Lord Daniel, nor had she seen him again during her brief stay at the estate.

She would likely not see him this time either, as he would no doubt be busy with his many mistresses. Handsome Lord Daniel Farnsworth was now the Duke of Lybrook.

★ ★ ★ ★

Daniel stepped out of his bath and into the towel held by his valet. He dried himself and held out his arms for the silk dressing gown. "Thank you, Putney," he said, taking a seat in his leather armchair for a shave.

The valet soaked a towel in a basin of steaming water, wrung it out, and wrapped it around Daniel's face. He tried to relax. He enjoyed a good shave, but right now all he could think about was the guests gathering below and how he had to begin his life as the Duke of Lybrook this evening.

Hosting a two-week house party at what was now his estate was a daunting concept. Thank goodness for his mother and Aunt Lucy. They were renowned hostesses and would see that everything went according to plan.

He felt a smile coming, but kept it at bay so as not to disturb Putney's shaving. Lady Amelia Gregory would be there. The attractive widow would no doubt be thrilled to warm his bed tonight. She could do marvelous things with her mouth. He stiffened.

Putney rubbed the last traces of shaving soap from Daniel's face and went to the wardrobe to prepare his garments.

"I think you'll find this acceptable." Putney held out a suit jacket of dark burgundy velvet and black trousers.

Daniel dressed and poured himself a small snifter of brandy.

"Do you require anything else, Your Grace?"

"No, Putney. You may go."

Putney bowed and left. Daniel drained the brandy in two gulps, left his chamber, and headed down the wide staircase to join the gentlemen who had congregated on the back terrace. *Here goes nothing.*

His father and brother had been good at this sort of small talk. Daniel had usually been debauching some willing widow or housemaid in a dark corner. His lips curved slightly upward at the thought. Those days were over, now that he was obliged to be the host of these blasted events. He pasted a smile on his face and joined the first group of gentlemen.

★ ★ ★ ★

Fatigued from their journey, Lily and Rose fell into a slumber after a maid had shown them to their guest chamber. After what seemed like only seconds, Lily awoke to a knock on the chamber door. Quickly she flew off the bed, searching for her gown on the floor. "Who is it?"

"It's us! Let us in!"

Lily ran to the door and threw it open. "Ally, Sophie!" She grabbed her cousins in a hug.

"Lily, dear, you're in your undergarments," Sophie admonished.

"Rose and I were napping. We were tired and our bags hadn't been brought up yet."

"They're right outside the door," Alexandra said. "Sophie and I can get them for you."

"Oh, don't be silly, I'll get them."

"Lily, do not step one foot outside that door in your undergarments." Rose sat up in bed. "Sophie and Ally can get our bags."

"My God, what is in this one?" Alexandra asked, lugging in a huge leather case.

"Those are my art supplies." Lily grabbed the bag. "Do be careful."

"Don't tell me you're going to paint during your stay here," Alexandra said. "There are going to be lawn parties, and rides, and fancy dinners, and balls."

"You tell her, Ally," Rose said. "She's absolutely determined not to have any fun at all."

"You have your fun, and I'll have mine. This estate is breathtaking. I intend to brush every bit of it onto paint board and describe every last foot of it in my journal."

"I think that sounds lovely, Lily," Sophie said.

Lily looked at her small cousin with affection. Sophie had thick golden hair and large hazel eyes that could mesmerize a person. Her younger sister, Alexandra, had chestnut hair, golden eyes, and a flamboyant personality. Gentlemen would no doubt be queuing up for Ally's favors this very evening.

Their mother was Lady Ashford's older sister, Iris, the Countess of Longarry. Their father, an abusive Scottish earl, had died two years earlier, his lifetime of reckless spending leaving them penniless. The Ashfords had supported them since then and planned to bring the girls out for their first season with Lily and Rose.

"We have the chamber right next to yours," Alexandra said. "And mother is way down the hall. Where are Uncle Crispin and Auntie Flora?"

"I have no idea," Lily said. "Rose and I were so tired from the trip that we passed out as soon as we got here."

"Hopefully they're far away as well. Then we won't have any problem sneaking around." Alexandra winked.

"Now you're talking." Lily laughed. "I plan to do my share of sneaking around as well."

"Really? Who do you have your eye on?" Alexandra plunked down on the bed next to Rose. "I saw some exciting prospects out on the terrace when we came in."

"She has her eye on Vermeer," Rose said.

"Which one is he?" Alexandra widened her eyes. "Please tell me he's not that dashing tall one with the auburn hair."

"Really, Ally, Vermeer is an artist," Sophie said. "Didn't you pay any attention to Miss O'Hara's lessons?"

"You want to sneak out to look at a painting?" Alexandra burst out laughing. "You are mad, Lily."

"I'm certainly not going to sneak out to be debauched by some randy lord." Lily opened her valise and began to unfold her garments.

"I am." Alexandra curled her cherry lips upward. "Perhaps two or three. Perhaps even the duke himself!"

"He'll most likely be debauching everything in sight, knowing his reputation," Lily said.

"You had better watch your own reputation, Ally dear," Rose warned. "If anyone sees you get compromised, you'll be ruined and no decent man will ever offer for you."

"Then I won't be seen." Alexandra's sandy eyes gleamed.

"Ally," Rose said. "You don't really want to go down that path, do you?"

"I've been a good girl all my life," Alexandra said. "I'm tired of wondering what it's like. I want to be kissed."

"Yes, it would be heavenly, wouldn't it," Rose agreed dreamily.

"It's not all that much," Lily said.

"Lily, you haven't been kissed!" Alexandra stood. "Do tell all!"

"I knew it!" Rose said. "Why didn't you tell me? Wentworth stole one, didn't he?"

"Yes, just once, last Christmas," Lily said. "But it was nothing. His lips were pasty and clammy. If that's kissing, I need no part of it."

"Any kiss is better than nothing." Alexandra closed her eyes. "I'm quite envious."

"Darling Ally, please don't be. And you are welcome to Teddy if you want him. He's Thomas's age, and he's not too bad to look at, although his hair is receding. He does have nice hands and a good strong build. Not the smartest peacock, but he's got a sizeable fortune."

"He sounds fine. Introduce us, will you, Lily?"

"I'd be delighted, if he's here. But if he's not, there will certainly be better prospects to choose from, especially for a girl as pretty as you with your vivacious personality."

"What about Sophie?" Alexandra asked.

"There will be plenty for Sophie as well. And for Rose."

"And for you too, Lily," Rose said.

"I am definitely not concerned about that." Lily embraced her cousins again. "I'm so glad you two are here. The four of us are going to have such fun. Now, about tomorrow. There's a lawn party scheduled for the ladies after luncheon. What do you say that we sneak off and explore the estate a bit?"

"I don't know, Lily," Sophie said, nibbling on her lower lip.

"The men will be gone on a hunt all day," Lily continued.

"No men at the lawn party?" Alexandra scoffed. "Then count me in."

"All right, Lily," Rose agreed. "It might be fun."

"If the three of you are game, so am I," Sophie said.

★ ★ ★ ★

Lily found, to her dismay, that the Wentworths were indeed at Laurel Ridge, and just her unfortunate luck, she was seated next to Theodore Wentworth at dinner. At least he was better than his lecherous uncle, Lord Ludley. On her other side sat Lord Victor Polk, whose height and silky auburn hair identified him as Alexandra's dashing knight. Thomas was seated across from her, between Regina Wentworth and a thin blond woman whom Lily did not recognize.

Both Wentworth and Polk took care of Lily, filling her wine glass and keeping the conversation lively as they feasted on Beluga caviar, vegetable chowder, poached cod, roast goose with apple-and-raisin dressing, creamed carrots and peas, and kidney pudding.

Polk's attentions flattered Lily. He was attractive and much more intelligent than Wentworth.

"I would be honored, Lady Lily," he said, "if you would save a dance for me at the ball."

"Of course. I would be delighted."

"The delight will be mine, I assure you. Tell me, where has Ashford been hiding you?"

"Hiding me?"

"I would remember you had we met before. I've seen your father and brother at many galas over the past few years."

"I'm afraid my father and brother are both quite

protective. This will be my first season."

"Are you looking forward to it?

Lily took a swallow of wine and set her glass on the table. "Not in the slightest."

Polk's light brown eyes shone with amusement. "My, you certainly know your own mind. Tell me, what have you got against the season?"

"My lord, I'm sure you have no interest in my opinion on that subject."

"You would be mistaken. Please, elaborate." He smiled.

Lily knew she should hold her tongue. But— "Frankly, my lord, I consider the whole London season to be nothing more than a thinly veiled meat market."

Polk erupted in a gale of laughter. "Without a doubt, you are the first person I have ever heard describe the season in that manner."

"Well it's true, isn't it?" Lily gestured, nearly toppling her wine glass. "Men and women window shopping for a mate as if they were looking for the most sumptuous chops in the butcher shop. It's barbaric."

"You're opinionated, aren't you? It's rather refreshing, actually."

"Just remember, you asked."

"Yes, I certainly did. And I agree with your assessment, although I think there are some who prefer the richest chops to the most sumptuous." His eyes twinkled. "May I offer you some more wine?"

"No, thank you, my lord. I believe I've had enough. You wouldn't want me to become any more loose-tongued, would you?"

"I can't think of a more pleasant way to spend the evening,"

Polk said, his smile a bit devious, "than with a loose-tongued lovely like yourself."

Lily's cheeks warmed. Was Polk still speaking about her opinions?

★ ★ ★ ★

Lily had chosen a gown of pale green for the opening ball that was fairly low cut. Thomas had shaken his head slightly when he came to the girls' chamber to escort them to the ball, but she didn't care. A maid had swept her dark hair into an elaborate chignon, leaving wisps of curls dangling around her face, framing her high cheekbones.

Thomas escorted Rose to the dance floor for a quadrille while Lily looked for a table. Before she sat down, Lord Wentworth approached her.

"Oh, Teddy, I'm so glad you're here. There is someone I would love for you to meet. Come with me." She took his arm and walked toward her cousins who had just entered, making the necessary introductions quickly and pushing Alexandra into Wentworth's arms for a dance.

When Thomas deposited Rose back at the table, Lily grabbed his arm. "Thomas, you must dance with me.

"All right, Lily. I never knew you were much for dancing."

"I'm not, but I need to keep Wentworth from asking me."

He laughed. "I see. Shall we, then?" He held out his arm and expertly led her in the next quadrille.

"Who was that lovely young woman sitting next to you at dinner?" Lily asked.

"The blonde? Her name was Emma Smith or Smythe. I can't remember."

"I see her over there." Lily motioned with her eyes. "You should ask her to dance."

"If I dance with someone else, how can I keep Wentworth from focusing on you?" He chuckled.

"I'll take care of Wentworth. I'm trying to get him interested in Ally."

"He's not good enough for you, but you'd shove him at Ally?"

"Don't be silly. He's not good enough for Ally either. But she wanted to meet him so I obliged. In fact, she's interested in meeting just about any eligible gentleman here. Do you have any ideas for her? And for Sophie and Rose?"

"I would suggest Lord Victor Polk, but he seemed quite taken with you at dinner."

"I think Ally would like to meet him also. Now, about Rose and Sophie."

"Good Lord, I'm no matchmaker." He looked around the dance floor. "There's Van Arden, his father is a viscount." He motioned to a gentleman of average height who was not exactly handsome, but had a striking head of pale blond hair.

"Hmm. He's too short for Rose, but he would do nicely for Sophie. Introduce them, will you?"

"Anything for you, dear sister."

"Now, you must find Rose a nice gentleman. I can't bear the thought of some rogue taking advantage of her."

"I'm not exactly comfortable with this, Lily."

"Yes, I know. You're just being overprotective, as usual. But wouldn't you like Rose to meet someone you approve of rather than some lecherous goat?"

"You have a point there. I'll introduce her to Lord Evan Xavier. He's quite intelligent, and I believe his intentions would be honorable."

"Which one is he?"

Thomas looked around. "He was here earlier. Don't worry, I'll find him. You'd recognize him if you saw him. He's tall with blondish hair, built like a tree trunk. He was an oarsman at school."

"Is he handsome?"

"I don't really know what you women consider handsome."

"Well, you're handsome, Thomas."

"Of course he can't compare to me." Thomas laughed. "But I don't think Rose will have any complaints. Now, if you're done telling me what to do, the dance has ended." He led her back to their table.

"Thank you, Thomas." Lily took a seat. "You dance divinely. Now, as soon as you make all the necessary introductions, I want you to ask Miss Smythe to dance."

"Aye, aye, Lily."

Lily sat, smiling, as the gentlemen came by and escorted her companions to the dance floor. When Thomas approached Miss Smythe, and her parents were busy dancing, she silently rose. No one would notice if she stole out of the ballroom in search of the Vermeer.

She crept along the back wall of the ballroom and headed to the double door that led out to the terrace. She'd sneak around to the front of the house and begin her quest there.

As she stepped onto the terrace, she delighted in a breath of fresh air. It was a gently warm night, and she had always preferred outdoors to indoors. Several couples chatted intimately in the shadows. No one seemed to notice as Lily crossed the terrace and descended the staircase to the lawn. Swiftly she walked around to the side of the mansion, giggling to herself. The manor was built onto the side of a hill. As she walked up the incline, she took care to stay in the shadows, away from the torch lights.

She smiled, humming to herself. This had been easier than even she could have imagined. In less than an hour, she'd gotten her sister, her brother, and her cousins out of her hair. Pleased with her success, she began to skip a little. She was almost laughing out loud when a pair of strong arms grabbed her and pulled her behind a large flowering bush. Before she could scream, a mouth clamped down on hers.

CHAPTER TWO

Lily pushed her palms against her attacker's shoulders, but his strength defeated hers and he pulled her closer to his body. She gasped at the hardness of his chest. At her slight opening, he dipped his tongue into her mouth and circled gently, exploring. She dropped her arms limply to her sides. He tasted of brandy, or was it port?

Run, Lily. Run!

Yet her feet seemed glued to the ground. Her pulse quickened as a stabbing flame surged between her legs. Her heart lurched as fear coursed through her, yet she found herself standing on her toes, trying to get closer, as warmth enveloped her entire body.

Slowly her captor released her waist and slid his hands down until they were clasping hers. He gently guided her arms around his neck without breaking the kiss. She feathered her fingers over the velvety skin covering corded muscle and moved downward to caress his broad shoulders clad in soft fabric. Was it velvet? She didn't know. She didn't care. But she was certain that his hard body was the most glorious thing she had ever touched.

What am I doing?

But her thoughts evaporated until only feeling remained. Oh, she had been wrong about kissing. This was heaven. Apprehensively, she let her tongue touch his, and he groaned softly. Her nipples stiffened and she pushed them into his chest. Something was making her want more. Was it his groan? The smooth stroking of his tongue on hers? She trembled as they tasted each other. She tilted her head upward to meet his mouth better and opened her eyes briefly.

In the edge of her vision, she saw a shadowy figure stop and then hurry away. The spell broken, Lily panicked. She was kissing a complete stranger. His tongue was in her mouth. He could be anyone, the local idiot for goodness' sake!

With all her strength, she removed her hands from around his neck, pushed at his shoulders, and tried to retreat.

"Wait!" He grabbed her arm and pulled her back, right into the path of one of the torch lights.

She looked up into the mesmerizing green eyes of Daniel Farnsworth, the Duke of Lybrook. Lord, he was still handsome, but not the pretty boy he had been. His beauty had matured. The edge of his jawline glittered with golden stubble, and his amazing eyes were deeper set and surrounded by tiny laugh wrinkles. His golden hair still flowed flawlessly past his shoulders. How might it feel against her fingers?

No! She gulped, willing herself not to stammer.

"Y-Your Grace?"

★ ★ ★ ★

Daniel looked down at the dark-haired woman whose mouth he had been ravishing. How could he have made such a mistake? She wasn't who he expected. Yet he had known, somehow. Her kiss had been different. Innocent and sweet.

Her lovely dark curls and eyes the color of aged cognac seemed slightly familiar, but he couldn't place her. Who was she—this maiden whose lips met his with a tender purity he had never known? He longed to take her in his arms again, to hold her, to kiss her. He wanted more of her. Much more.

But that was not to be. He had to apologize and let her go. It was the decent thing to do. Even he drew the line at seducing innocents. Most of the time, anyway. He was the duke now. He had responsibilities.

The pulsing inside his trousers convinced him otherwise. "Oh, bloody hell," he said aloud, and pulled her body into his again.

She responded, and his heart pounded so hard he thought it would leap from his chest.

"Yes," he whispered, "give me your tongue, love."

Sweet, so sweet. He breathed deeply and inhaled her scent—spice cake and mulled wine. Wonderful. Slowly he guided one of her hands to his head and laced her fingers through his hair. Her other arm reached around his neck and caressed the muscles of his shoulders and back. He slid his hand from her waist, up the gentle curve of her spine to her nape, tilting her head farther back. He slid his lips away from her mouth, across her cheek and to her ear, tracing her lobe with his tongue, her ivory skin smooth as Oriental silk under his lips.

"I want to touch every part of you," he said, rasping.

She shuddered and pushed into him. Yes, good. She wanted this too. He trailed his lips across her cheek, her sigh a delicate whisper against his skin. He moved to her throat, found her pulse point, and nuzzled it gently. He slid his tongue down farther and dipped in between her breasts. Such a soft, plump, rosy bosom—the satin skin heaven against his tongue. Her dress hid the fleshy crimson of her nipples—like cherry bonbons but so much sweeter. How he wanted to suck them, pinch them. Bite them until she screamed.

He pressed his groin into her and groaned. God, she felt good against him, a perfect cradle for his manhood. He grabbed her bottom and pulled her closer.

Too far. Her lovely body tensed against his. Yet he didn't let her go. He couldn't. He nibbled at her lips, teasing them, sucking them.

A few breathless moments later, she pushed him away.

"Your Grace, have you lost your mind?"

"Yes," he murmured, sucking in a breath and pulling her back to him.

She turned her head away, and his tongue slid across her satin cheek.

"Let me go!" She pushed hard and broke his grasp, and then she lifted her skirts and ran toward the front of the mansion.

Daniel wanted to follow her. He wanted to grab her and carry her up to his bedchamber. He wanted to undress her, sink into her body, and make her his. His arousal ached in his trousers. Slowly he slid to the ground, snagging his velvet jacket on the stones of the building. He buried his head in his hands. Good God, he didn't even know her, yet his reaction to her was one he had never expected. He hadn't thought there was anything new to experience with women.

He had been wrong.

★ ★ ★ ★

When Lily reached the front entrance to the mansion, she leaned against the doorway before entering, her pulse racing. Her legs trembled as she forced them to bear her weight. She tried to regain her composure, but after a few moments, she realized it was a lost cause. All she could think of was his silky blond hair between her fingers, his soft full lips on her neck and between her breasts, his tongue exploring her mouth. His ravishment had permeated every cell of her body, centering in the damp heat between her legs. The sensation alarmed her, but she wanted more. More of him. God help her, she had enjoyed it.

She forced back a shudder and opened the front door. Lily walked until she found the ladies' retiring area. She entered and sat down on a stool to view her reflection in the looking glass.

Her lips were swollen and dark from the duke's passionate kisses. Her hair had come through fairly well, although it was a bit disheveled. Her hands still shaking, she fussed at it until she felt it acceptable. *Dear God!* Her breasts were pink and swollen and about to tumble out of her dress. She warmed as she remembered the sweet tickle of the duke's tongue in her cleavage. She fidgeted with her bodice, tucking her bosom back in as far as the cut would allow. Had she asked for this? Thomas hadn't approved of her low cut gown.

When another woman entered the room, Lily nearly jumped off her stool.

"My dear, are you quite all right?"

The dark-haired woman wore a pale blue gown that showed a lot of bosom. She was tall and pretty. Lily didn't recognize her.

"I'm fine, thank you."

"Forgive my rudeness. I'm Lady Amelia Gregory. And you are?

"Lily. Lady Lily Jameson."

"Of course, Lord Ashford's daughter. What a lovely thing you are. It's a pleasure."

"The pleasure's mine." Lily stood, still a bit dizzy, and turned. "If you'll excuse me."

"Not so fast." Lady Gregory reached out and touched Lily's arm.

"I beg your pardon?" Lily yanked her arm away.

"It may interest you to know that I saw you in a compromising position with His Grace a few moments ago."

Lily forced back a swallow and tried to sound nonchalant. "That doesn't particularly interest me."

"No doubt you're wondering why he grabbed you as he did." Lady Gregory smiled and let out a little yawn. "You see, he mistook you for me. It was rather dark outside, and you and I seem to be of similar size and coloring. He asked me to meet him there."

"And you went willingly?"

"Of course." Lady Gregory sat down on a chaise longue and smoothed her skirts. "My, you're an innocent one. He and I were going to get—shall we say—reacquainted this evening. We haven't seen each other since he left for the continent a year ago."

Who was this woman? That smile was so fake. Lily blew out a breath. "And I should find relevance in this statement because?"

"I can see I may have underestimated you, dear." Lady Gregory patted the seat next to her. "Believe me, the duke made a mistake. He's not at all interested in you."

Lily remained standing. "He seemed interested to me." Her heart lurched as she remembered how the duke had pulled her back into his embrace after he had seen her face.

"As I told you, he mistook you for me."

Lily gave a terse smile. "Well, I couldn't care less anyway. I'm not the least bit interested in him."

"Of course you're not." Lady Gregory's acid tone was sardonic. "This must be your first season. No young debutante would want to land the Duke of Lybrook. How foolish of me to think it. Well, get it out of your mind. You're not going to stand in my way of becoming a duchess."

Lily let out a breathy chortle. "I have no interest in becoming a duchess. If you were acquainted with me at all, you would know the truth of that."

"Forgive me if I have a difficult time believing you, dear."

"Believe what you want. You're welcome to him." Lily moved forward to leave, but couldn't help adding, "I wonder, though, if you're so intent on becoming his wife, why you didn't bludgeon him into a commitment years ago?"

Amelia chuckled, shaking her head. "You are daft. He was a second son. Not even a lowly viscount. I was married to an earl. Why would I want to lower my station?"

"How charming." Lily rolled her eyes. "Look, Amanda—"

"It's Amelia. But I prefer to be addressed as Lady Gregory."

"I would certainly address you as such if you were a lady."

Lady Gregory's face reddened. "Who do you think you are?"

"No one of any consequence." Lily waved her hands in front of Amelia's face. "I have no designs on the duke. You may certainly have him. Now if you'll excuse me—"

"Just one minute." Lady Gregory stood up in front of Lily, blocking her exit. "I can be very nasty when I don't get what I want."

"So can I. And right now, I want to leave this room."

Lily pushed Lady Gregory aside and walked briskly out into the hallway. The nerve of her. She headed toward the staircase, but Lady Gregory grabbed her arm.

"You know, if I can't have the duke, I might look around at other prospects. Your charming brother, for instance."

"A lowly viscount?" Lily said, mocking. "Why on earth would you bother?"

"Darling, your brother is a *first* son, heir to one of England's wealthiest earldoms, and he is a delectable specimen."

Rage boiled beneath Lily's skin. "You stay away from him."

"Just something for you to keep in mind. I'd love to be able to call you sissy."

Lily broke free and headed toward the ballroom. One more second and she was likely to claw Amelia's eyes out, and over what? A case of mistaken identity and a kiss? At least she didn't have to worry about Amelia spreading the news of her passionate embrace with Lybrook. If it ever got back to Thomas and her father, they would force Lybrook to offer for Lily, and that would ruin Amelia's plan.

Lily took a deep breath and descended the stairs into the ornate ballroom. Her parents were on the dance floor, as was Aunt Iris. Rose was dancing with Xavier again, while Alexandra and Sophie were seated at a table with Wentworth. Thomas sat at another table with Miss Smythe. Lily ambled toward them.

★ ★ ★ ★

Daniel entered the ballroom after having taken a brief respite in his bedchamber. He made a quick detour to the table where his mother and aunt sat and bowed to them, murmuring an apology for his tardiness. Then he walked to the refreshment table and grabbed a glass of champagne. He had never been a heavy drinker, but damned if he hadn't imbibed more than usual in the past few days. He looked up as Victor Polk approached him.

"Lybrook, where have you been?"

"Here and there." Daniel drained the champagne and reached for another glass.

"Steady, old boy, the night is still young."

Daniel ignored Polk and glanced around the room. There she was, sitting with Jameson and an attractive blond girl. She was laughing heartily, moving her hands as she talked, having a good time. Had she forgotten their interlude already?

"Lybrook, aren't you listening to me?" Polk asked.

"I'm sorry. What did you say?"

"I said Lady Gregory is in quite a dither. She's been searching for you for the past half hour."

"Lord." He had forgotten about Amelia. He had no desire to see her now. Odd how one kiss could change so much. "Help me evade her, will you?"

Polk shook his head. "Count me out. I always thought you were a fool to get involved with her in the first place. She's bad news."

"She had her use at the time, but I can truthfully say I'm finished with her." To his astonishment, he meant every word. "Polk, do you see that dark-haired girl sitting with Jameson?"

"Yes, that's his sister, Lady Lily."

"Of course, Ashford's daughter." The lovely young girl in the alcove. "I knew she looked familiar. I met her years ago. She was just a child."

"She's no longer a child, Lybrook."

"I can see that. She's attractive, don't you think?"

"Attractive?" Polk chuckled. "The woman's a goddess. Quite a little spitfire, too."

"Spitfire? Why do you say that?"

"I sat next to her at dinner. We had some interesting conversation. She's very opinionated."

"Do me a favor, will you? Ask her to dance."

"No problem. I was going to anyway."

"No, you don't understand," Daniel said. "I want you to ask her to dance, and I'm going to cut in."

"Why don't you ask her yourself, then?"

"Because I have reason to believe she will decline my invitation. But if I cut in on you, she'll have no choice but to dance with me."

"Why would she turn you down? You're a duke."

"Let's just say she might and leave it at that."

"What the devil did you do to her?" Polk's ears reddened a bit.

Damn, did his friend carry a torch for this woman?

"Nothing, nothing. Just do as I ask. Or do I have to bring up that old debt about saving your life back at Weston?"

"When in hell will that damned debt be repaid? You've been holding it over my head for fifteen years. It was just a silly fistfight."

"With three ham-fisted oarsmen, Polk. They would have bloody killed you. You never have learned how to keep your big mouth shut."

"Fine, fine, I'll ask her, and you can cut in." Polk relented. "But I'm warning you, if she prefers me over you, I'll fight you for her. This one is worth it."

I don't doubt it.

Polk walked toward Lily's table, sat down for a moment, and then took her hand when the next waltz started. Daniel adjusted his gloves and began to walk toward them. Polk was holding her a little too closely. A stab of jealousy erupted like a knife in Daniel's gut. It was a new emotion. He had never felt it before. If one woman left him, ten others were willing to take her place. He didn't like the feeling, and he liked even less the smile that Lily was bestowing upon his friend.

He took a deep breath and tapped Polk on the shoulder. "May I?"

"Of course, Your Grace." Polk bowed politely, playing his part well.

Daniel's stomach darted as he led Lily's left hand to his shoulder and took her in his arms. Why was he nervous around a woman?

"My lady, I wish to apologize for my abominable behavior earlier."

"You simply mistook me for someone else," Lily said. "It happens."

"Why would you think that, my lady?"

"I just assumed so. Since we haven't been formally introduced, you couldn't have meant to..."

"Perhaps I did." Daniel summoned his best rakish grin. "Perhaps I saw you and wanted you."

"I suppose that is possible, knowing your reputation."

He winced. "I deserved that one. The fact is, I *was* waiting for someone else. But I can't say I'm sorry it turned out to be you."

He twirled Lily into an ornate step and was impressed when she followed fluidly. She felt perfect in his arms, as though they were one body moving to the elegant music.

When the waltz ended, Daniel didn't let go of her, couldn't force his gaze away from her cognac eyes. "My lady," he said softly, "If there's anything I can do for you...anything at all...to make up for my disgraceful behavior, please—"

"Might I have the pleasure of the next dance?" Polk interrupted.

"Yes, of course." Daniel let go of her reluctantly, scowling at his friend.

As Polk waltzed away with Lily in his arms, Daniel clenched his fists. She was smiling at him, damn her.

To cut in on them again would be bad form. But he couldn't help himself, he was going to do it. As he began walking, someone grabbed his hand. He turned to look into the flushed face of Amelia Gregory.

"Darling," she whispered wickedly, "I'm so sorry I didn't meet you earlier. I was unavoidably detained. Perhaps we could enjoy our little reunion now?"

"I don't think so, my lady," Daniel said. "I must stay at the ball. I am the host."

"You weren't worried about your hosting duties earlier."

"I am now." He shook his arm loose from her grasp.

"What has gotten into you, Daniel? An hour ago you couldn't wait to debauch me on the side of the manor."

"Lower your voice," he commanded. "And stop using my Christian name."

"You never mind me using it in the bedchamber." She slid her hand inside his jacket and caressed his chest.

"For God's sake, stop that!"

Amelia removed her hand abruptly, her face tense, but then she eased her lips into a smile. "Your Grace, I feel a bit of a headache coming on. I shall have to retire. And you know, my chamber has been so dusty. I could hardly breathe in there this afternoon. I'm afraid I just can't abide the thought of sleeping there."

"I'm sorry it doesn't suit you. I'll send a maid to give it an extra cleaning on the morrow."

"But what shall I do tonight?" she asked with mock innocence. "I fear I shall have to find an alternative place to sleep. But don't you worry a smidgeon about me. I'll find a bed. Somewhere." She winked and then slowly turned and walked toward the door of the ballroom.

Christ. Now he would have to find somewhere else to sleep. He turned his attention back to Polk and Lily. They left the dance floor and sat down at the table with Lord Jameson and the blond girl. Lily was laughing gaily, talking with her hands again. As she smiled up into Polk's admiring gaze, another twinge of jealousy speared Daniel. Damn it.

Polk rose, walked to the refreshment table, and brought back two glasses of champagne for himself and Lily. They sat, talking, while Jameson and the blonde got up to dance. Daniel thought of joining them, but what would he say to her?

Polk was his oldest and closest friend, yet at the moment Daniel wanted to jam his aristocratic nose into the nearest wall and then carry Lily off like a pirate's prize.

God, he wanted to kiss her again. Just thinking about it aroused him. He grew stiff, but the release he craved...

Amelia. No doubt she was naked, lying in his bed. Bloody hell, a bird in the hand and all. He turned and walked swiftly out of the ballroom.

He entered his bedchamber stealthily, removed his clothes, and slipped under the cool sheets where Amelia lay.

"What took you so long, darling?"

He didn't answer. He wasn't interested in the niceties this evening. Quickly he moved on top of her.

"Easy, lover. I can see you're impatient. It has been a long time, after all. But I want to please you. Have you forgotten how good I am at the preliminaries?"

"Don't talk." He reached between her legs, parted her intimate folds, and plunged his fingers into her depths.

Amelia gasped. "I'm not quite ready for you, Daniel. Give me some time, and it will be better for both of us."

"I said don't talk." The sound of her voice bothered him.

He removed his hand from between her legs and rolled away from her. It was Lily's voice he wanted to hear. Lily's body he wanted to feel under his. Never before had he thought of one woman while he was with another.

He breathed heavily, the ache between his legs pulsating in a blind heat. He was barely aware of Amelia moving on top of him. She wet her fingers with her tongue and slid them back and forth across her pussy, moistening herself to receive him. She grasped his cock with one hand and rubbed the tip back and forth against her opening, sighing softly. Slowly she began to ease herself onto him.

"No, Amelia." He grabbed her around the waist and easily lifted her off. "I'm sorry. I don't want to do this."

"What is the matter, darling? Aren't you feeling well?"

"It's not that. It's just..."

"Of course, whatever you like, my love," she said. "Just hold me for a while." She snuggled against his chest and laid her head in the crook of his arm.

He stiffened. "I'm sorry," he said. "I...this is hard for me to say."

"Go on, dearest. We have the whole night ahead of us."

"Amelia, I did ask you to meet me outside. I take full responsibility for that."

"I'm so sorry that I was detained. Did it anger you?"

"No, of course not. I'm sure you had a good reason for... that is..."

"Daniel, do get on with it," she barked. Then, "I'm sorry. I didn't mean to snap at you. It's just that I've missed you so much."

Though they had shared intimacies of the body, no real feeling had ever existed between them. Still, Daniel had no wish to hurt her. He could let her stay. He could sleep with her, but he lacked the desire to do so. It was a new feeling, something he had never imagined. He almost felt he was being unfaithful. But why? He had shared a few passionate kisses and one dance with a beautiful young woman. That was all.

"Amelia. I'm sorry to tell you this, but I wish to end our liaison."

"What?" She jerked away from him.

"You heard me. I wish for you to leave my bedchamber. I don't anticipate requiring your company in the future."

"Daniel, if it's something I've done..."

"No, no. It's nothing you've done. It's my fault. I'm the one who has changed. I no longer wish to have you in my bed."

"After all we've shared, you would simply cast me aside?"

"You know we were never faithful to each other. Why are you reacting this way?"

"Perhaps I *have* been faithful to you. Have you considered that possibility?"

"Really, Amelia. I was gone for a year. I know your appetites."

"Of all the... How can you insult me that way?"

Daniel began to lose patience. "Insult you? For God's sake, this is probably the most we've spoken to each other since we met. We never had any relationship other than in bed, and it is not my wish for that relationship to continue."

Amelia got out of bed, strode slowly across the chamber to the leather armchair where her garments lay, and began to dress. "You know, tomorrow night when you're lonely, don't bother coming to me. I will likely find a gentleman who appreciates what I have to offer. I already have my eye on someone. Perhaps you know him. Lord Jameson? He is quite devastatingly handsome, and I do believe he will be receptive."

Lily's brother. Lily's brother who was obviously taken with the blond woman who had monopolized him all evening. Clearly Amelia was bluffing, trying to hurt him. Daniel didn't blame her for the attempt.

"By all means. I hope you do find someone. I wish you nothing but happiness, Amelia. However, I think it might be best if you left Laurel Ridge on the morrow."

"You can't be serious! You invited me here, Daniel!"

She was right of course. He had invited her, and she had done nothing to merit being sent away. "I spoke in haste. Of course you don't have to leave. Please make yourself welcome, and I hope you enjoy the rest of your stay."

"Fine." She walked to the door, her dress unbuttoned in the back.

"Wait, I'll fasten you," Daniel said.

"Please, don't bother. I'll go straight to my chamber." She slammed the door.

Daniel turned over, burying his face into his pillow, clenching his hands into fists. His unsated erection throbbed.

He imagined a pair of soft white hands caressing it, ruby lips enfolding it.

"Lily," he groaned aloud. "Lily."

CHAPTER THREE

Lily woke early the next morning. She smiled to herself, remembering the ball. She had enjoyed it, to her surprise. Lord Victor had been charming company, although she didn't wish to encourage him. Somehow, she had to get him interested in Alexandra.

And the duke. His kiss and his dance edged their way into Lily's mind more often than she desired. Consciously, she banished them.

Lily brushed out her hair and plaited it, letting the long braid hang down her back. She dressed in a morning gown of pale orange and put on her ankle boots. The men would no doubt be meeting to begin their hunt. She decided to give them a few more moments before descending. Most of the women would still be abed due to the late hour of the ball last evening. Lily intended to take her art supplies and do some painting. She gathered her leather case that held her watercolors and paper. She took out a pint-sized jar, filled it with water from the basin, and capped it and put it in her case. She dropped her writing journal into the case as well. Then she left the room quietly. Rose was still breathing steadily in slumber.

She enlisted a young servant to carry her supplies and walked toward the alcove. Servants were hurrying about on the front lawn, setting up tables and chairs for the ladies' lawn party that afternoon. In about ten minutes, she found the rocky path she had walked across eight years ago, and in the distance the stony alcove beckoned. The bench was still there, although foliage had grown over parts of it.

Lily dismissed the servant and hummed softly to herself as she set up her easel, placed a watercolor board upon it, and tied an apron around her waist. She opened her jar of water and saturated the paper. Delving in to the case again for her colors, she spied the painting she had brought from home. She looked beyond at the landscape she had painted. Remarkably, it hadn't changed much in eight years, except no color bloomed now. It had been early autumn during her last visit. She put the painting back in her case and decided to start fresh. She continued humming as she mixed color for the sky, which was scattered with wispy white clouds. A bird twittered in the distance, and Lily stopped in mid stroke. She jotted a few sentences in her journal describing the sounds in the alcove and then went back to her painting.

★ ★ ★ ★

Daniel stood several yards back. He smiled as he watched Lily paint, write, paint, and write. He'd first seen her years ago, in this very spot. She had been lovely, her dark hair and eyes promising true beauty as she matured. She had not disappointed. She dipped her head a bit as she mixed more color, and then she added some lush green to the light blue of her painting. Her strokes were deliberate, leaving the color in silky caresses on the paper. She turned again to her journal and wrote for a few moments, and then went back to painting. She changed to a thin brush and drew some delicate brown lines on her board.

Daniel stole forward. "My lady."

She turned, startled. He recalled with a smile how she had stood up eight years ago, spilling her tin of water. She remained seated this time.

"Good morning, Your Grace. What are you doing here?"

She sounded remarkably calm at his presence. For some reason, this bothered Daniel.

"It *is* my estate," he said.

"Why aren't you on the hunt with the others?"

"I have some business to attend to this afternoon, so I decided to skip the hunt."

"What on earth are you skulking about for then? I didn't think men of your station were inclined to rise before noon."

Daniel chuckled softly. "It seems you have some rather interesting ideas regarding men of my station."

"You haven't done anything to make me cast my notions to the wind." Lily reached for her journal.

"Perhaps I can change your mind about some of your generalizations," he said. "What are you writing?"

"Nothing much. Just descriptions really. I find that my painting and my writing often go hand in hand."

"Really? Which do you prefer? Painting or writing?"

Lily turned her gaze to the horizon. "I'm not sure I could say. I suppose I can never decide, which is why I do both at the same time."

Daniel regarded her with amusement. "I don't think I've ever known anyone like you."

The porcelain skin on her neck pinked. "You don't really know me."

Good Lord, she's beautiful. "I'd like to."

The pink on her nape turned to crimson. "You would, would you? I suppose I should be flattered. However, I'm disinclined to associate myself with a gentleman—and I use the term loosely—of your reputation."

An insult. Not many ladies would dare. She was a delight! Daniel reached to touch her. Her physical charms were overwhelming to any man, but what enticed him most was her loose-tongued sharpness. Clearly she cared little for propriety. He dropped his arm back to his side and ignored her comment.

"My lady, please, I must ask you again for your forgiveness for my behavior last evening."

"Don't give it a thought, Your Grace. I'm sure I'm not the first innocent maiden who found herself entrapped in your snare."

"I wish you would stop joking."

"I'm not joking."

"Oh." Daniel stepped backward. Oh, she was audacious, this one. And so beautiful and intriguing. "Then if you would allow me to make it up to you in some way…"

Lily put down her journal and stood, turning to face him. She wiped her hands on the apron covering her skirt. Daniel's skin heated as her cognac eyes pierced his. She opened her mouth, but no words emerged.

"Yes?" he urged.

She bit her lip. "Your Grace, there is something that you could do for me."

"Anything, my lady."

"I would like to see your art collection." She spoke quickly, her voice softening with each catch of her breath. "It's rumored to be one of the finest in England, and my brother told me that it could only be viewed by private invitation. I have a passion for art, Your Grace, and Vermeer is one of my favorites. You do have a Vermeer, do you not?"

He grinned. "I do."

"I know this must seem very forward, but I've been excited about this trip to Laurel Ridge for quite some time. To actually see a Vermeer! The thought of being close to something that he touched. I suppose this must sound crazy to you, but, well, to tell you the truth, I had planned to find it myself..."

"So you thought you'd do a little investigating, did you?" He smiled, enjoying her nervousness.

"No, of course not." She blushed. The rosiness crept down her neck to the swells of her plump bosom. "Well, yes, actually."

"Is that by any chance what you were doing last night, when I...caught you?"

Lily looked to the ground. "Yes, I suppose it was. I stole onto the terrace and was planning to go around to the front entrance and sneak through the house until I found it. Everyone was at the ball, so I figured it was a perfect time to have a look."

"You would have found some beautiful pieces, but I'm afraid the Vermeer would have eluded you."

She looked up. "Why is that?"

"Because I keep it in a very special place. A place you wouldn't have dared to look."

"Where?"

"My bedchamber." He couldn't help himself. He gave her his best rakish grin.

"Oh." Her dark eyes radiated disappointment. "I suppose I shall never see it then."

"Nonsense. I would be happy to show it to you." *Oh, I would indeed.*

"I can't possibly go to your bedchamber. It would be highly improper." She bit her lip again.

That soft plump lower lip, so satiny against his own last night... *Damn*. His cock twitched. "My lady, you don't strike me as a woman who would let convention keep you from something you want."

"I don't know why you feel it necessary to insult me, Your Grace." Lily reddened again, but she spoke with eloquence. "After all, you are the one who has behaved abominably."

"You are right, of course, and I meant no insult." He touched her arm lightly and his cock jerked again. "But my lady, it's just a painting, and it happens to hang in my bedchamber. If you would like to see it, I will show it to you. I did promise to do anything you wanted to make up for my unforgivable behavior last night."

"Oh, I do so want to see it."

"Would it help if I gave you my solemn promise to keep you at arm's length the entire time we are there?"

"I'm not sure I would believe such a promise."

"Just as well, since I'm not sure I can make it." He winked at her.

Lily widened her beautiful eyes. "Goodness..."

"Come with me," Daniel said. "I will escort you to the house, and it will be my pleasure to show you the Vermeer. It's been a long time since a woman has wanted to come to my bedchamber for something other than—"

"Your Grace, please."

She was absolutely lovely when she blushed. He waited a few seconds, hoping her passion for Vermeer would win over convention.

"All right, Your Grace." She took his offered arm. "May I leave my art supplies out here?"

"I'll have someone take care of it. They'll be delivered to

your chamber."

"Actually, give me just a minute. I'll get things in order. I don't want to leave my journal sitting out here, and this painting isn't finished yet, obviously. I would like to...but I can't possibly finish it today, can I? By the time we get back, the light will have changed significantly. Damn."

Daniel smiled at her curse. She didn't seem to notice that she'd said it.

"I may as well put this all away now," she continued. "I'll have to come back out tomorrow at the same time."

"If you would like to complete your work, we can see the Vermeer later." Daniel ran his finger lightly over her forearm. God, he loved touching her. "I can think of nothing I would rather do, actually, than watch you paint."

Lily whisked her arm away. "Surely you have better things to occupy your time, Your Grace."

"Not really." He leaned against the bench as she covered her watercolor palette.

"As much as I would like to finish, I really want to see the Vermeer. So I shall continue this on the morrow." She hastily packed her supply case. As she bent to slide in the unfinished painting, the edge of another piece caught Daniel's eye.

"What is that one?" he asked.

"Oh, this? I actually painted this same scene when I was last here. I brought it with me to see how the landscape had changed. However, it seems my perception is what has changed."

"May I see it?"

"I suppose, if you want to. But my technique wasn't really up to par then. It's not very good."

"Let me be the judge of that." He regarded the painting.

"My lady, this is truly lovely. I remember you painting it. Do you recall our first meeting?"

Lily blushed again. "I believe so. I was just a child."

"I remember thinking that you had a remarkable gift. I can see that I was correct."

"Th-Thank you," she stammered. "But I'm a much better painter now. That work is just, well, yes, it's pretty, I agree, but—"

"Nonsense, it's wonderful. May I?" He pulled out the unfinished watercolor and compared the two. "Yes, your technique has definitely improved, but this one shows your talent when it was raw and untamed. There's an innocence to it, yet a wildness as well."

"I'm...glad you appreciate it, Your Grace."

"I do, my lady. Perhaps you should return to Laurel Ridge more frequently and paint the same scene. It would be incredibly interesting to see how your perception changes over time."

"Certainly, I would...love to return sometime. I'm sure my family would appreciate another invitation." She fidgeted. "May I have the painting? I'm almost finished putting everything in order. I cannot wait to see the Vermeer." Lily put both paintings away.

"Please, allow me." Daniel took her supply case but set it on the bench. He moistened his thumb in his mouth and rubbed it across Lily's jawline. Her skin was warm and oh so soft.

"Your Grace?"

"You have the most adorable smudge of blue paint on your lovely face."

There went the rosy flush again. "If it's so adorable, why

are you removing it?"

Daniel warmed and gave a half smile. "Are you flirting with me, my lady?"

"Your Grace, of course not."

"Folly. I was hoping you were." Daniel lifted her supply case and led her out of the alcove toward the main house. "You know, I don't usually escort a lovely lady to my chamber during midmorning. What will the servants think?"

Lily cleared her throat. "I would appreciate discretion, Your Grace."

"Of course, I was only teasing. No one will know that you've been to my chamber. I promise you."

★ ★ ★ ★

When they reached the house, Daniel handed Lily's supplies to a servant with orders to deliver them to her chamber and then led her through the dining hall and kitchen where cooks were busy preparing the luncheon. She felt extremely conspicuous, but no one seemed to notice them. He led her up a back stairway to his suite on the third floor.

They entered a large sitting room decorated in an eastern style. A large sofa covered in a fiery red brocade graced one wall. An intricate Oriental rug covered the floor and was so plush that Lily's shoes sank down at least an inch as she stood on it. Two leather armchairs surrounded a mahogany reading table, and two tall elegant barristers' bookcases lined one wall, housing gilt-edged leather-bound volumes. Oriental prints adorned the walls, framed beautifully in black lacquered wood. Lily stopped, her feet sinking into the soft fibers beneath her, and looked around the room, taking it all in. Daniel nudged her forward to a door on the far wall, and she entered his bedchamber.

His four-poster bed was solid cherry draped in burgundy silk. An elegant sitting window housed a chaise longue and settee, both covered in a burgundy brocade. A small table sat between the two seats. On it were several crystal bottles filled with a dark liquid. Probably brandy, Lily thought. A lush leather armchair sat opposite the bed, next to a door that undoubtedly led to a lavatory with modern plumbing. For some strange reason, Lily was curious to see the duke's bath chamber. She must have been staring, for he came up behind her, lightly touched his hands to her waist, and slowly turned her to the left.

"This," he whispered into her ear, "is, I believe, what you wanted to see."

Lily gasped. The gilt-framed painting graced the wall, positioned so that it was visible from the bed. The picture was of a maiden, gowned in vivid crimson, holding a crucifix and cleaning blood from a dead man behind her. Her expression was one of serene contemplation, despite the vile task she undertook. Lily moved closer to the painting, reaching toward it.

"Don't worry," she told Daniel. "I won't touch it. I know better. I just want to... God, it's wonderful. I want to look closely at his strokes."

"I know what you mean. It's almost a psychic touch, isn't it? You can feel the texture in your mind if you put your fingers close to it."

"Yes, exactly!" He understood. The duke actually understood how she felt. Lily gazed, drinking it in. "Who is it, do you suppose?"

"St. Praxedis. It's one of Vermeer's earlier works. There are some skeptics who don't think it can be attributed to him, but there has never been any doubt in my mind."

"St. Praxedis...from the early Catholic Church?"

"Yes, she was elevated to sainthood for her services to the dead bodies of the martyrs. Do you see how she's holding the crucifix as she cleans the blood from the body? That symbolizes the martyr's blood mixing with the blood of Christ."

"My God, he was a genius," Lily whispered. She couldn't tear her eyes away. "I wish I could paint like that."

Daniel moved closer behind her and wrapped his arms around her waist, encircling her. Lily absently settled her hands on his and continued to admire the painting.

"Have you ever tried oils?" Daniel asked.

"No, but I've always wanted to. My father has had a hard time indulging my artistic side. He would rather I stitch samplers and find a husband. He allows my dalliance with watercolor; however, he feels that oil painting is for more... masculine endeavors. I was never allowed to try them." She leaned back against him. The nearness of his hard muscled form warmed her through. His breath tickled her cheek. Being in his arms felt...good.

"That's a pity," he said. "I'd love to see what you could do with them."

"So would I, Your Grace."

He gently turned her around to face him. "Daniel," he said softly.

"I'm sorry?"

"I want you to use my name. My Christian name."

"Oh, I couldn't. It wouldn't be proper—"

Then his mouth was on hers, slowly sliding over her lips,

coaxing them open. He nipped gently at her lower lip, teasing her with his tongue. She sighed as he licked her softly. She was kissing him again. In his bedchamber. She should be fleeing, but her legs wouldn't move. Didn't want to move...

He trailed to her cheek and covered it with soft fluttery kisses that felt like the wings of a butterfly, and then slid to her ear and nipped lightly on the lobe.

"Say my name," he whispered. "I want it to drip from your ruby lips like a fine Bordeaux. I want to feel the silky caress as you whisper it against my neck. I want to hear you sob it into my mouth as I kiss you. Please, Lily. Say my name."

She shuddered. His husky voice made her knees tremble. Was it possible that underneath this renowned blackguard lurked the soul of a poet? Or was this just a practiced technique in seduction? As he slid his lips over her neck and face and her heart thumped wildly, she couldn't bring herself to care.

"Daniel," she moaned softly. "Oh, Daniel."

He groaned. "Oh yes, love. Kiss me."

Despite her better judgment, she responded with innocent eagerness, finding his mouth with hers and letting her tongue wander apprehensively into his warmth. He took her tongue, mated it with his, sucking it gently and then freeing it to explore him. She let it roam over his full lips, sucking them and biting them gently, as little moans escaped from her throat. His lips were firm yet soft on hers, and he tasted of honey. Mmm, delicious. Her blood boiled as his lips meandered over her cheek to her neck.

"God, you smell so heavenly." He covered her smooth skin with kisses. "I haven't been able to think about anything but this since last night. I couldn't eat. I couldn't sleep. All I wanted was to see you again."

He pressed his lips to her neck and covered it with gentle little bites while he roamed his fingers over her hips and up towards her breasts. Gently he slid his hands over her bosom. She gasped as her breasts swelled and her nipples tightened into hard little knobs. He trailed kisses down to the neckline of her gown and then back up to her lips again. Lily panted, trying to get closer to him. When his arousal nudged against her body, a stabbing desire ran through her womb.

"Lily," he whispered. "Please, Lily." He urged her toward the bed.

No! This was no love-struck adolescent stealing kisses. This was the Duke of Lybrook, rake extraordinaire and seducer of women. Her heart pounded against her sternum. How had she let this get so far? She pushed Daniel away, the suction of their kiss breaking with a loud smack.

"I can't do this." She backed away from him, keeping her hands behind her. She fumbled for a table or a chair, anything to help maintain her balance.

"I didn't mean to frighten you." Daniel edged toward her slowly.

"Your Grace, I came up here to see your painting. I-I... apologize for any part I may have played in this...mistake. I..."

"It's not a mistake. None of it has been a mistake. Please don't back away from me."

"I..." She couldn't finish.

He stood close to her, staring at her with those wonderful eyes. As if it had a mind of its own, her hand shakily reached up to his honey locks, smoothing them. God, his hair was beautiful. It was the color of burnished gold, with highlights of amber, brown, and just a few silvery strands near his temples. It felt like raw silk beneath her fingers.

She snatched her hand away. "I'm sorry."

"Don't be sorry." He took her hand. "You can touch me. I want you to touch me."

She pulled her hand away. "No, I can't. I...need to leave. Thank you, Your Grace, for showing me the Vermeer. I'll never forget it. It was one of the most precious things anyone has ever done for me." She turned toward the door.

Daniel touched her arm lightly. "Please don't go," he said, his voice low and husky. "Will you have lunch with me? I'll have a tray sent up."

"It's not lunchtime." She closed her eyes and took a deep breath. His warmth pressed against her back. "Please, you must let me go."

"Do you want to go?"

"I want..."

She trembled as he placed his hands on her shoulders. She wanted him. She couldn't help herself. Something about this beautiful, dangerous man called to her in a way she never thought possible. Unfamiliar emotion and desire flooded her body, her soul. She wanted more of his kisses. She wanted his hands on her skin...her bare skin.

She turned to face him. "I don't know why you want me," she said, willing her voice not to crack. "I'm likely to be a frightful bore for you."

His green eyes sparkled. "Love, there is nothing boring about you."

"What I mean is...for a man of your experience...an untried maiden would be..."

He chuckled softly.

"Damn it, you know what I mean!"

"Lily, I want *you*. I've never wanted a woman this much."

He crushed her to him and inhaled. "God, you smell good. What scent is that? I've never smelled anything like it before."

"It...it's just clove oil," Lily said, escaping from his grasp. "I get it from the apothecary. I can't abide those expensive French perfumes. They make me feel like a powder puff. So I just dab a little clove oil..."

He chuckled again, the skin around his eyes crinkling.

"What is so funny?"

"Nothing. I'm sorry. You're just...you're not like any other woman I've known."

"I should hope not." She tapped her foot. "Likely the women you're acquainted with are mostly strumpets."

"Touché. Perhaps it's time I elevated my standards a bit."

"And...you want to elevate them with me?"

"God, more than anything."

"Then you should know," she said, her pulse racing, "I-I'm not like most women my age. I want different things. I'm looking forward to the coming season about as much as a case of the pox. I have no desire to marry, as I have little use for men."

Daniel's full pink lips curved into a half smile. "I wasn't proposing marriage, love."

Lily's skin heated. "Of course not. I didn't mean to imply that you were."

"As for your feelings about men—" He winked. "Is it that you prefer the fairer sex?"

Clearly the duke expected to embarrass her. She was quite aware of the writings of Sappho and others and knew some women and men preferred the same sex for intimacy. Lily was inexperienced, yes, but not naïve. She let out a husky giggle. "No, Your Grace. I assure you I have even less use for women. I can't abide the bubbleheaded idiots who fawn at my brother's feet, and at yours."

Daniel laughed softly. "I see, then. If you don't want a season or marriage, what do you want, Lily?"

She closed her eyes and inhaled. "I want to paint and write and travel. I want to sail around Venice, dine in Paris, spend an entire week in the Louvre. I want to stroll through the vineyards in Burgundy. I want to listen to Mozart in Vienna, climb a mountain in the Swiss Alps. I want to buy silk in the Orient and swim in the Mediterranean Sea. I want to see everything Vermeer ever painted."

When she opened her eyes, Daniel was grinning at her.

"Damn it, I don't have to explain myself to you."

He moved toward her and cupped her face in his hands. "You don't have to explain anything to me." He kissed her mouth lightly, caressing her cheeks with his thumbs. "I want you just as you are." He kissed her again. "My God, you're beautiful."

"Thank you," she murmured. Jumbles of thoughts crowded through her mind. She wanted to stay with him. It was improper. She wanted his golden hands on her body. She would be ruined. Her virtue was at stake. But did it matter? She didn't wish to marry. Yet she wanted every experience life had to offer. Sleeping with the duke was just one more experience, yes? Who better to introduce her to the pleasures of the flesh than a man she was attracted to and who probably had the knowledge and experience of ten men?

But it would hurt. And people might find out and shun her. Her family deserved better.

She looked down at her feet. "I'm afraid."

"Lily, look at me." He tilted her chin up to face him. "You

have nothing to fear from me. I promise you."

"It...will hurt."

"It may. But I'll do everything I can to help you. It doesn't have to be unpleasant."

"I-I will require discretion."

"Of course. No one will know. You have my word."

"And I don't want to... That is, I have no desire for you to get your brat on me."

She regretted the harsh words, but they didn't seem to faze him.

"Don't worry. I can take care of that."

"How?"

"Just leave it to me. There are several ways to—"

"I don't want to know," Lily interrupted. "Just take care of it. Lord, I can't believe I'm going to do this."

Daniel pulled her gently into his arms. "I'll be so good to you. I'll take care of you. I want to give you pleasure unlike either of us has ever known. Kiss me." He guided her lips to his.

As she melted into him, she was vaguely aware of his hands working the buttons on the back of her gown and easing it down over her shoulders until it was in a heap on the floor. He turned her around gently, untied the strings of her corset, and carefully removed her stockings and her drawers. Soon she stood before him wearing only her chemise, which left nothing to the imagination.

"You're absolutely lovely," Daniel whispered.

He turned her away from him again as he slowly lifted her arms, caressing them lightly, and eased the chemise over her head. He leisurely ran his fingers over her arms, bringing them back to her sides, and then slid one finger up the curve of her spine and back down. She shivered. He untied the ribbon that held her long hair in a braid and gently untangled her thick locks. They fell into waves around her shoulders. He turned her back to face him.

"I want you so much," he said, his bewitching eyes taking in every inch of her. In one swift movement he gathered her into his arms and carried her to the bed, where he laid her down gently on the silky burgundy.

He undressed himself, leaving his garments in a heap on the floor next to the bed. His stomach was lean and rippled, his chest covered with a smattering of tawny curls. His arms were strong and muscular, and his shoulders, oh, his shoulders. How she wanted to run her hands and her tongue all over the sleek tan warmth of them.

As he came to her, she widened her eyes. His cock was thick and hard...and huge. She wrapped her arms around herself, shivering.

He grinned and winked at her. "It will fit," he whispered.

Then his mouth was on hers again, and he sank his tongue into her and moaned softly. His sweet honey flavor devoured what little was left of her resistance. She couldn't get enough of the silkiness and fire of his mouth. She sucked on his tongue, trying to taste every part of him. He moved his lips along her cheek, to her ear, down her neck, nuzzling and nipping her gently, and then not so gently. When he reached her breasts, he cupped them in his large hands and stared at them for a moment.

"Beautiful," he said, his voice smoky.

He buried his face between the soft mounds, running his thumbs over her nipples. Slowly he covered them with kisses, easing toward one rosy circle. He licked it gently, swirling his tongue around her nipple until it was a tight bud. *God, so good*... Then he softly breathed on the wetness, and a sweet chill rushed straight to her womb.

"Please," Lily heard herself moan. "Please."

Daniel took the nipple into his mouth, licked and sucked it lightly. Lily shuddered and arched against his hard body, grasping the silk of his hair, pulling him closer to her. He kissed his way over to the other nipple, sucking and tugging.

"Daniel, please!"

"Slowly," he whispered. He trailed his lips down her abdomen to the triangle of glossy black curls. Gently he parted her with his fingers. "Tell me, love, is the rest of you as sweet as your succulent kisses? Your gorgeous breasts?"

"I-I don't know what you mean."

"Innocent angel," he murmured. "Let me show you."

She gasped as he parted her legs and pushed her knees up. "Wet," he said. "So wet for me."

"W-Wet?"

"Your pussy is wet. It's normal, love." He smiled between her legs. "It means you want me as much as I want you."

Then he was kissing her...there. She'd heard of such things, but a lady wouldn't... It was disgraceful really. Try as she might, though, she couldn't bring herself to stop him. As he swirled his tongue around the entrance to her body, he breathed fire into her.

"You're so sweet," he said, "and so amazingly pink and pretty. God, I want you like I've never wanted anything."

Lily arched as he found a place that made her head spin. She quivered and moaned as his tongue danced over her hot flesh. More, she wanted more.

"Please."

She had no idea what she was asking for, but he seemed

to understand. Her tissues stretched as he filled her with a finger and stroked languidly in and out. The stretch, though uncomfortable at first, soon had Lily writhing as her body adjusted to the fullness. As his fingers danced inside her, ripples of flame ignited across her skin. Lily curved against him, grabbed his satiny hair, and pulled his face closer as pleasure rang through her in a rapturous wave of ecstasy. She cried out his name as she surrendered herself, while he continued to lick her and stroke her, nursing her through the waves. When a euphoria settled over her, he stopped, moved upward, and kissed her mouth slowly and deeply. The fruity musk on his tongue was different. *Her.* She melted into his kiss, her own flavor an intoxicating sensation.

"Oh, Daniel," she whispered. "I had no idea."

He stroked her cheeks with his lips. "My God, I love the taste of you, the smell of you, your touch, your kisses." He nipped her earlobe. "Let me inside you, Lily. I'll be so gentle. I'll make it good for you, I swear it."

His hard cock poked against her thigh. The desire to have him inside her body overwhelmed her. "Yes, yes," she whispered. "Come inside me. Please."

Daniel led her hand to his hardened shaft. She grasped its length, spreading her legs and leading it to her entrance.

"Rub it over your wetness, love." He groaned. "That's it, get it good and slick." He clenched his teeth. "I'm going to enter you now. You tell me if you want me to stop. I don't want to hurt you."

"I don't want you to stop." Lily gritted her teeth, bracing herself for the pain.

He entered her slowly. She grabbed his shoulders, loving the feel of his hard muscle, as he slid all the way into her. Full.

So full. The invasion hurt a bit, but not nearly so much as she had feared. Daniel's shudders and groans of pleasure seemed much more important than the small amount of discomfort Lily felt. She arched against his hips, drawing him deeper into her body.

"Are you all right?" Daniel asked.

"I-It's so big. I'm so full." Her words were a breathless rasp.

"Do you want me to stop?"

God, no. "N-No. Don't stop."

"Oh, thank God." Daniel's body crushed against hers, nearly knocking the air out of her lungs.

"I c-can't breathe, Daniel."

"I'm so sorry, love." He adjusted his body. "Better?"

"Yes, yes," she whispered. "Show me what to do."

"Just kiss me."

He clamped his mouth onto hers and began to move within her, pulling himself out then pushing back into her in a rhythm she met with her hips.

"So sweet, so tight," Daniel said against her neck.

The burning of his intrusion slowly turned from ache into pleasure as he nudged her sensitive peak with each sensational thrust. Her whole body throbbed, and soon the waves of pleasure rippled through her again. As she sobbed her climax, he thrust mightily, his entire body pulsating against her in a blazing explosion.

"Lily. My God, *Lily.*"

CHAPTER FOUR

Daniel slowly turned onto his side, cuddling Lily in his arms, gently pulling her leg over his hip, their bodies still joined.

"Sweet Lord," he said.

Lily let out a nervous giggle. "I guess men do have their uses." She laced her fingers through his hair.

He laughed softly and kissed her nose. "Go to sleep, love."

★ ★ ★ ★

Lily awoke to the noonday sun streaming through the bay window in Daniel's bedchamber. Should she feel regretful? Ashamed? Oddly, she felt only relaxed.

She sat up in bed and turned to feast her eyes on the man lying next to her. He was on his back, one arm strewn across his eyes. Oh, he was beautiful. Timidly she reached over and ran her fingers through the tawny curls on his well muscled chest. When she reached a nipple, it hardened beneath her touch. She feathered her hands down lower, traced a circle around his navel, and laced her fingers through the dark blond curls of his private area. His sex hung loosely, looking so different than it had during his arousal. She touched the softness apprehensively and then shyly removed her hand. Turning her head to look at his beautiful sleeping face, she found his green eyes open, smoldering as he looked at her.

"Don't stop," he said.

"Forgive me." Warmth crept over her skin.

He chuckled softly. "There's nothing to forgive. I told you, I want you to touch me."

She looked toward the window. "It must be nearly noon. The luncheon starts at one, and my sister and mother will be expecting me. I have to go."

He reached for her hand and entwined their fingers together. "You have an hour. Stay with me. In fact, skip the luncheon. Have lunch with me. We can dine here."

"I couldn't possibly. Besides, I...need a bath."

He gave her a half smile as he stroked her thumb. "I'll bathe you."

"Daniel..."

"I told you I would take care of you. There might be some blood. Let me bathe you."

"My God..." A bath seemed so intimate. Yet hadn't they already shared the ultimate intimacy?

"Is that a yes?"

"I suppose so. What have I started?"

"Nothing that I have any intention of stopping." He waggled his eyebrows. "Then we'll dine together, here."

Her heart pounded. "What about the luncheon?"

"Will your mother and sister really miss you?"

Lily shrugged. They would most likely think she had lost track of time painting. It happened often. "Probably not. But I do have to leave after lunch. I promised to spend time with my sister and my cousins. We're going to skip the lawn party and..."

"And what?"

"Have some...fun." She looked away.

"Doing what, pray tell?"

"I don't really know yet. But we'll find something."

"I have no doubt of that." Daniel kissed her fingertips, stood up, and walked leisurely to the door leading to the bath chamber. "Stay there, love," he said, his gaze wandering over every curve of her body as she sat on the rumpled comforter. "I want to remember how you look right now. Your lips are the color of a ripe cherry, still swollen from our kisses. Your breasts are the most lovely I've seen, round and plump, with the most perfect little crimson berries that harden under my tongue."

"Daniel..."

"And your hair. I love your hair. It's so soft and dark, almost black, with little glints of brandy here and there. Mmm, your legs, so long and shapely, wrapped around me, and between them, the most luscious little—"

"Dear God." Lily looked down. Her breasts were as red as she imagined her face to be.

Daniel grinned. "Vermeer himself couldn't do you justice right now."

Lily squirmed on the bed, the tender spot between her legs burning. "You shouldn't talk like that."

"Hush. I'm going to run your bath. I'll call you when it's ready." He walked, naked, to the bath chamber.

She heard the rush of water as he filled the tub. *I could be happy here.* She lounged lazily on the bed. *If I never left this chamber again, I think I could be content.* Such musings surprised her, given her desires for art, writing, travel, so she banished them quickly from her mind. She couldn't get attached to a man like Daniel. He had a renowned sexual appetite and would never be satisfied with just one woman. But for this one day, she would let him care for her. They had shared something intimate and beautiful, and she didn't regret a moment of it.

"You can come in now," he called.

She padded quickly to the door of the bath chamber and gasped. Gold-veined marble walls encased a large room, in the center of which stood a giant porcelain tub with lion's claws for feet. To her surprise, Daniel was already relaxing in it.

"I thought I was going to bathe," Lily said.

"Of course you are. This tub is plenty large enough for two. You wouldn't deny me the pleasure of bathing with you, would you?"

"I haven't denied you any pleasures so far today, have I?" She couldn't help smiling.

"Come to me," he said.

She stepped into the tub. The water was warm and soothing as he nestled her back against him.

He touched her between her legs. "Does it hurt?"

"Not too much," she said. "Just a little residual soreness. The warm water feels heavenly."

He reached for a bar of scented soap and a soft cloth. He wet the cloth in the water, rubbed the soap on it, and placed it between Lily's legs. "Let me wash the blood from you. I'm so sorry to have caused you pain."

"You didn't." She gave a nervous laugh. "That is, I didn't mind."

"I'm glad." He wrung out the cloth and placed it on the side of the tub. He grabbed the soap again and smoothed it over Lily's body, caressing her with its lather.

"Mmm," Lily said, breathing deeply, "that's nice."

She opened her eyes and took in the sights of the chamber. The golden faucet was in the shape of a lion's head. A basin stood on a pedestal, also made of creamy white marble. A small door beyond led to a water closet, she assumed. "This is a beautiful bath chamber, and so modern. How long have you had it?"

"It's all new actually," Daniel said. "My mother had all the master bath chambers redone with the most efficient plumbing available after my father died. I was surprised to find it all when I returned from the continent."

"It's just decadent." Lily closed her eyes and inhaled the natural scent of bodies in warm water. "I don't know when I've enjoyed a bath more."

"Is that due to the modern plumbing, or the company?" Daniel smoothed his fingers over her breast and pinched her nipple lightly.

She swallowed. "I guess I couldn't have one without the other."

She angled her face toward him and he caught her lips in a delicate kiss. Carefully she turned around so she was facing him, her legs straddling his.

"If you're going to sit on me like that, I may have to take you again."

She ignored his comment and gazed into his eyes. "You know, you have the most amazing eyes I have ever seen. They're almost the color of emeralds, but not quite. There's a touch of blue in them, but not enough to call them teal or turquoise. I can't really describe the color, which is quite maddening, actually. There's almost an undertone of...violet, if that makes any sense. Violet, yes, and a midnight blue. It's like someone took an emerald, added just a touch of amethyst to it, and then melded it with a sapphire, but only on the bottom." Lily ran her thumbs lightly across his eyelashes. "So beautiful." She pulled him toward her and touched her lips lightly to his temple. "If I had some oil paints, the first color I would try to mix is the color of your eyes."

Daniel stared at her. He started to speak, but she continued, lacing her fingers through his hair.

"And your hair. It's so rich and thick. The color is like the afternoon sun shining through those high wispy clouds. I see highlights of burnt gold, and amber, and chestnut brown, and just a touch of silver."

"The silver is grey, Lily."

She reveled in the silk of his hair entwined in her fingers. "It feels like soft suede. I love how it falls in waves and touches your shoulders." She smiled and paused for a moment. Then, "I want to wash it for you."

"What?"

"Did I stutter? I said I want to wash your hair."

Daniel shook his head, smiling. "You are, without a doubt, the first woman who has ever asked that of me."

"I never claimed to be like any of your other women." Lily batted her eyes. "Now, may I wash your hair or not?"

"I could never deny you anything, love," Daniel said.

"Wonderful." Lily reached over and grabbed the pitcher from the wash stand next to the tub. "Now close your eyes."

Daniel obeyed as Lily poured warm water over his head until it was saturated. She grabbed a dry towel and dabbed his eyes. "You can open now." She took some soft soap in her hands and rubbed it into a lather between her palms. "Now, now, this won't hurt a bit." She smoothed the soap onto his head. Gently she massaged him, his wet locks sliding between her fingers. Her breasts rubbed against the wet hair on his chest, forcing her nipples into erect nubs.

Daniel closed his eyes and groaned. "You have sensational hands, Lily."

"So I've been told." She smiled.

He jerked against her. "You have?"

"By my art instructor, you cad!" She threaded her fingers through his hair one last time. "There, I think it's clean now. I love the feel of your hair, Daniel." She reached for the pitcher again. "Close your eyes. It's time to rinse." She drenched his head with warm water until the last trace of soap was removed. Gently she toweled his eyes. "All done. I bet your hair hasn't been that clean in ages."

Daniel stared at her, his eyes rife with mischief. She looked down. The ends of her long hair were slick with moisture and clung to the swell of her breasts.

"Your turn," he said, grabbing the pitcher and filling it with the warm bath water.

"Daniel, no!" Lily shouted, trying to scramble away from him. "My hair is long and thick. It will never dry in time!"

"Too late!" He poured the water over her head. He wiped her eyes and rubbed into her hair. "Your hair is so long." He added more soap, pulling it through to the ends of her tresses. "You've taught me something today, Lily. I never knew hair washing could be such an erotic experience."

"No doubt you find something erotic in every experience, Your Grace," Lily said, laughing.

He pushed her away slightly. "I don't ever want you to call me that again. At least not when we're alone."

"I was only teasing."

He gently pulled the suds through her hair and into the tub. "I love the way you say my name, Lily. I want to hear it all the time. Lean back now. I'm going to rinse your hair in the bath."

He eased her down until her head was floating on the

surface of the bath water. With one hand behind her back, steadying her, he rinsed the soap from her hair with the other. When the water was clouded with lather, he pulled her to him.

"Kiss me," he said.

Lily slid against his chest as her mouth found his. Daniel's arousal prodded against her as she straddled him, and she rubbed against it. Suddenly she couldn't kiss him hard enough, deep enough. She let her tongue wander into the deep recesses of his mouth, exploring every hidden crevice while grinding her pulsing sex against his hardened shaft. He groaned as she teased and stroked. She was near climax when a knock on the door startled her. She broke the kiss and looked up, quivering.

"That's just our lunch," Daniel said gruffly. He pressed his mouth to her cheek. "I'll make this up to you, I promise. Stay here. Don't come out until I call you." He left the tub, toweled himself off, and grabbed a dressing robe from a hook on the wall, closing the door of the bath chamber behind him.

Quietly Lily stepped out of the tub, smiling. What would Daniel do about his raging erection when he answered the door? No doubt the servants would act as if it were totally normal. For Daniel, it probably *was* totally normal. She wrapped herself in a dry towel, found another for her hair, and began wringing the moisture from it. It would never dry in time to meet Rose and the others for the afternoon. She would have to braid it wet and hope no one noticed.

Daniel opened the door and handed her a velvet dressing gown similar to the one he was wearing. "You look delectable in that towel, but I think you'll be more comfortable in this."

"I need to borrow a comb." She dropped the towel and put on the robe. "If I let my hair dry like this, I'll never get the snarls out."

"Of course." He grabbed a comb from a nearby shelf. "Here, allow me."

"You don't have to..."

"I want to. Your hair is beautiful, Lily."

"My hair is wet, Daniel. Ouch!"

"Sorry, love. I'm not used to combing long hair."

"All the more reason why you should let me do it." She took the comb from him. "I'll only be a minute." She quickly finished and replaced the comb on the shelf. "Shall we?"

Lunch had been set on a table by the bay window. Lily sat down and looked out onto a spectacular view of the luncheon on the front and side lawn. "Lord, my mother and my sister are down there."

"All the ladies are down there. It's nearly one. They'll be gathering for lunch and then for the lawn party afterward."

"Gossiping and talking of other frivolous nonsense, of course."

He filled a plate and handed it to her. "I hope you're hungry."

"Famished, actually. This looks delicious." She speared a quail egg with her fork and popped it into her mouth. "It looks like a pleasant afternoon. I love April, especially when it's warm like it is this year."

"Do you ride?" Daniel asked. "It's excellent weather for riding."

"I love animals, and I've always wanted to ride more," Lily said, "but I abhor riding sidesaddle. It's dreadfully uncomfortable. I never really understood it, anyway, and frankly, now that I have a keener, shall we say, understanding, of male anatomy, it seems to me that men should ride sidesaddle and women astride."

Daniel's laughter rang out like holiday bells. "Lily, I can't recall when I've had a more enjoyable time. I didn't know it was possible to have this much fun with a woman outside the bedchamber."

"We're still *in* the bedchamber," she said.

"You know what I mean. In fact, I don't think I've ever relished a woman's company more than I have today."

"You flatter me, Daniel. You'd better watch out, or I'm liable to take you seriously."

"I am serious."

She smiled at him. He was likely feeding her one of his many practiced lines, but her heart thumped anyway. The reasons for Rose's and Ally's interest in the opposite sex was becoming clearer. She cleared her throat. "Back to riding. My sister, Rose, is an excellent rider. She doesn't mind riding sidesaddle. Sometimes I take Thomas's gelding out and ride astride on his saddle. With his blessing, of course. If my parents knew, they'd probably lock me up."

"I'd like to take you riding."

"We'd need a chaperone."

"We'll take Thomas with us, or your sister."

"My twenty-year-old unmarried sister is hardly a suitable chaperone." Lily laughed aloud.

"What's so funny?"

"I'm talking about a suitable chaperone whilst I'm lunching, nearly naked, with a duke in his bedchamber. It's absurd, is it not?"

"Not to me. Now, about riding."

"Do I have to ride sidesaddle?"

"You can ride any way you want."

"That's very kind of you. Of course, you know I would

refuse if you made me ride sidesaddle." She laughed again.

"Damn it, Lily, I don't care what you do. As long as you do it with me."

Clearly he was joking, but she decided to ask for the world. "In that case, may I see the rest of your art collection? I'll need a private invitation."

"Of course, anytime you wish."

Even under the heavy velvet, her skin warmed. She was enjoying herself more than she ever thought she could with a man. They shared an easy banter unlike anything she had experienced. Nothing about being with him seemed awkward, which surprised her, given they hardly knew each other. He was very nearly perfect, but for his past. *But we only have today.* She could live with that. She had to.

She gazed out the window once again. The ladies took their lunch on the white wrought iron tables set up on the lawn. She frowned at the sight of Lady Amelia Gregory. She had to keep that woman away from Thomas.

"Daniel," she said sweetly.

"Yes?"

"Who prepares the seating charts for dinner?"

"My mother and Aunt Lucy, I suppose. Why do you ask?"

"I was wondering if you could do something for me."

"Anything."

"Well, I want to make sure that certain people are seated next to certain other people at dinner tonight. Is that possible?"

"Perhaps. Why do you care? Is there someone you wish to be seated with?"

"No, not me. I was wondering if my sister could sit next to Lord Evan Xavier. She seemed quite taken with him last night at the ball, and he with her. And Thomas seems quite enamored with Miss Emma Smythe."

"Is she the blond woman he was with last night?"

"Yes, do you know her?"

"I recognize the name. She's my banker's daughter."

"I had the pleasure of meeting her last evening. She's charming and intelligent. Frankly, my brother's taste in women hasn't always been so discriminating. Is there another attractive young woman with a brain who could sit on his other side?"

Daniel smiled and shook his head, but said nothing.

"Well, I'll think on it," Lily continued. "I don't want him seated next to Regina Wentworth. She's been trying to drag him to the altar for months, and truthfully she's a ninny. And keep that horrible Lady Amanda Gregory away from him too. She'll do anything to snag another title. As for my cousin, Alexandra, Lord Wentworth seems slightly interested in her, although she can do better. I'd prefer that he be kept away from me also. He's been trying to court me for the last year, and I'm not at all interested." Lily's mind raced with deviltry. "In fact, put Wentworth next to Amanda Gregory."

"It's Amelia Gregory, Lily."

"I don't give two figs what the doxy's name is, Daniel. Just keep her away from my brother. Put her next to Wentworth, and find some old lecherous codger for her other side. Now, for Alexandra, perhaps you could seat Lord Victor next to her."

Daniel spoke slowly. "Polk seems taken with you, Lily. You spent a lot of time with him last night."

"He's very nice and I did enjoy his company, but as you know, I'm not in the market for a husband. I think he and Alexandra would get on well, and she finds him quite attractive."

HELEN HARDT

"So you're not at all interested in Polk?"

"Not in the slightest."

"I'm glad to know that," Daniel said, smiling.

"No need to worry. Now, can you do all that, Daniel?"

Daniel shook his head and laughed.

"What is so funny?"

"You are adorable, do you know that?"

"Don't change the subject. Can you take care of this or not?"

"Lily, do you really expect me to remember everything you just said?"

"Of course. What's so difficult about it?"

"Why don't I just have the seating chart sent to your chamber later for your approval?"

"There's no need to tease me. I'm only asking for a simple little favor."

"Simple?" He chuckled. "I'll take care of it."

"Thank you." She leaned over and brushed her lips against his cheek. "Lunch was fabulous, but I really must go now." She stood and walked to where her clothes lay in a heap on the floor. "Could you help me with my corset and gown?"

"I'd rather help you out of them."

"I'm already out of them."

"Then stay out of them. Come back to bed with me."

"Didn't you say you had business to attend to this afternoon?"

"Yes, and I do, but I'd rather stay here with you. I did promise to make up for our unfortunate interruption in the bath." He eased the dressing gown off of her shoulders, caressing her arms as it fell to the ground.

"Oh..." She sighed. "No, I have to go. I must get back to my chamber and change into an afternoon dress. Goodness, what am I going to do about my hair?"

"Wear it down. It will dry in the afternoon sun, and you'll look ravishing." He stroked her nipples lightly with his thumbs.

"Stop that, I can't think." She reluctantly pushed his hands away. "And I couldn't possibly wear my hair down. I'm twenty-one, not twelve." She paused, regarding his handsome face. "How old are you, Daniel?"

"Thirty-two, though around you I feel no more than nineteen."

"Is that a compliment?"

"Yes, love. It is."

"Then thank you. I think." She turned again. "Now, please help me. I do have to go."

Daniel rose and strode toward her. "If you must."

When she was dressed, he turned her to face him and gently kissed her. Then he put on his own clothes. "I'll escort you to your chamber. We'll be discreet."

"I would appreciate that."

He pulled her close. "May I come to you tonight?" he whispered, his breath caressing her neck.

She trembled, her knees weakening. "You can't. I share a chamber with my sister."

"Then you come to me."

"Daniel...I..."

"Please."

"How could I possibly?"

"I'll figure something out. I'll come get you, or send someone for you."

"No. No one can know."

"There are servants here who are trustworthy. I'll take

care of it."

He kissed her lips, gently prying them open, taking her tongue with his. Lily reached for him, smoothing his still damp hair, caressing his muscled shoulders. As Daniel moved his mouth to her neck and nuzzled her with soft kisses, she inhaled the fresh clean male scent of him, pressing herself closer to his hard masculine body. Her nipples tightened and her sex throbbed. She still wanted him. But she had to say no.

"There is no need to prolong this affair, Daniel. I cannot come to you tonight."

"Lily, please."

"I've now had the experience of being in your bed. And I'm sure you have...other engagements."

"If you're sure, Lily. But I reserve the right to try to change your mind."

"You won't," she said, and walked swiftly out into the hallway.

CHAPTER FIVE

Lily changed into a light beige afternoon dress with a pattern of small green-and-white polka dots sprinkled across it. Her hair had dried considerably more than she had anticipated, so she sat while the maid braided it and pinned it into an attractive coiffure. Pleased with the results, she dismissed the maid and headed downstairs and out to the lawn. The ladies were finishing their dessert, a plum torte with Bavarian cream. She found her mother seated with her sister, aunt, and cousins.

Bending to kiss her mother's cheek, she said, "I'm so sorry to be tardy, Mummy."

"Where have you been, Lily?" the countess asked.

"You know me. I went out this morning to paint, and I lost track of time. I'm so dreadfully sorry."

"Aren't you hungry, dear?" Aunt Iris asked.

"Not at all. I had a rather large breakfast. I couldn't possibly eat another morsel until dinner."

"Would you at least like some dessert?" Rose asked. "This plum cake is delicious."

"No, thank you. I'm fine, really." She sat down in an empty chair next to Rose. "What have all of you been up to this morning?"

"I played the pianoforte in the main parlor for a while," Rose said. "I'm working on that new Beethoven piece, and Her Grace said I should use the pianoforte as often as I like. Sophie and Ally read while I played."

"That sounds enchanting," Lily said. "What about you, Mummy?"

"Auntie Iris and I visited with Her Grace and Miss Landon a bit. Did you know that Miss Landon and Auntie Iris were best friends as girls?"

"No, I didn't. Auntie, why have you never mentioned that before?"

"Oh, I don't know. I had too much else to think about when the earl was alive, I suppose. It was good to talk to Lucy again."

"Tell me, do you know why she never married?" Lily asked.

"Yes, she was head over heels in love with an Irish sailor. They were betrothed, but he died at sea. Lucy's father never approved of the match and made no secret of the fact that he was glad Nolan had perished. A month later, Her Grace married the duke, and poor Lucy was forgotten."

"How sad," Alexandra said. "She never met another man that she wanted to marry?"

"No, never," Iris replied. "Her Grace made a place for Lucy here, so she could escape their parents. She has lived here since, and she and I lost touch eventually."

"I'm so glad you've gotten reacquainted," Rose said. "How is it that you first met Miss Landon?"

"She and I are the same age. The Landons had a London townhouse near ours."

"Is Her Grace older or younger than Lucy?" Sophie asked.

"Older. She's fifty-four."

Lily did some rapid calculations in her head. That meant she had been twenty-two when she had Daniel.

Aunt Iris continued, "We all spent time together when

our families were in London. Her Grace was being courted by an earl when she was seventeen, and the three of us used to follow her around and spy on them." Aunt Iris laughed. "She was actually quite good about it. Lucy and I were fifteen, and your mother but eleven. What fun we had!"

"An earl?" Lily said. "What about the duke?"

"The earl had his heart set on someone else, actually. He broke Her Grace's heart, and he didn't marry until many years later. Her Grace married the duke when she was twenty. They had known each other for only a week. The duke approached Her Grace's father, and a betrothal agreement was reached before Her Grace had even met the duke."

"I wonder why the duke chose Her Grace," Rose said. "He probably could have had whomever he wanted."

"Maggie—I mean Her Grace—was exotically beautiful," Aunt Iris continued. "Her hair was dark blond and her eyes the most remarkable emerald green. Her hair is lighter now, but she's still a handsome woman for her age. Her intelligence was well known also. Most likely the duke thought she would bear smart and handsome heirs, which she did, of course."

"That's fascinating," Lily said. "Whatever happened to the earl she was in love with?"

Aunt Iris grinned. "He married your mother."

Lily widened her eyes into saucers. "You're joking. Mummy!"

Lady Ashford smiled. "I was just a child when your father was courting the duchess. We renewed our acquaintance about six years later, when I was seventeen. By that time Her Grace had been married to the duke for two years. She had already produced an heir and was expecting another."

Daniel. Lily smiled to herself, imagining the beautiful boy slumbering in Her Grace's belly, with hair more tantalizing than his mother's and eyes like no other.

"You look dreamy, Lily," Rose said. "What are you thinking about?"

"Nothing," Lily said abruptly.

"It is incredibly romantic," Sophie said.

"What's so romantic about it? The duke forced Her Grace to marry him."

"Actually, Her Grace grew to love the duke," Aunt Iris said. "They had a happy marriage. She was devastated when the duke and Morgan were taken from her last year. Thank goodness Lucy was here to take care of her. The duke—that is, the new duke—was no help at all."

"You shouldn't speak ill of our host, Iris," the countess said.

"You're right of course, Flora. I'll say nothing more."

Lily fought a strong urge to defend Daniel. Suppressing the odd feeling, she nodded to Rose.

"Mummy," Rose said on cue, "do excuse my interruption, but we—that is, the four of us—would like to walk about the estate a bit."

"That's fine," Lady Ashford said, "unless you have an objection?" She nodded to Aunt Iris.

"Oh, to be young again," Aunt Iris sighed. "Do go ahead. But stay out of trouble."

"That means you, Lily," the countess said.

"Mummy, whatever do you mean?" Lily asked.

"You know very well what I mean. Have a good time, then."

The girls giggled as they walked away.

"I noticed our brother dancing with a lovely blonde last

evening," Rose said.

"I had the pleasure of talking to Emma and Thomas last night, Rose," Lily said. "I am thrilled with their friendship."

"She must be perfect then," Rose said. "You're terribly hard on the girls Thomas associates with. Now tell me"—she turned to the others—"what shall we do? Did you find any spectacular places while you were out painting this morning, Lily?"

Lily fought a smile as she thought of the spectacular place she *had* found—Daniel's bedchamber. "I spent most of the time in one place, and it's more for painting than for fun. Let's explore a little. This estate is absolutely beautiful. I do think I love it more than our own. How did all of you enjoy the ball last night? Did any of you meet anyone interesting?"

"I danced with your Lord Wentworth twice," Alexandra said.

"Please, he's not *my* Lord Wentworth. You may certainly have him."

"I'm not sure I want him." She lowered her voice to a whisper. "He stole a kiss on the terrace."

"No!" Rose said. "I can't believe it."

"Believe it. And you were right about kissing, Lily. His lips were sticky, and he tried to push his tongue into my mouth."

Rose and Sophie gasped.

"I was only talking about kissing Wentworth, Ally," Lily said. "I'm sure that we can't judge all men by his efforts." She smiled to herself. How right she was!

"Why on earth did you go to the terrace with him?" Sophie asked.

"Curiosity, I suppose. I won't do it again."

"Still, I'm a little jealous, even if the kiss wasn't to your liking," Rose said. Then, "Oh, that reminds me. Lord Evan asked me to go riding with him tomorrow. I was hoping you could go along, Lily, as our chaperone."

"Me?"

"Of course," Rose said. "You're older than I."

"By only eleven months, and I'm unmarried."

"Goodness, Lily, since when are you so sensitive about convention? It's just a ride during a house party. Dozens of others are likely to be about."

"Of course I'll go along," Lily said. "I take it you found Xavier acceptable then?"

"Yes, I had a lovely time."

"Did he take any liberties?" Alexandra asked.

"Goodness, Ally," Sophie said. "Is that all you think about?"

"Well?" Alexandra asked again.

"No, but he did ask me to call him by his Christian name. Isn't Evan a lovely sounding name?"

"Yes, it is," Sophie said. "Oh, look. There's a little lake up ahead."

"We've been talking so much that I haven't been paying a bit of attention to the scenery," Lily said. "But I love the idea of a lake. Maybe we can go wading."

"Or swimming!" Alexandra said.

"Dear Ally," Lily laughed. "I admit the idea intrigues me, but it's only April. It's a delightful afternoon, but the water will be cold. We'd likely freeze to death."

"No harm in checking, is there?" Alexandra ran toward the lake. "Last one there has to kiss Wentworth!"

"Goodness, we'd better all hurry," Lily said, giggling. "Trust me, you don't want that fate."

By the time they reached the lake, Alexandra had already kicked off her shoes and stockings and was pulling up her skirts and heading toward the water. She dipped her foot in. "You're not going to believe this. It's actually *warm*."

What had appeared to be a small lake was actually a large pool, fed by a stream of water cascading from a jagged grey rock formation. Steam rose from the surface of the water, coiling upward in cloudy drifts. Lily hurriedly removed her shoes and stockings and dipped her foot in. "It *is* warm. How can that be, do you suppose?"

"Likely it's an offshoot from the hot springs in Bath," Rose said. "They're not far from here."

"I see why Lord Evan adores you, Rose," Lily said. "You're so bright. That must be so."

"Then swimming is definitely on the agenda." Alexandra turned her back to Lily. "Here, undo me."

"This is highly improper." Sophie said.

"Ally, Sophie is right," Rose said. "Anyone could come by and see us."

"Nonsense," Lily said. "The men are all on the hunt and won't be back for hours yet. And the women are at the lawn party. Besides, we've been walking for almost an hour, and how many people have we seen along the way?"

"None, but..." Sophie fidgeted.

"There you are, dear." Lily loosened Alexandra's corset and turned around. "Now you do me."

"Lily, we don't have towels," Rose said tentatively.

"True," Sophie said, "and our undergarments will be wet. We simply mustn't—"

Alexandra smiled and raised her eyebrows. "Then we'll swim in the *nude*."

Sophie clasped her cheek. "Where do you get such ideas, Ally?"

"I read, Sophie. A little gem called *The Ruby*."

Lily warmed as Alexandra loosened her corset. She'd heard of *The Ruby*, an underground paper that published erotic stories. But how on earth had Ally seen it?

"What is *The Ruby?*" Sophie shook her head. "Never mind. I don't want to know."

Alexandra laughed. "I'm sure you don't. But we're perfectly alone here. And if we don't wear any garments, we can dry in the sun before we put our clothes back on."

"We should at least keep our undergarments on," Rose said.

"By all means, if it makes you feel better to have a soggy chemise and drawers, then do so," Alexandra said, "but I'm going in naked."

"So am I!" Lily tossed her dress in a heap and stepped out of her corset and drawers.

"Lily, at least keep your chemise on," Rose said.

"For goodness' sake, Rose, there's not another person within sight."

Lily lifted the delicate garment over her head and ran into the water where Alexandra was already splashing around. The warm waves flowed over her naked form like a sensual embrace. Her mind wandered to the bath she had shared with Daniel that morning, but she shooed the thought away. She drifted over to Alexandra, where the water was nearly five feet deep. Her breasts floated on the surface as she splashed her cousin.

"Wouldn't it be wonderful," Alexandra said, grinning, "if some young men came by right about now?"

"That would be embarrassing, Ally." But Lily couldn't help giggling.

"No, it would be hilarious," Alexandra continued. "They would be embarrassed beyond measure. They would see us frolicking about like two naked water nymphs, laughing and splashing each other. They would probably fall right off their horses!"

Lily turned to where they had left their clothes. "You were kidding, weren't you Ally? I see a horse yonder."

"Oh my." Sophie gestured to them. "Stay under the water. If he comes close enough to see, duck your heads at the same time." She pulled Rose away behind a cluster of large trees.

"Who could it be other than some servant out and about?" Lily said.

"You're probably right," Alexandra agreed. "Let's just keep our treasures under the water until he goes away."

"Oh dear God." Lily gulped.

The beautiful hair she had washed and caressed earlier drifted in the slight breeze. Daniel sat atop a majestic black stallion. He wore a brown riding outfit and his shirt was open at the neck. His hair blew softly in the warm April breeze.

"What is it, Lily?" Alexandra nudged her arm. "Do you recognize him?"

"I'm afraid so. It's the duke."

"I'm going to faint," Alexandra said.

Lily steadied her cousin. Their secret would be safe with Daniel, she was sure, but she didn't know how to tell Ally without divulging her affair. "He probably doesn't see us. Come on, let's just move over here, towards the rocks, until he goes away."

Daniel rode closer, guiding his horse around the piles of

clothing. He looked out into the pool. Ally was turned away, but his eyes met Lily's. She gave him a quick nervous grin. His head rolled back in gales of laughter as he turned his horse around and rode away. When she could no longer see him in the distance, she poked Ally. "You can turn around now. He's gone."

"He saw us," Alexandra said. "I heard him laughing."

"He couldn't have known who we were. Our backs were turned. There's no need to worry."

"He may have recognized you, Lily. I saw you dancing with him last night."

Lily's skin heated, though not from the steaming bath. "While he was dancing with me, he wasn't looking at my back. How would he recognize me?"

Rose and Sophie returned as Lily and Ally stepped out of the water.

"It was the duke!" Sophie said.

"Yes, we know," Lily said. "I'm sure he didn't know who we were."

"He's so handsome," Ally gushed.

Lily looked away. "Of course, he's attractive, but you know his reputation."

"I think I could overlook a reputation to dance with such a delectable man," Alexandra said dreamily. "How was he?"

Lily jumped backward. "What do you mean by that?"

"As a dancer, of course, you ninny. What did you think I meant?"

Lily's heart hammered against her chest. "He...he's marvelous on his feet. Better than Thomas even."

"How did you come to dance with him?" Sophie asked.

"He cut in on Lord Victor, actually. I'm sure he was just

being polite."

"Dear, it's more polite *not* to cut in," Alexandra said. "He obviously wanted to dance with you."

"We only danced once. That's hardly anything to get worked up about."

"Of course not," Sophie said. "But we should keep an eye on him. Maybe he has decided to court a woman honorably. He is a duke now, after all. He'll need an heir."

"He isn't going to get one from me." Lily brushed the droplets of water from her arms and torso, shaking from the chill of leaving the bath's warmth. Or was she shaking for another reason?

Dear Lord, what have I gotten into?

★ ★ ★ ★

Daniel was still chuckling when he returned to his stables. He should have known Lily would find the hot pool. The sight of her had been almost too much. He hadn't been able to see her lovely body under the water, but oh, he had imagined it. If the other woman hadn't been there, he would have stripped off his clothes and jumped in with her. And then he would have shagged her until they were both sated and exhausted.

What an amazing woman she was. Beautiful, yes, but he had never lacked the company of beautiful women. No, it wasn't her beauty that fascinated him.

He couldn't recall when he had been in a more pleasant mood. He hummed to himself as he put his saddle away and brushed Midnight's coat. Midnight snorted, and Daniel grabbed an apple from the bushel basket next to his stall and fed him. "There you are, old boy."

"Hello, Daniel."

He turned to see Amelia Gregory holding her nose.

"My goodness, doesn't anyone ever clean up in here?"

"This is a stable, Amelia. If the smell of horse shit offends you, I suggest you stay out of here."

"I missed you at the luncheon today."

"There were no men at the luncheon. Why in the world would you think I would be there?"

Amelia didn't reply. Instead, "Why didn't you go on the hunt?"

"I had some business to attend to this afternoon that required my immediate attention."

"Did it go well?"

"Yes, very well." He smoothed the curry comb over Midnight's flanks. "If you don't mind, Amelia, I must attend to my horse."

"Don't you have servants for that?"

"I prefer to take care of Midnight myself."

"Do you mind if we talk while you groom him?"

Daniel cleared his throat. "I'd rather not. I don't think there is anything more that needs to be said between us."

"But there is, darling. I have wonderful news." She reached toward him. "I have decided to forgive you."

"Forgive me? For what?"

"For tossing me out on my arse last night, dear. Obviously something was bothering you, and I should have been able to read you better. It's all my fault really. I want you to know that I still want to be with you, and when you're feeling up to it, I want you to come to me."

God. He hadn't expected this. "I'm sorry, Amelia. I won't change my mind. I no longer desire your company."

"How can you say that, after all the pleasures we've shared? I thought we had a relationship."

"Relationship?"

"Of course, I haven't always been faithful to you, darling, but you've hardly been faithful to me, either. Still, we both knew we would end up together someday, did we not?"

"I knew nothing of the sort. I never wanted a relationship, nor did you. At least that's what you led me to believe. Our liaison was purely physical, and although it was enjoyable, I no longer wish to pursue it."

Amelia reached up to caress his cheek. "I don't believe a word of that, Daniel. You and I were meant to be together."

No spark from her touch. Nothing. "I'm afraid you're wrong."

She moved forward, her mouth only inches from his, her breath blowing quick puffs of air against his lips. "You know that no one else can make you feel as I do."

Daniel grabbed her wrist. "Amelia, don't do this."

"I would do anything for you, you know. If there's anything we haven't tried in bed, although I can't imagine that there is, I'll do it for you. Just tell me."

"This has nothing to do with our antics in the bedchamber."

"Please, Daniel, don't throw me aside. I can make you happy. Have you forgotten?" She lowered her voice to a husky rasp. "I'll ride you hard and fast until you're grunting and groaning. I'll suck your cock until I'm blue in the face—"

He quickly tore her hand from his face. "Amelia, it's over."

Her face twisted into rage. "You are a scoundrel, Daniel."

"My lady, I've been called worse by better women than you."

★ ★ ★ ★

Amelia flounced out of the stables, seething. Oh, she'd show him, one way or another. He was hers, and by the end of this wretched house party, he would bloody well know it.

CHAPTER SIX

Lily and Rose returned to their chamber, sneaking up the servants' stairway to avoid Lily being seen with wet hair and slightly damp clothes.

Rose yawned. "I'm incredibly sleepy. We were up so late last night at the ball, and now all this ruckus this afternoon. I do believe I will nap for hours. I don't know how you were able to drag yourself out of bed so early this morning, Lily."

"My love of art knows no bounds."

Rose yawned again, stretching herself out on her bed. "My love of sleep knows no bounds." She closed her eyes.

Lily lay down on her own bed. She couldn't ever recall being quite so content as she was at this very moment. Life was too short not to extract out all the pleasure one could. Should she reconsider her decision not to go to Daniel tonight? He obviously wanted her, and she wanted him. They had no future, but she didn't want a future with him anyway. *Carpe Diem*, as her Latin tutor used to say. Seize the day. *And the night*, she thought, giggling to herself.

She padded to the door when she heard a soft knock. A maid stood there, holding a large leather case. "Shh," Lily said, holding her finger to her lips. "My sister is sleeping."

"His Grace bid me bring this to you. When you're done with it, you're to leave it outside your chamber door."

"His Grace? What in the world?" Lily said, as the maid scurried quickly away.

Lily sat down on her bed and opened the portfolio. Inside was the seating arrangement for dinner. Each name had been inked with a quill onto a small square of parchment that stuck without adhesive to a felt surface. It was an ingenious system. Seating could be changed at a moment's notice. But why had Daniel sent it to her? Surely he didn't mean for her to prepare the seating arrangement for the entire population of the house party. What would the duchess say? There were four tables, each seating fifty.

Flabbergasted, she studied the arrangement as it was. Well, there was certainly room for a lot of improvement. Rose was seated next to Wentworth. That would have to go. She moved the small name cards around. Daniel did send this to her, after all. He had said he would take care of it. Perhaps he really didn't remember everything she had asked. She had been speaking rather quickly.

First things first. Amelia Gregory had to be far away from Thomas. Lily sat her at the outer table, the one farthest from the duke's. On one side she placed Wentworth, and on the other she decided on Lord Ludley, Wentworth's bachelor uncle. He was bald and portly and he tended to salivate excessively. He was known to frequent brothels and debauch unwilling women whenever possible. Perfect.

Turning to the next table, Lily arranged Rose next to Xavier. She sat Thomas on Rose's other side and Emma next to him. That would keep Thomas and Rose both focused on their own choices. At the next table, she maneuvered Alexandra next to Lord Victor Polk and Sophie next to Van Arden.

That is that. She closed the portfolio, but opened it again quickly. She had almost forgotten to look at her own situation. She was seated at the same table as Ally, between two men whose names she didn't recognize. Hoping the duchess knew what she was doing, she left it as it was.

She took a quick glance at the duke's table. Her parents and Aunt Iris were seated there. She closed the leather case, quietly opened the door of her chamber, and set it against the wall outside. Rose was snoring lightly, and Lily's eyes blurred. She lay down on her bed and closed them. Visions of Daniel appeared in her mind, and she smiled as she drifted off to sleep.

★ ★ ★ ★

Rose and Lily awoke in time to wash and dress for dinner. Rose chose an off-white gown that highlighted her fair skin and peachy complexion. Lily wore soft plum satin, with a plunging neckline that drew attention to her ample fullness.

"Why you have your gowns cut so low is beyond me," Rose said.

"Because it looks good on me. It's stylish too. You're always telling me I should follow the dictates more closely."

"You might try leaving a little more to the imagination."

"Mummy approved all of our gowns, Rose. What more do we need?"

"Mummy wants you to catch a husband, Lily. I'm sure she flaunted her own charms in her day."

Lily giggled. "Yes, she may have. I had no idea that Papa was so enamored with her that he jilted the duchess."

"You heard Auntie," Rose said. "Papa didn't court Mummy until several years later."

"Just the same, perhaps he saw something in her when she was young. It's possible."

"I suppose." Rose sighed. "The romance of it all... I do

hope I meet someone like Papa or the duke someday."

"The duke?"

"The old duke, of course," Rose said. "Lord Evan is charming, but he's a second son. He'll never come into a title of his own."

"That's silly, Rose. The title doesn't make the man."

"Of course, you're right. I suppose we had better go down now."

"I'm right behind you." Lily snatched her reticule and followed Rose out of the chamber.

Downstairs they met their parents in the main parlor. Thomas was there also, beaming as he conversed with Emma. He looked up as Lily entered and frowned slightly at her neckline. She rolled her eyes and strode toward him.

"Thomas, how was the hunt?" she asked.

"I enjoyed it very much. But it sounds like you had an equally enjoyable day. Miss Smythe was just telling me about it." He winked.

"Emma?" Lily said, her voice wavering.

"I ran into Lady Alexandra earlier." Emma smiled. "Don't worry. I left out the good parts."

"What good parts?" Thomas asked, turning back to Emma.

Lily laughed. "Oh, Thomas, some things are between girlfriends only. Shall we go into dinner?"

"It would be my honor to escort you both in," Thomas said. "I'll be the envy of every man here, with two such lovely ladies on my arm."

Thomas found his seat next to Emma and held out her chair for her. "I'll be back. I need to escort Lily to her seat."

"I think I'm over at that next table, Thomas." Lily gestured.

"Across from Ally."

They said a quick hello to Alexandra and Lord Victor as Thomas guided Lily to her seat.

"I don't see your name here, Lily. You must be at another table."

"That's impossible," Lily said. "What on earth?"

"Let's look around then," Thomas said. "Maybe you're at my table."

Lily's name was nowhere to be found there, so they moved to the outer table. *I suppose it would serve me right to have to sit at a table with Amelia Gregory.* Thank goodness, her name wasn't there.

"Thomas, I don't know what's going on." Lily feared for a moment that she might have forgotten to put her own name card back on the chart, or perhaps it had slipped out of the portfolio when the maid fetched it from outside her chamber.

"There's one table left," Thomas said.

"But that's the duke's table. I couldn't possibly..."

He took her arm and led her over. Her mother and father were already seated, as was Aunt Iris, the duchess, her sister, and several others. Lily gawked when Daniel entered. He looked absolutely magnificent in full ducal regalia, a deep red velvet jacket, black silk cravat, and black trousers that highlighted the tight musculature of his legs. His beautiful hair was pulled back in a queue. Her heart leaped.

He approached Lily and Thomas. "Good evening, Jameson, my lady. Jameson, may I have the honor of escorting your lovely sister to her place?"

Thomas's smile was fake, but he nodded. "Of course, Your Grace."

Daniel smiled down at Lily. "I think this is the first time

I've seen you with clothes on today," he whispered.

Lily's skin blazed. "I had clothes on when I was painting," she whispered back. "What have you done? I'm supposed to be at the other table."

"Did you really think I would let you have total control of the seating?" He smiled. "You're sitting next to me." He led her to the head of the table.

"What will people think? This is highly"—she searched for the right word—"controversial."

"No one will notice. Or care, for that matter. My mother and Aunt Lucy approved the seating arrangement after you and I both improved it. You're the daughter of the Earl of Ashford. It's perfectly proper for you to sit at my table."

"But..."

He pulled out her chair. She looked around the room before she sat down. He was right. No one glanced their way. Except for one person seated at the outer table. Lady Amelia Gregory was glaring at her. Lily smiled tersely in Amelia's direction and sat down to the right of Daniel's place at the head of the table. On her other side was the Earl of Madison, his wife, and then her own parents. Madison was well known to be hopelessly devoted to his wife, so he would likely pay no attention to Lily. Seated on Daniel's other side was the dowager Countess of Bourough, an elderly woman who was hard of hearing, and next to her was her companion, Viscount Pomeroy, a widower ten years her junior who acted as her escort in return for her generously lavishing her fortune on him. Interesting choices. If Lily hadn't known otherwise, she would have thought Daniel had arranged the seating so that he would have no choice but to focus his attention on her.

Appetizers of pâté de campagne and foie gras were

followed by a clear beef consommé, which was light but tasty. As Lily ate her soup quietly, the Earl of Madison spoke over her to Daniel.

"We missed you on the hunt today, Your Grace."

"I'm sorry to have missed it," Daniel replied. "I was otherwise engaged."

"Business, I suppose?"

"Yes, but after my business concluded early in the afternoon, I took Midnight out on a ride. It was a most pleasant excursion. I saw some splendid rare wildlife."

Lily swallowed a spoonful of soup and nervously choked back a giggle. She reached for her napkin.

"Are you quite all right?" Madison asked her.

"Yes, thank you, my lord," Lily said into her napkin. She reached for her goblet of claret, took a sip, and looked sideways at Daniel. His beautiful eyes gleamed at her, and his full lips were curved into a puckish grin. Madison had turned his attention back to his wife.

She couldn't help herself. "Tell me, Your Grace, could you describe the wildlife?"

"Such rare and exotic creatures are seldom seen in these parts, my lady," Daniel said. "Had I a sketchbook on my person, I would have stopped and tried to put the beauty to paper."

Lily nearly jumped out of her seat. "You sketch, Dan— Your Grace?"

"I do indeed, my lady. Do you?"

"Yes. But I prefer painting."

"So you are interested in art, then?"

"I'm utterly passionate about it, Your Grace."

"Then it would be my honor to show you the art here at Laurel Ridge. We have a marvelous collection. Would you care to accompany me after dinner?"

She smiled. "You know I would."

"Fine then. I'll come fetch you after my cigar and port."

Lily started on her second course, a poached salmon with a creamy dill sauce, and looked around the table. Daniel had been right. No one seemed to notice their conversation. Daniel engaged her, asking about her life in London and at the Ashford estate in Hampshire. The subject somehow came to the previous Christmas, and the kiss Wentworth had stolen.

"It was awful, really," Lily said. "I didn't think I wanted to kiss anyone again after that."

"Have you changed your mind?" he asked, his voice low.

She nodded, smiling. "Tell me a little about your family, Your Grace."

"Well, you know my father and brother are gone now."

"Yes, I'm so sorry about that. It must have been very hard on you and your mother. Were you close to either of them?"

"Not especially. I was closer to my mother. My father spent most of his time with Morgan, because he was the heir. Morgan was completely educated in the management of the estate and the affairs of the House of Lords and would have made a fine duke. Now the title has been thrust upon me, and I'm wholly unprepared for it."

Lily stared at Daniel's handsome face. Worry lines creased his forehead. Odd that she hadn't noticed them before. How could such a formidable man sound so unsure of himself?

"You seem to know what you're doing," she said.

"At least my bankers and stockbrokers do, and that's encouraging. And my mother is very intelligent and was always involved in the affairs of the estate. I've learned quite a bit from her. You remind me of her, actually."

"Do I?"

"Yes, she defied convention herself in her day. No woman should have been involved in such business affairs, but my father valued her opinion and sought her advice frequently."

"I always knew I liked her." Lily smiled. "Did you know that her sister and my Auntie Iris were best friends when they were girls?"

"No, I didn't."

"Neither did I until this afternoon. Evidently they lost touch over the years." Lily lowered her voice. "And do you want to know something else?"

"What, love?" Daniel whispered.

"My father once courted your mother."

Daniel smiled mockingly. "Really?"

"You knew that?"

"I did."

"Just think, if they had married, neither one of us would exist," Lily said.

"I'd rather not imagine a world without you in it." Daniel squeezed Lily's thigh under the table. "Do you want to know something?"

"What?"

Daniel lowered his voice until it was barely audible. "I've been thinking about you all day."

Lily's blood turned to molten nectar, and her heart pulsated wildly. Warmth crept up her breasts to her face.

"You look amazing in that dress, but I know you'll look even more delicious out of it."

Lily squirmed as moisture penetrated the thin fabric of her undergarments. "You must stop talking like that."

"Why? No one's paying attention to us."

"Because, it makes me feel all..."

Daniel grinned. "That's the idea."

★ ★ ★ ★

After dinner, Lily relaxed with the girls on the front terrace, enjoying coffee and dessert, while the men retired to the back terrace for cigars and port. The others pounced on Lily.

"How did you manage to get seated next to him?" Alexandra asked.

"I'm not exactly sure." At least that was the truth.

"He seemed to enjoy your company," Sophie ventured. "It looked like he was conversing mostly with you, from what I could see."

"It was either that or try to talk to Lady Bourough, who is deaf as a stone, or Lord Madison, who can't keep from drooling over his wife."

"Who cares?" Alexandra said. "You got to sit with him. Is he agreeable?"

"He's very nice. And charming, as one would expect given his reputation with the ladies."

"Not to mention, devastatingly handsome," Alexandra added.

"Yes, there is that," Lily agreed. "Tell me, Ally, how did you get on with Polk at dinner?"

"He was agreeable, but I actually preferred Mr. Landon, who was on my other side. He's a cousin of the duke."

"Really?"

"Second cousin actually. His father and Her Grace are cousins. He owns several businesses here and in America. It sounds like he's worth a fortune."

"Ally, don't go barreling after a heavy purse," Sophie warned. "There are more important things."

"We can't sponge off of Aunt Flora and Uncle Crispin forever, Sophie," Alexandra said. "And damn it, I don't want to be poor."

"No one does, dear," Sophie said. "But there are more essential matters, like love. Do you really want to end up in a loveless marriage with a tyrant like Father?"

"Of course not, and if any of us are lucky enough to find a love match, I'll be the first one to hoot and holler in glee. But in the meantime, I'm willing to settle for money, especially if he's handsome, which Mr. Landon is."

"Well, as long as you have standards," Sophie said, her tone sardonic.

They conversed and laughed until a maid approached them. "My lady?" she said to Lily.

"Yes?"

"I was bid to bring you to the library."

"Whatever for?"

"His Grace wants to see you."

"Oh." How would she explain this to the others? "He's going to show me the estate's art collection. I nearly forgot. Will you all excuse me?"

They all stared at her wide-eyed.

"Would any of you like to come? Laurel Ridge is supposed to have some of the finest art."

Alexandra beamed. "No, no, dear. We'll wait right here for you. Do tell us all about it when you're done."

"You will have a chaperone, won't you, Lily?" Sophie said.

"I'm sure His Grace has it all arranged." Lily stood. "Do enjoy your evening, then."

Lily followed the maid back into the house and dismissed her. Walking quietly through the entrance hall, she paused to glance inside the enormous dining room where servants were cleaning up after dinner. She continued down the hallway, looking for the library, but stopped when she came to a looking glass hanging on the wall by a small table. She quickly assessed her appearance, biting her lips, pinching her cheeks, and tucking a few stray hairs behind her ears.

"Good evening, love."

"Goodness," she said, nearly jumping. "Do you just appear out of thin air?"

Daniel smiled. "Come with me."

"Wait a moment," she said. "Shouldn't we have a chaperone?"

"Does anyone know you're with me?"

"My sister and cousins."

"Ah. And I assume one of them was your nude bathing friend?" Daniel's eyes sparkled.

"My cousin. Alexandra."

He winked. "I think our secret is safe with them."

He led her farther down the hallway to an enormous two story room filled with books and art. The overhead chandelier had been lit, and the soft velvety lighting cast brightness upon shelves and shelves of books. Lily breathed in the alluring scents of leather and parchment. She loved reading nearly as much as art, and this room was a treasure trove.

"This is magnificent." She hurried toward the rows and rows of beautifully bound volumes. Books of history and books of law, volumes of poetry and Greek mythology, novels, reference volumes, and religious treatises. Lily ran her fingers over rows of books, taking in their texture and warmth. "If I had the time, I'd devour everything in here."

"I thought you wanted to see art this evening," Daniel said.

"Oh, I do. I just never imagined seeing so many books at once. This simply dwarfs the library at our estate."

"Feel free to borrow anything you'd like while you're here."

"I intend to. I'm going to finish my painting tomorrow morning, and then I'm going to curl up under a tree with a good book. Doesn't that sound heavenly?"

He smiled. "It actually does. In the afternoon, though, I'd like you to go riding with me."

"Of course, I'd love to." Then, "Oh, Lord Evan asked Rose to go riding, and I think she wants me to go along. I'm sorry. I forgot."

"That's not a problem," Daniel said. "We'll all go together."

"I don't know." Lily chewed on her lip. "Are you sure we should go with others? They might think you're courting me."

"Perhaps I am." His gaze met hers.

Lily laughed aloud. "You're too funny, Daniel. If you were courting me honorably, you wouldn't have taken me to bed. And if I'd wanted to be courted, I wouldn't have gone."

Daniel looked away. "I suppose you're correct about that. I've never courted anyone before anyway. I'm not sure I even know how to go about it."

"I think you would probably do fine. You're quite charming. Any woman would be thrilled to have you court her."

"Even you?" He gave her his lazy half smile.

The warmth of a blush crept over Lily's skin. "Well, I... You certainly are appealing, naturally. And we seem to get on well enough. But I don't have to remind you that you have a rakish reputation, and of course, you know I'm not looking for courtship of any kind."

"You've made your point, Lily." He spoke gruffly. "But I see no harm in going riding with your sister tomorrow. I'll speak to Xavier about it in the morning."

"That sounds fine. Oh, Daniel!" Lily spied a portrait of two small boys on the far wall of the library. She hurried toward it to examine it more closely. The boys didn't look to be more than four or five, and they were both beautiful, one with light chestnut hair and brown eyes, the other with blond hair and green eyes. "My God, that's you, isn't it?"

"Yes, that's Morgan and me in 1825. I remember sitting for that damned portrait when all I wanted to do was play."

Lily reached to explore the texture in her mind. "The technique is wonderful. It's beautifully done, but the artist didn't get the color of your eyes quite right, did he? It's signed MLF. Who is that?"

"Morgana Landon Farnsworth. My mother."

"Really? She is quite a talent, isn't she, even if she didn't do your eyes justice."

"The eyes look all right to me," Daniel said.

"How can you say that? Your mother is gifted, to be sure, but she made your eyes green."

"My eyes *are* green."

"Well, yes, but your eyes are unique. They're not just garden-variety green. They're deep and expressive, with hues of forest and blue and violet. I'll have to try to recreate the color, if I can ever get my father to allow me to have some blasted oils." Lily sighed softly. "My, you were a beautiful child. I just want to reach out and pinch those adorable little cheeks!"

"You're welcome to pinch any part of me, Lily." He grinned rakishly and put his arms around her.

"Daniel! Anyone could walk in."

"I'm not sure I care," he said, nuzzling her hair.

"You are a rogue! Now let go of me and show me some more art."

"All right." He led her to a beautiful oak table and pointed to an ornate coppery red vase. "This is from China, the Ming dynasty. It's dated around 1500."

"It's lovely. I've heard of Ming vases. They're quite valuable aren't they? Are you sure it's safe to have it sitting out here?"

"This is a reproduction. The actual vase is in the estate's safe. My father agreed with your assessment, especially when Morgan and I were young. Sometime maybe I'll show you the real one."

"I'd love that."

She followed him to a portrait of an older gentleman.

"Do you know who this is?" he asked.

"Yes, I think so. It's George Washington, the first president of the colonies."

"It's the United States, love. Since last century, remember?"

She gave him a friendly smack on the arm. "Who painted it?"

"An American artist named Gilbert Stuart. My father got it when he went to America shortly after the turn of the century. Many peers faulted him for hanging it here, but he always admired the Americans and their courage and fortitude. He said they offered a great lesson in pride and perseverance. This painting reminded him of that."

"Your father sounds like a wise man."

"He was. About some things. I'm hoping some of it rubbed off on me along the way. Here, this one I think you'll like."

They stopped in front of a full-length portrait of his parents, the Duke and Duchess of Lybrook. "This was commissioned shortly after they were married. My mother was actually pregnant with Morgan at the time, but the artist depicted her otherwise."

Daniel's father, Charles Farnsworth, the sixth Duke of Lybrook, was built like his son, tall and strong with broad shoulders and lean hips. His hair was a light chestnut, and his eyes the color of cinnamon. His face had the same fine lines and strong jaw that Daniel possessed. Morgana, the Duchess of Lybrook, was as Aunt Iris had described her, exotically beautiful, with hair that rivaled Daniel's and eyes the color of clear green emeralds.

"I can see where you get your good looks, Daniel," Lily said. "Your parents are both spectacular."

"Yes, I can't say they never gave me anything, can I?"

The facetious comment confused Lily, but she said nothing as Daniel led her to a glass-knobbed door between the rows of shelving on the wall opposite the door they had come in. He took a key out of his pocket and turned it in the lock. "Now, if you'll follow me."

Lily's heart nearly stopped. It was another library, but this one was a gallery dedicated solely to art. The giant chandelier illuminated a room filled with treasures. Paintings hung on the walls, sculptures stood on the floor, and vases and smaller statues graced several cherry tables. "Oh Daniel!" She grasped his arm. "I can't believe this!"

"Don't get overly excited. About half of these paintings are my mother's work, and she was never a big name in the art world."

"You silly, art isn't about names. It's about beauty and

emotion." She whirled around, trying to take it all in.

Daniel patiently led her through the room, showing her each individual piece and explaining the history behind it and how it had come into his family. Lily gushed over paintings by Van Dyck and Rembrandt, and was particularly taken with a copy of Leonardo Da Vinci's *Mona Lisa* that the duchess had painted.

"This was the only time she ever copied someone else's work. She was so taken with the portrait that she spent a month in Paris so she could go to the Louvre and look at it every day. She would spend about an hour each morning studying it and then go back to her chamber and paint. I've seen the real one, and my mother's is remarkably accurate."

"It's amazing," Lily said. "I must see the Louvre someday. I can't even imagine what a thrill it will be."

"Let's go tomorrow, then," Daniel said with a smile.

"All right. I'll pack my valise." She gave him a quick hug. "This has been a fantastic evening. Thank you so much for showing me everything."

"I have several more pieces I'd like for you to see, but they're scattered around the estate. Would you like to save them for another time?"

Lily lifted her hand and caressed the curve of Daniel's jaw, his night beard rough against her palm. "You know, I never thought I'd say this, but I don't want to look at another piece of art tonight."

"What do you want to do, love?" he asked, taking her other hand in his.

More than anything in the world, she knew what she wanted. And damn the consequences.

"I want to go to bed," she said. "With you."

CHAPTER SEVEN

Lily sighed as she entered Daniel's bedchamber. A fire had been started in the grate, casting a delicate glow about the room and illuminating St. Praxedis's lovely face in an incandescent beauty. The table in the window was set with a small platter of fruit and chocolate, and an uncorked bottle of wine and two glasses stood next to it. Two tapers lit the small banquet.

"Oh my," Lily said. "That's lovely." Then, turning to Daniel, "One might think you assumed I'd come with you."

"I just believe in being prepared, love."

"And I suppose, had I refused, you'd have found a willing substitute?"

He moved toward her and cupped her face in his hands. "I don't want anyone but you tonight, Lily. Had you refused, I'd have blown out the candles and gone to bed." He led her to the table. "Come, sit with me. I want to feed you."

Lily's heart raced. Daniel had the most remarkable way of using words to make her feel absolutely giddy with desires. Years of practice, no doubt. She pushed the conjecture from her mind. She wanted to enjoy the moment. She started to sit down on the settee where she had taken lunch, but he pulled her away.

"I said sit with me." He sat down and pulled her into his lap. He took the bottle of wine and poured two glasses. "This is Château Beychevelle, 1831. I think you'll find it to your liking."

"I'm afraid I know very little about wine."

"Then I shall teach you." He held up the glass. "Smell this."

"What?"

"Stick your cute little nose into the glass and smell it."

She complied.

"Now, what did it smell like?"

"I'm not sure I understand."

"Was it smoky, or floral, or fruity? Those are just some examples. Here, try again."

"Daniel, I feel like an utter fool," she said, but she tried again anyway. "I don't know. It's fragrant."

Daniel chuckled. "Of course it's fragrant, Lily. What does the fragrance remind you of?"

She smelled the wine once more. "It reminds me of berries."

"Swirl it in the glass," Daniel said, showing her. "That releases the aromas a little more. Now smell it again."

"Berries still. A little...wood, perhaps? Maybe some cinnamon?" She swirled and smelled again. "This can't be."

"What?"

"I'm getting..." She stuck her nose far into the glass, touching it to the wine. "Coffee, Daniel. It has a slight coffee smell."

Daniel kissed the drip of wine off of her nose. "I knew you'd have a good nose, Lily. As an artist and writer, you have heightened senses of sight, hearing, and touch. It's not surprising that your sense of smell is enhanced also." He swirled the wine in the glass, closed his eyes, and took a long sniff. "I do believe you're right. It does remind me a bit of coffee. But I'm smelling the cinnamon and berries much more on the surface. You did amazingly well for your first time."

"What now? Do we just smell it, or are we going to drink it?"

"We're not going to drink it yet," he said. "We're going to taste it."

"What's the difference?"

He held the glass to her, smiling. "Take a sip, but don't swallow. Let it rest on your tongue for a moment."

She obeyed.

"Now swish it around a little. Let it coat every part of your mouth. Good. Now swallow slowly if you can. Each part of your mouth will register a different part of the wine's complexity. There, what did you think?"

"It was... I don't know. Warm, a little spicy in the back of my mouth. But on my tongue it was fruity, like layers of dark grapes. And blackberries. And currants."

"Very good."

"Aren't you going to taste it?" Lily held the glass to him.

"Of course."

He took the glass from her, set it on the table, and kissed her gently, prying her lips open with his tongue. He glided smoothly over every inch of her mouth. She was breathing heavily by the time he lifted his head.

"Definitely blackberries and cinnamon. But mostly my favorite flavor of all. You."

"You are a wizard with words, Daniel," she said dreamily, her pulse racing. "It's no wonder women have been falling all over you for so long. You're a master of lines."

"That wasn't a line."

"Oh, that's an even better one." She closed her eyes and let out a soft breath.

★ ★ ★ ★

Daniel gazed at her beautiful face. Her lashes were so long that they touched her cheeks when her eyes were closed. So very beautiful. How could he convince her he was telling the truth? That he wasn't simply feeding her lines that were tried and true? Her complexity and intelligence captivated him. She had awakened feelings in him that he didn't know he was capable of having. He touched her cheek gently.

"Open your eyes, love. I want you to taste something else." He reached onto the table for a chocolate. "Have you tasted chocolate bonbons before?"

"Papa brought some from Prince Albert's exposition in London a few years ago. They were wonderful."

"Then I know you'll like these. This is a dark chocolate truffle from Belgium." He held it to her mouth. "Take a small bite."

"Mmm, delicious. I've never tasted anything like it."

"Now a sip of wine," he said, holding the glass to her lips.

She moaned softly. "My, that's absolutely sublime."

Daniel kissed her again, swirling his tongue around hers and capturing the lingering richness of the chocolate and the crisp, dry fruitiness of the wine. "Oh yes. Sublime."

Lily leaned into him and whispered in his ear. "Are you actually going to eat or drink anything, or are you just going to taste it all on me?"

"I had planned to partake with you, but I like your idea better." He kissed her again, deliberately and sensually, his cock hardening beneath her. Slowly he unfastened the back of her gown.

She giggled, but her body tensed against him. "Not so fast.

Now that you've introduced me to this divine confection, do you really think I'm going to be satisfied with just one little bite?" She reached for another truffle.

"My love, you'll find that the more you experience of the finer things in life, the more you'll want." He eased her gown over her shoulders. He took a truffle, rubbed it between her breasts, which were bulging out of her corset, and licked the chocolate from her warm body. Her skin was like silk under his tongue.

Lily held a glass of wine to his mouth, smiling down at him. He sipped slowly, his gaze never straying from hers.

"Lily, you are the most amazing woman I know."

"Thank you." She put the wine down. "And you, Daniel, are..." She took a truffle, rubbed a thick coating of chocolate on his lips, and kissed it off. "The *only* man I know." She burst into a fit of giggles. "In the biblical sense that is. You make me do such wicked things."

"I don't think you're completely under my influence." He unpinned her hair and let the dark waves cascade down her back. "I don't recall having anything to do with you swimming naked in the hot pool this afternoon." He fondled her bare shoulders—Lord, such soft skin. "Whose idea was that, pray tell?"

"Actually, it was Ally's. Although I didn't exactly resist. I told you we would find some fun, didn't I?"

He erupted in laughter. "And I told you I didn't doubt that you would. Although it didn't occur to me that your fun would entail you frolicking about naked. If it had, I never would have let you out of my sight. I should have known you would find the pool."

"Rose thought it might be an offshoot from the waters in

Bath." Lily reached for her wine to take another sip.

"It is. It's very relaxing and pleasant, as I'm sure you found out."

"We weren't relaxing. We were playing. Then we were hiding from you. The girls were mortified when you showed up. I knew you wouldn't divulge our secret, but I had no way of letting them know that."

"If you had been alone, I would have stripped and been in there with you in about three seconds." His cock surged under her. God, he wanted to bed her. Now. He took another sip of wine when she held the glass for him.

Lily rolled her head back and giggled. "That would have been wicked."

"But fun, yes?"

"I suppose so."

She leaned down and pressed a kiss to his cheek. A simple, innocent kiss that plummeted straight to his groin.

"I'm almost sorry I wasn't alone, although Ally and I had a marvelous time." She reached for another chocolate and took a small bite. "I dare say we won't be able to visit the pool again unless there's another day like today, when most of the guests are otherwise occupied."

"You can visit the pool anytime you want," he said, "with one condition."

"And that would be?" She gave him another sip of wine.

"You have to take me with you." He grinned and squeezed her breast.

"Well, all right." She grabbed a cluster of grapes from the platter and fed one to him. "Mmm. You know, the last time I was at Laurel Ridge it was September, I believe. I took a walk through the vineyards and couldn't resist the lovely bunches of grapes. They were so tiny. So I picked one and ate it, but it was completely full of seeds. These are wonderful, though." She popped another into her mouth.

"The grapes in our vineyards are for making wine, Lily. They're not meant to be eaten."

"How interesting. How do you get all the seeds out?"

"I don't actually know. I'm sure it requires sophisticated equipment."

"You don't make wine here?"

"No. We sell our grapes to other vineyards."

"You seem to have a keen interest in wine, and you have your own vineyards. Why haven't you tried to make some?"

"I wouldn't know the first thing about it."

"You have a brain, Daniel. You could learn." She fed him another grape.

He grabbed the cluster of grapes from her. "I thought I was supposed to feed you." He pushed one between her lips and lifted the glass for her to take a drink.

"You're changing the subject."

"And I'm doing a smashing job of it." He grabbed a strawberry and held it up for her to take a bite. "Don't swallow yet." He held up a truffle. "How is that?"

"Mmm. Wonderful. You try."

"If you insist." He moved toward her mouth.

"That's not what I meant—"

He kissed her delicately, extracting the strawberry and chocolate flavors from her mouth with slick strokes of his tongue. "Delectable. Now try a sip of wine." He held it to her lips.

"I could get used to this," Lily said breathlessly, touching his hair. "Sitting on your lap, being fed chocolate and fruit and wine. I feel like Cleopatra. I'm not sure life can get any more pleasurable."

"Oh, it can," Daniel said, sliding his lips along the side of her neck.

"Nice," she said dreamily. "But we've already done that. And it couldn't possibly be any more pleasurable than it was the first time."

"My sweet, naive angel," Daniel said, his entire body pulsating with need, "it will get better and better, I promise."

Lily looked down at him with fire in her eyes. "Show me."

He stood up with her in his arms. He kissed her passionately as he removed her clothes, plucked the remaining pins from her hair, and laid her on the bed. He disrobed and joined her, taking her into his arms and kissing her, slowly at first, and then more intensely.

"I'm going to taste every inch of you tonight, Lily." He ran his tongue along the outer edge of her ear and gently nipped her lobe.

"Oh, that's nice," she said.

He moved to her eyelids, covering them with light touches of his lips. Her eyes fluttered under the attack and she moaned his name softly.

Then to her nose, her cheeks, her other ear, her neck—he explored each separate place with his lips, ravishing her as if she were his first taste of a woman, while his cock throbbed. He caressed and kissed her arms and hand, swirled his tongue on the inside of her elbow and breathed on the wetness, delighting in her shudder.

"My love, you are so breathtakingly beautiful. The finest artists in the world could not have created such perfection." He kissed each of her fingers, sucking them into his mouth and caressing them with his tongue.

When he moved to her breasts, she groaned as he kneaded them gently and then brushed them with his lips, teasingly avoiding her nipples.

"Daniel, please."

He sucked on the skin underneath one nipple. "Yes?"

"I...I..."

"Is this what you want?" He tugged on one nipple lightly.

"Yes, oh yes. Please, Daniel."

God, how he loved to hear her say his name. He sucked gently, and then harder. Her fingers threaded through his hair, pushing him into her breast. His erection pulsated, but he calmed it. He wanted to concentrate on her. He let the nipple go with a soft pop.

"Do you like that, Lily? When I take your nipple between my lips? Does that feel good to you?"

She sighed. "Yes. Oh yes. It's wonderful."

He lavished attention on the other nipple, teasing and tickling it to a hard knob, and then replaced his tongue with his fingers as he moved lower on her torso. He lightly pinched both nipples while he swirled his tongue in small circles on her belly, around her navel. He paused when he reached the patch of dark curls.

"Oh, Daniel," she moaned. "Please."

"Patience, love." He gave her wetness a quick nip, the tang of her juices like nectar on his tongue. He was tempted to eat her, but he wanted to explore her, taste every part of her. He licked the sensual plumpness of her hips and thighs, to her calves, to the instep of her foot. He kissed each of her toes and then gently turned her over on her stomach and started working his way back up. He paused in the inside of her knees, moving his tongue in lazy, wet circles, making her wriggle beneath him. Then he blew softly on the wetness, and she arched off the bed. Her hands became fists and she grabbed the silk comforter and moaned his name. His cock nearly burst.

He moved upward, gently biting the backs of her thighs, the round cheeks of her bottom. He paused and licked her pussy in one languid, sensual stroke.

"Now, Daniel. Please."

"Not yet." He slid his tongue over the curve of her back, until he was at her neck, sucking and nuzzling gently. His swollen cock pushed against her thigh. "What do you want, love?" he asked softly, his voice hoarse.

"I want you. Inside me. Please, Daniel."

"Not yet, Lily. I want to feast on you." He spread kisses and nips down her back and then gently moved her legs forward until her bottom was propped up. He parted her intimate folds, delicately stroking them with his fingers. She was so wet. *God, so wet.*

"You have the prettiest, sweetest, most perfect pussy I have ever seen." He smoothly slid his tongue inside of her, mimicking the sexual act, skillfully fingering her swollen nub. Her honey tantalized his tongue, sweet and spicy at the same time.

"Please, Daniel, please." The pillow muffled her voice.

He teased her, took her almost to climax and then stopped and licked her in long lackadaisical strokes. The tight rosebud of her anus beckoned him, and he touched his tongue to it.

She shuddered beneath him, but didn't stop him. *Oh, thank God.*

He licked the opening gently, slowly, all the while fingering her swollen clitoris. Would he ever take her there?

That tight forbidden heaven? He suddenly wanted it more than he wanted his next breath—to fill her everywhere. His cock throbbed and threatened to release.

"Daniel, my God."

He couldn't tease her any longer. He had to let her come so he could get inside that warm wet pussy. He moved down to her clitoris and sucked hard while he pushed two fingers into her heat. He plundered her body with such drive that she rolled from one orgasm into another, bucking up against him, shuddering and squealing. Her muscles clamped around his fingers. His cock hardened even further.

"Daniel, no. I can't take any more." Yet still her hips moved with him.

His power to please her intoxicated him. He moved forward, touched his lips to her back, her neck, her hair. He could wait no longer.

He plunged his cock into her pussy from behind. God, she was perfect. So tight, so beautiful. He found a rhythm and pumped into her harder, faster. "You make me so hard, Lily. So, so hard."

He reached beneath her and stroked her clitoris as he thrust his cock in and out. Soon she slid into another climax, and he followed her, spilling his seed inside of her with spasms so powerful and intense he wasn't sure he'd survive it.

"Yes, Lily, yes." He thrust and he thrust, until he had given her all he could.

He pressed a soft kiss to her shoulder and fell to his side, taking her with him. Lily snuggled against him. They lay together for several moments.

"Daniel," she whispered. "I have to go."

"No." The idea of her leaving him was too unbearable for

words. "Stay with me."

"I can't."

"Please. Sleep in my arms. I want to wake up with you and make love to you. I want to feel you next to me all night. Stay."

"Oh, Daniel." She sighed and turned her body to face his.

"Go to sleep, my love. You'll need all your energy if we're going to the Louvre tomorrow."

Her lips curled into a soft smile against his chest, and then she drifted peacefully into oblivion, her heart beating softly against him.

Daniel stroked her silken hair, her sweet breath blowing in shallow puffs against his chest. How could she mean so much to him in so little time? Gently he moved her head to the satin pillow and gave her a chaste kiss on the cheek. Her eyes fluttered softly beneath her ebony lashes. He rose gingerly, so as not to disturb her, went to the table, and poured himself another glass of wine. He padded to his night table and lit a candle. The soft glow illuminated Lily's lovely face. He reached into a shallow drawer, drew out a sketchbook and a soft lead pencil. He sat down on the bed and began to sketch the exquisite beauty before him.

★ ★ ★ ★

Lily woke later to find Daniel's lips sliding over hers. He sat on the edge of the bed, clad in his dressing robe. "Lily," he said softly. "Wake up. Our breakfast is here."

She sat up abruptly. "Breakfast? My God, what time is it?"

"About eight." He held up a dressing robe for her. "Put this on and have breakfast with me."

"Eight o'clock, you say? I guess it's all right. Rose rarely rises before ten." She took the robe and headed to the bath chamber. "I'll only be a moment."

She took care of her needs quickly and returned to find Daniel sitting at the small table in the window. He stood and led her to her chair, and then sat down and poured her a cup of tea.

"How do you take it?"

"Just like that." She lifted the cup and inhaled the rich fragrance of the steamy liquid.

"You're a woman after my own heart, Lily. I can't abide sugar and cream in my tea either." He placed a filet of smoked salmon, a scone, some lemon curd, and fresh fruit on a plate and handed it to her.

"Thank you," she said. "I'm quite hungry."

"Of course you are." He grinned. "You used a lot of energy last night."

Lily smiled shyly. "We can't keep this up, you know."

"Why not?"

"You have compromised me beyond repair, Daniel."

"Then why not keep at it?" He grinned. "It makes little difference to your virtue at this point."

"That's not the issue," Lily said.

"What is the issue, Lily?"

"It's that..." She sighed. Every minute she spent with him would make leaving at the end of next week much more difficult. She would think about him, wonder what he was doing and with whom. He would replace her quickly and forget all they had shared. She had known from the beginning what kind of man he was, yet she had gone to him willingly. No strings. No regrets. She still didn't want marriage. Especially not to a man who could never be faithful to her. She had started this for experience. And she had gained experience tenfold.

"What, love? You can tell me." He stroked her arm.

His touch set her ablaze. "Oh, I don't know. It just doesn't seem right, that's all."

"It seems very right to me."

"I didn't mean that it didn't *feel* right. It feels very..."

Daniel kissed her hand. "You're not going to get away from me that easily, Lily. I plan to monopolize your time for the rest of this house party. Then we shall see what happens after that."

After that? What did he mean? That they'd continue their illicit affair, or that she would become his mistress? Not in a million years. "Daniel—"

"Plus, you promised to go riding with me today."

"Yes, I know. I want to, Daniel, but—"

"No 'buts,' Lily. You already said you'd go."

She looked into his eyes and couldn't find the strength to fight him. She wanted to be with him. Leaving him would be so... But why think about that now?

"Yes, I'll go."

"Of course you will. Now eat your breakfast like a good girl. And no more of this ridiculous talk. Here, have some more tea."

"I should get back to my chamber soon," Lily said.

"Yes, I'll take you back after breakfast. Then you can change and get to your painting. I'll go to the bachelor house and find Xavier and arrange for our ride this afternoon."

"All right, Daniel."

They ate the rest of their breakfast in silence, but it wasn't awkward. Nothing about being with Daniel seemed awkward, which was a big part of the problem. Lily gazed out the window, sighing, pushing the thoughts of leaving Laurel Ridge from her mind. When she had finished the last crumb on her plate, she asked, "Am I to sit with you at dinner again tonight?"

"Of course. There's no one else whose company I prefer over yours. Don't you wish to?"

"I'd like to."

"Good." He smiled. "Come on. I'll help you with your clothes." He pulled her to her feet and embraced her. "Oh, Lily," he whispered, barely audibly. "What am I going to do when you leave me?"

"The same thing you always do," she said, her tone cynical. "You'll find a replacement in no time."

"Don't say that." He brought his mouth down on hers.

He kissed her violently, thrusting his tongue into her and taking her mouth in an angry passion. He dug his hands into her arms as he moved his mouth down her neck, kissing her and biting her, grabbing her shoulder and wrenching the dressing robe from her in one swift motion.

"Daniel."

"I want you, Lily, right now," he growled. "Put your arms around me."

She obeyed. He lifted her, not gently, into his arms, as easily as one would a child, and shoved his cock into her.

"Kiss me," he commanded.

She gasped from his thrust as his mouth crushed down on hers, taking and demanding. He pushed into her body again and again. Lily shivered and moaned, clinging to him as he drove into her mercilessly.

"You mean something to me, Lily." His voice came in grunts as he pumped into her. "Tell me you know that. Tell me."

"Yes, Daniel." She trembled, nursing waves of bliss, clutching his heated body. He was being forceful. Violent, even.

But she wanted him. Ached for the pleasure of his thrusts. Her breasts dripped with sweat as she crashed like a tidal wave into the depths of pleasure. She cried into his neck, her lips sliding against the saltiness of his dampened skin.

Daniel drove into her with a final surge. His body shook as he pushed himself deep into her pussy. "God, Lily, you hold my cock so tightly. Oh. My. God!" He moved toward the bed and set her upon it as he released.

★ ★ ★ ★

Several moments later, as his breathing returned to normal, Daniel had a sudden urge to drop to his knees and beg Lily's forgiveness for taking her so roughly. Slowly he regained his sanity, and to his surprise, she was rubbing his back gently, quietly whispering comforting words. Eternally grateful that she wasn't running as fast as she could away from the sight of him, he whispered, "Thank God."

"Thank God for what?" she asked softly.

"That you're not angry with me." He blinked back a tear.

"No, Daniel, I'm not angry. I suppose I should be, but I..." She inhaled sharply. "Well it's no use denying it, is there? I enjoyed it." She continued to caress him in soothing circles.

"Please, tell me you're not hurt."

"I'm fine."

"I could never forgive myself if..." His voice cracked.

"It's all right. I promise you it's all right."

He moved away from her body. Red marks the size of his hands marred her perfect arms. How could he have been such a monster? A tear fell down his cheek.

Lily smoothed it away and reached up to kiss him. "Tell

me what this is about. What is troubling you?"

How could he tell her when he didn't know himself? His emotions were in turmoil. He couldn't concentrate. He barely recognized the person he thought he was. All he thought about was Lily. She was consuming him like a blazing fire sweeping through a dry forest. He stood up, his legs barely able to support his weight. "I'm going to run you a quick bath," he said. "I'll call you when it's ready."

In the bath chamber, he turned the faucet and placed his hands under the fall of water, letting its heaviness slide over his skin, cleanse away his guilt. Damn. It would take more than water. When the tub was full he called to Lily.

He picked her up gently and set her in the tub.

"Aren't you going to get in with me?"

He shook his head and proceeded to gently bathe her as though she were a delicate child.

She held out her arms. "Come, Daniel. Please."

"You want me, after what I just did to you?"

"Yes. Come bathe with me. It's all right."

What had he ever done in his godforsaken life to be worthy of such tenderness? He joined her in the tub, sitting behind her and pulling her back against his chest. He caressed her smooth skin, relishing the intimacy with this extraordinary woman who had somehow squirmed her way into his ironclad heart. How was he going to let her go?

"I don't deserve this," he said softly.

"Nor do I," she said, her voice filled with compassion. "But we may as well enjoy it while we can." She turned to face him and kissed him warmly, granting him grace without condition.

He had never felt so whole.

CHAPTER EIGHT

Daniel and Lily dressed slowly, the tense air between them gradually returning to normal. They crept stealthily down to the second floor to Lily's chamber. The hallway appeared deserted, and Daniel pulled Lily to him and kissed her.

Lily returned the kiss and moaned softly. Daniel was an enigma to her. She had found a chink in his armor this morning, and she wasn't sure what to make of it. She broke away. "I do need to go to my chamber."

"I know." He led her to her door. "I'll see you this afternoon." He kissed her temple.

Suddenly the door to her chamber swung open, and Rose stood before them in her nightgown, her blond hair in a tumbling mass around her shoulders. "Lily, where in the devil have you—" Her gaze moved to Daniel standing behind Lily. "Your Grace, what in the world? Get out of here before someone sees you!" She grabbed Lily's arm and yanked her into the chamber, shutting the door quickly and quietly. "You have some explaining to do."

"I guess I do." Lily sat down on her bed. "I'm sorry if I worried you."

"You did. When you didn't come back to the terrace last night, I had to make excuses to Mummy and Papa."

"What did you tell them?"

"I told them you went to bed because you were feeling poorly, due to your...monthlies."

Lily giggled. "That was smart."

"Yes, I thought so. Neither Papa nor Thomas mentioned you again all evening. I kept Mummy at bay by pretending to check on you from time to time."

"Thank you, Rose. I'm sorry I put you in that position."

"Yes, you owe me. And I'll start collecting right now. What the hell have you been doing?"

Rose's curse shocked Lily. Her sister never spoke like that.

"And I want the whole sordid truth."

"I'm not sure where to start."

"At the beginning." Rose sat down beside Lily. "If you expect my cooperation for the remainder of this house party, you owe me that much."

"Yes, you're absolutely right." Lily told her sister everything, happy to finally confide in someone. She began with the kiss on the side of the mansion and ended with her return to the chamber a few moments earlier, although she left out the details of their lovemaking. That was between Daniel and her, and she didn't want to share it.

"Oh, Lily, I admit that it sounds absolutely enchanting," Rose breathed, closing her eyes, but then she opened them quickly. "But you've been compromised. You're ruined. What are you going to do?"

"We've been discreet, Rose. No one will know. And you know that I don't give two figs about finding a husband anyway."

"I'm not sure you've been all that discreet," Rose said. "The duke's attention to you at dinner last evening was apparent to everyone, I'm afraid. And this morning, what was he thinking? He brought you back here in broad daylight." Rose paused, her brow furrowed. "It's almost as though he wanted to get caught."

"That's ridiculous, Rose. He wants discretion as much as

I do. If we were caught, Papa might force him to marry me, and believe me, that is the farthest thing from Dan...er, the duke's mind."

"Are you certain about that?"

"Yes, of course. I'm not such a complete ninny that I've forgotten what kind of a man he is."

"What about you? Do you have feelings for him?"

Heat rose to Lily's cheeks. "I...I believe I care for him." Her voice cracked, and she steadied it. "I can't help it. But that doesn't change who he is. I know he's been an utter scoundrel. But I enjoy his company, and he seems to enjoy mine. We have some common interests. I'm having fun, that's all."

Rose's gaze turned sorrowful. "Lily, I don't want to see you get hurt."

"I won't. Believe me, I know what I'm doing. I have no intention of marrying any time soon." Lily stood and turned. "Unfasten me, will you? I want to put on a morning dress and continue with my painting from yesterday. What are you going to do this morning?"

"I'm going to work on my Beethoven for a bit, I think. Are you going to be able to come along with Lord Evan and me on our ride this afternoon?" Rose finished unbuttoning Lily's gown and untied her corset strings.

"Yes, absolutely. In fact, Daniel asked me to go riding, and he suggested we all go together. Isn't that a perfect solution? We'll have built in chaperones."

"Daniel? And I suppose he's using your Christian name as well?"

"Yes, he asked me to, and I saw no reason not to allow it."

"And he's taking you riding."

"Yes, of course. He asked me yesterday."

"Dear Lord," Rose said. "I'm afraid he may be more serious about you than you think."

"Don't be silly," Lily said. "You and I both know his reputation."

"We shall see what we shall see." Rose left it at that.

★ ★ ★ ★

Lily finished her painting, pleased with the results. She headed back to the main house to return her art supplies to her chamber, after which she planned to browse in the library and choose a book to relax with for the rest of the morning. As she entered, a large brown crate and several white canvases sitting at the foot of her bed drew her focus. Her name was written in elegant script on a sheet of parchment sealed with the Lybrook crest. Her hands shaking, she opened the note and read it, admiring the masculine scrawl.

Lily,

I can't wait to see what you create with these. Make Vermeer proud.

Yours,

D.

She knelt beside the crate. The nails had been loosened so she could remove the top easily. She gasped. The box was filled with tubes of oil paints, brushes and other tools, a color mixing palette, and several jars of various spirits. At the bottom was a book about oil painting. She grabbed it and opened it. No need to visit the library now. This would be her reading material for the rest of the morning.

"Oh, Daniel," she whispered. "You're so completely wonderful."

She closed her eyes and sighed. How could she show him her appreciation for this most thoughtful of gifts? She took the watercolor she had just finished out of her leather case. It had turned out beautifully. She had signed it with a simple "L" in script, and then the date, the way she signed all of her paintings. She removed the painting she had completed eight years prior. The "L" had a girlish curl to it, and the technique was "raw and untamed," as Daniel had put it. Still, he had seemed charmed by the painting, and she wanted him to have it. She would give him both pieces. Perhaps he would remember their time together, and she would rest easier knowing that a little part of her stayed at Laurel Ridge when she left.

But...was it appropriate for her to gift him with the paintings? In fact, was it appropriate for her to even accept his gift?

She laughed aloud. Of course it wasn't. But she had slept with him. That certainly hadn't been appropriate. The oils beckoned her. She had to accept them. And she so wanted to give him her paintings.

She picked up her journal, tore a page from it, and dipped a quill in ink to write a short note.

Daniel,
Thank you so very much for the loveliest gift anyone has ever given me. Please keep these paintings to remember our time together. I will never forget you.
Lily

Was that too personal? She tried again.

Daniel,
I love the oils. Thank you so very much. Please accept these paintings as my gift to you.
Yours,
Lily

No, that wasn't right either. She ripped another sheet out of her journal and began scratching the quill once more.

Daniel,
Thank you for the lovely gift. I can't wait to get started.
Lily

That was better. Short and to the point, with no room for second guessing. She wouldn't mention the watercolors, she would just attach the note to them. He could decide for himself what her gift to him meant. She delivered her gift discreetly to Daniel's chamber, leaving it against the door, and then sneaked down to the first floor and walked outside into the beautiful April day. When she found a tree that suited her, she sat down beneath it and opened her new book.

★ ★ ★ ★

Daniel found Lily sitting under a giant oak, absorbed in a book.

"Good afternoon," he said, smiling.

Her body visibly tensed. "My goodness, you must stop sneaking up on me like that," she said. "You're liable to send me into conniptions."

Daniel laughed. "You were so engrossed, I doubt you would have noticed a cyclone. What are you reading?"

Lily held it up for him. "It's the book about oils that you gave me. I just love it, Daniel. I don't know how to thank you for the gift."

She held her arm out to him and he sat down next to her. She looked around, and then gave him a moist kiss on the lips, setting his skin ablaze.

"There is so much information here. I'm so excited."

Daniel stared at her, and for a moment he thought he would give his entire fortune to keep that unfeigned look of happy excitement in her glowing dark eyes. "I'm glad you like the paints, Lily."

"Oh, I do. They're just perfect."

"Are you ready to go riding?" He played with her hand, entwining their fingers together.

"Already? I haven't had any lunch yet. What time is it?"

"Two in the afternoon."

"Goodness, I must have forgotten to eat. That's my downfall, you know. I get so involved in reading, or writing, or painting, that sometimes I'm oblivious to all else. I've missed many a meal in my day."

"I don't have to worry about you getting plump on me, do I?" He winked at her. "Come on, let's go to the kitchen. I'll have one of the cooks make you a sandwich."

"Are you sure there's time?"

"Yes, Xavier and your sister are meeting us at the stables at half past. Come on." He helped her up, crushing her body against his for a moment.

Daniel took Lily to the kitchen for her sandwich and then waited in the foyer while she changed into her riding habit.

"I'm sorry it took me so long." She rushed down the stairs. "Now we're running late, aren't we?"

"They'll wait for us."

Lily took his offered arm and they walked to the stables. Rose stood in the distance with Lord Evan. She held a small black puppy, and several others panted at her feet.

"Lily!" Rose cried, "look at what we found!"

Lily broke from Daniel's arm and started running toward Rose. A tiny brown puppy ran to Lily, whimpering to be held. She knelt down and picked up the dog, cuddling it to her face. "Rose, where did they come from?"

"They were here when we got here. I wonder where their mother is?"

Daniel reached them, relishing the joy on Lily's face. "She's behind the stables," he said. "This particular bitch likes to nest there when she's breeding. She won't stay at the kennels. The pups are nearly weaned, so they come and go as they please."

Lily continued to hug the puppy, looking down at the others. "They're all black and yellow, but this one is brown. She's the color of milky chocolate. No, brandy. She's the exact color of that brandy Papa favors, Rose."

"She's the runt of the litter, Lily," Daniel said, "and the only brown one."

"What kind of dogs are they?"

"St. John's dogs, from Newfoundland. My father started breeding them years ago. Her siblings will be excellent hunting dogs, but I'm afraid this one is just too small."

"Nonsense, she's perfect." Lily laughed as the puppy licked her nose. She set the puppy down and gave her bottom a shove back toward her brothers and sisters. The pup turned back around to Lily, reaching her small paws up and whimpering. Lily picked her up again. "My goodness, you certainly like attention, don't you?" She giggled. "I just can't put you down.

You're too precious!" She kissed the puppy's head.

"Lybrook," Lord Evan said amiably, as Rose picked up one of the yellow pups, "I think we've been jilted. These two seem to prefer the company of tiny drooling four-legged creatures over us."

"Can we interest you in large four-legged creatures at least?" Daniel said. "I can't promise you that they'll drool, though they might snort a bit."

Lily and Rose laughed. "Yes, I suppose we came here to go riding didn't we, Lily?" Rose said. "Lord Evan picked out a mare for me from the horses he brought. She's absolutely beautiful. Which one are you going to ride?"

"I haven't the slightest idea, but His Grace did promise that I didn't have to ride sidesaddle." She smiled at Daniel.

"I have a sister who doesn't like to ride sidesaddle either, my lady," Evan said. "She says it's extremely uncomfortable."

"It is for me also, my lord, but wait until you see Rose ride," Lily said. "She's a natural."

"Are you?" He turned to Rose. "Then I'm looking forward to this ride all the more. Shall we see if Lionheart and Beatrice are saddled?" He held his arm to Rose.

"Certainly, my lord. We'll see you in a minute, Lily, Your Grace."

Lily turned to Daniel. "I'm not the rider Rose is. Pick a gentle one for me, will you?"

He smiled. "How would you like to ride Midnight?"

"Your stallion? Have you completely lost your mind?"

"You can ride with me. My parents had a saddle for two made because my mother, like you, wasn't a natural rider, but she enjoyed animals so she rode with my father. We can use that."

"Is it sidesaddle or astride?"

"Astride for me, of course, side for you, I'm afraid. But my mother found it comfortable because she didn't have to worry about controlling the horse. My father took care of that."

"Do you think it's appropriate for us to ride that way? Given the...circumstances?"

"What circumstances would those be? We're chaperoned. There's no harm."

"It's already clear that Lord Evan thinks you're courting me, Daniel."

"It is, is it?" He smiled at her. She was so adorable when she was pretending to care what others thought. He knew the truth.

"Well, of course it is."

"Is he courting your sister?"

"Of course not. This is just a simple friendly outing. She would have told me if he... He probably hasn't spoken to our father..."

Daniel lifted the large leather saddle. "What is the difference between what they're doing this afternoon and what we're doing?"

"Well, they're riding separate horses."

"Because Rose loves to ride. You may certainly ride your own horse, Lily, but you seem uncomfortable with the idea."

"I'm not uncomfortable exactly. It's just that I don't really want to ride astride with others. I've always done it alone, and my dress will ride up my legs, and—"

"In that case, maybe you should have your own horse. I wouldn't mind looking at your legs all afternoon."

"Daniel..."

"Come now, this isn't the decision of the century. I love to ride, and I want to share it with you. It seems the easiest way for me to do that is for you to ride Midnight with me."

"All right, if you think it's suitable."

"I think it's perfectly fine. And I'll get the added pleasure of being close to you." He stole a quick kiss. "I've missed you."

"You just saw me this morning."

"I know." He kissed her once more. "You wait here for Xavier and Rose. They'll be coming around from the guest stables. I'll saddle Midnight."

★ ★ ★ ★

Lily settled against Daniel's chest as Midnight trotted away from the stables. Rose and Evan rode side by side, behind them. Daniel held the reins with one hand, keeping his other arm around Lily's waist. Snuggling back against him felt warm and wonderful. He was right. She was much more comfortable this way. So comfortable, in fact, that she wanted to lean against Daniel's hard muscled chest forever. God help her.

"We're coming up to a jump, Lily," he said into her neck. "Should I warn your sister?"

"Goodness, no. She can jump in her sleep. Watch her. You'll be amazed."

Midnight took the two foot jump with ease and Lily was hardly jarred. Daniel turned to the side to watch Rose, and then Evan, handle the jump expertly.

"You are certainly graceful on horseback, my lady," Daniel said to Rose.

"Thank you, Your Grace. I suppose it's my compensation for not being blessed with Lily's artistic talent."

"Don't listen to her," Lily said. "She may not be able to

draw a straight line, but she plays the pianoforte like an angel. Music is just another type of art, Rose. I myself never had the patience for it."

"I would love to hear you play sometime," Evan said.

"I've been playing in the main parlor most mornings. I'd like to ask Her Grace if I could play the grand in the conservatory. It's magnificent."

"Play it anytime you wish," Daniel said. "In fact, why don't you play for the three of us sometime?"

"I couldn't possibly. I don't have anything prepared."

"Aren't you working on that Beethoven?" Lily asked.

"The key word is 'working,' Lily. It's not ready for an audience."

"Don't believe a thing she tells you," Lily said. "She has a beautiful repertoire."

"Fine then," Daniel said. "Shall we say tonight after dinner? About eleven in the conservatory?"

"I-I'm not sure..." Rose stammered.

"She'd be delighted," Lily said, laughing. "Now let's see some more of this beautiful estate. And do pick up the pace, Daniel. I'm not made of china, you know. I want to ride!"

"All right, Lily," he said. "You asked for it."

He urged Midnight into a gallop, and Lily laughed with the pure exhilaration of the ride. Daniel slowed Midnight when they came to an ornate cast iron gate off the trail.

"Where does that lead?" Lily asked Daniel.

"It's a garden. Would you like to see it?"

"Yes, of course. Is anything in bloom this time of year?"

"You'd be surprised." He turned to the others. "Lily wants to take a look at the garden. Would you two care to join us?"

"Of course," Rose said, turning to Evan. "If it's all right

with you, my lord."

"Fine with me," he said. "Is there a hitching post?"

"Yes, right here." Daniel motioned. They dismounted and saw to their horses. Daniel opened the gate. They stepped inside and Lily and Rose both gasped. The garden was like a maze, with leafy shrubbery arranged in intricate formations. A few white benches sat nearby, and several little pathways led into the heart of the greenery.

"It's so much bigger than I imagined," Lily said. "It's enchanting, like a labyrinth. Whoever dreamed up such a place?"

"My grandmother," Daniel said. "She envisioned an oasis to attract fairies and gnomes and the like. She was a bit odd in the head, but a great duchess."

"I definitely need to bring my paints here," Lily said.

"Would you care to walk a little, my lady?" Evan offered his arm to Rose.

"That would be lovely."

Lily started to follow them, but Daniel held her back. "Let them go alone."

"I can't," Lily said. "I'm her chaperone. Rose is innocent."

"So were you a few days ago."

"I was never the innocent that Rose is. I read."

Daniel chuckled softly. "Let them have some time. They seem to like each other."

"If you think best," Lily said. Once Rose and Evan were out of sight, she tilted her head upward and sought Daniel's mouth with her own.

"Easy, Lily, or I may have to rip off your clothes and have you right here."

"Control yourself." Lily laughed, kissing him again.

He turned his face from her. "I want you so much right now. If you keep kissing me, I may not be able to stop. You know what I'm capable of."

"Yes, and I like what you're capable of." She pressed her lips to his neck, inhaling the salty scent of his skin.

He grasped her shoulders, pushing her away from him. His eyes were smoky and sunken.

"Daniel?"

"Come sit with me, Lily. I want to talk to you." He led her to one of the small benches.

"What is it?"

"I want you to know that I...care for you, and I'm so sorry about what happened this morning."

"Is that what this is about?" Lily touched his cheek. "You don't have to apologize. I'm not angry."

"I was so rough with you."

"Daniel, I wanted you." Lily was bewildered. "Did I scream? Did I try to get away from you? I went to you willingly, like I always have."

"You are the last person in this world I want to hurt."

His face was twisted in so much anguish that Lily wanted to clasp his head to her bosom and comfort him as though he were a child.

"I swear to you that it won't ever happen again. Why did you let me do it?"

She met his gaze. "Because you...seemed to need me. You were so emotional. I wanted to help."

Daniel looked away. "I just... When you said I would replace you... Damn it, Lily, I don't know what's going on with me."

Lily stroked his hair. "You shouldn't keep your emotions

bottled inside you. It's not healthy. You've been through so much in the past year. Have you ever let yourself mourn for your father and your brother?"

"I won't speak of that," he said abruptly.

"All right. I understand." She reached for his cheek and pulled him back around to face her. "But if you ever change your mind, you can talk to me. About anything. I mean that."

He wrapped his arms around her and drew her head to his chest, kissing the top of her hair.

Lily snuggled into his warmth. "Everything will be fine, Daniel," she said. "I promise, everything is fine."

CHAPTER NINE

Lady Amelia Gregory adjusted her skirts as the well-endowed stable boy pulled up his trousers. She didn't know his name, and she didn't care. "Stay here," she said. "Don't follow me out."

"My lady, I'd like to—"

"For God's sake, don't talk. I certainly didn't come here for conversation."

"But—"

"I got what I came for. You were acceptable. Now stay here, and don't leave for at least fifteen minutes."

"I'll go out the back way." The boy turned and walked away.

"Suit yourself." Amelia hurried to the door of the stables and peeked out. Three horses were approaching. "Oh, bloody hell."

Two of them headed left toward the guest stables, and one came toward her to the main stable. Midnight, carrying His Grace and that little twit, Lily Jameson. Amelia seethed. *Not interested, my arse. The little fool can't wait to become a duchess.*

Amelia quickly turned around and headed for the back door of the stable, but it was too far away. She ducked into a stall behind a brown-and-white mare and watched through a small crack in the wood.

"Come in, Lily," Daniel said. "Stay and talk to me while I

take care of Midnight."

"Don't you have grooms to take care of him?"

"Yes, but I like to do it myself."

"I understand. He's a beautiful horse, Daniel."

Daniel? She called him Daniel? The little harlot.

"Thank you so much for today," Lily continued. "I don't think I've ever enjoyed riding more."

"Neither have I."

"May I help you with him?"

"Certainly." He handed her a brush. "Take this and smooth out his mane, while I take care of his feet."

"I absolutely love animals." Lily ran the brush through Midnight's mane. "Dogs are my favorite, but horses are a close second. They're such beautiful and noble creatures. I wish I were a better rider."

"You just need to get more comfortable." Then he laughed. "You want to know what I think?"

"What?"

"I think you spend the majority of your time painting and writing, and you've never given yourself the chance to learn to ride properly."

"Rose has tried to teach me, but I'm hopeless."

"Nonsense. You responded well today."

"That's only because you were controlling Midnight. If I had been riding alone, you would have seen that—" She paused. "You're not buying any of this are you?"

"Not a word," he chuckled, shaking his head. "You have excellent instinct, as I saw today, plus it's obvious that you enjoy horses. I could teach you, and you'd be riding like Rose in no time."

"Would you really teach me?"

He finished with Midnight's hind feet and strode toward her, taking the brush from her hand. "Love, I would do anything for you. Don't you know that by now?" He grabbed a different brush and gave it to her. "Now we'll do his coat. You do this side, and I'll do the other. Here, I'll show you."

Amelia fumed, hidden. He had called her *love*. That ridiculous little twit, who "couldn't care less" about being a duchess. Lily had no doubt set the course in motion long before she arrived at Laurel Ridge. *I'll ruin her*, Amelia thought. But that wasn't possible. All they had done was go riding together, with chaperones. *Damn*. She could make something up, though, something deliciously scandalous. Of course, if she did that, the little fool's father, the earl, would no doubt force Daniel to marry her, and Amelia would have no chance at Daniel's title. Besides, why resort to lying when she could do something much more fun? The little bitch had a very handsome and very available brother. Amelia had already threatened to seduce Lily's brother, so why not go through with it?

Amelia smiled to herself, but her contentment was short lived, as the brown-and-white mare dropped a large clump of manure on her shoe.

★ ★ ★ ★

Lily and Rose barely awoke in time to dress for dinner. They were among the last to enter the dining room and be seated. Lord Evan rose and offered each of them an arm, guiding Lily to her seat.

Daniel took her arm. "Thank you for delivering her, Xavier," he said. "I'm sorry, Lily. I didn't see you come in."

"That's perfectly all right." She glanced around the room.

No!

Lady Amelia Gregory had somehow snagged the seat next to Thomas, which was supposed to be occupied by Emma. Lily turned to the outside table. Poor Emma was nestled between Wentworth and his uncle.

"Lily," Daniel said, "I want to thank you for—"

"What on earth is going on?" she interrupted in an urgent whisper.

"Nothing. What are you talking about?"

"Somehow that dreadful harpy Amelia Gregory is sitting next to my brother. And poor Emma is caught between Wentworth and his lecherous salivating uncle. Why did you change the seating?"

"I didn't. I told Aunt Lucy to keep it the same as last night."

"You have to do something, Daniel. I won't let that bitch get her claws into my brother."

"Lily," he said calmly. "There isn't anything I can do right now. Knowing Am...er...Lady Gregory, she will make a horrendous scene if I try to change her seat in front of all the guests. It will completely disrupt the meal. But I'll take care of it tomorrow. It won't happen again, I promise you."

"You said you'd do anything for me! Look at Emma! She can't even move her arms because Ludley is so...rotund. He'll probably drool all over her crumpets, and then try to squeeze her thigh under the table. And Amelia will...oh, I can't bear having her for a sister-in-law!"

"Lily," Daniel whispered, "you need to lower your voice. It's just dinner. Your brother has more sense than to make Lady Gregory your sister-in-law."

"You didn't have enough sense to stay away from her. What makes you think Thomas will? He's a man after all, who does the majority of his thinking with his—"

"What do you mean I didn't have enough sense to stay away from her?"

She didn't want to tell him about her conversation with Amelia, so she resorted to rumor. "Good Lord, Daniel, everyone knows." She looked quickly over her shoulder. "Emma is already dodging Ludley. My God, he'll use every tactic to try to grab her breast. He's been doing it to me for years."

"Lily, Lady Gregory never meant anything— He's been doing *what?*"

"What? Oh, Ludley. Yes, I've been diverting his roaming hands forever. I wasn't so successful the first time. I was not but fourteen, and—"

"Fourteen?" Daniel's voice lowered, his teeth clenched. "That sick bastard. I'll pummel him. By God, I'm going to boot him off this estate."

"Oh, for goodness' sake, don't bother." Ludley and his meandering hands were the least of Lily's concerns at the moment. "Just take care of this seating problem. Please."

"Lily, I can't. My mother would never forgive me. She would be incredibly embarrassed to have her dinner interrupted with such a trivial—"

"It is not trivial!"

"Not to you, love, but to her. I'm so sorry. I'll make this up to you."

"Daniel, this is the absolutely worst thing in the world!" Lily whispered urgently.

Daniel caressed her thigh under the table. "Please calm down. I'm sorry this has you so upset. But don't you think you're being a bit melodramatic? Your brother and Emma are fond of each other. That won't change because of an unfortunate seating choice. Why don't you talk to Emma after dinner. If she says Ludley acted inappropriately in any way, you have my word he will be sent packing."

"Melodramatic? How could you..." Daniel's caress under the table did feel good. Lily started to relax. "Yes, I will talk to Emma, and I don't expect we'll be seeing Ludley on the morrow. As for Amelia Gregory, if she so much as touches my brother—"

"Jameson can take care of himself, Lily. He wouldn't appreciate your interference anyway. I'm right, aren't I?"

"I suppose so, but I don't care. I'll burn in hell before that little doxy gets hold of him." She took a few deep breaths, the tension in her leg subsiding a bit. A *little* bit.

"Are you all right now?" Daniel asked.

"Yes, I'll be fine. Where's my wine?"

"Allow me." He filled her glass and handed it to her. "My, all that surliness, Lily. You're so worked up. Your skin is rosy all over. It makes me want to..."

Lily tried to stay angry, but she couldn't help smiling. "Later," she said. "And you're going to pay for this incident." She took a sip of wine.

He beamed. "I can't wait."

★ ★ ★ ★

Thomas was disappointed not to be seated next to Emma. He had grown quite fond of the lithe blonde and was beginning to believe Lily was right about finding a woman of intelligence. As the daughter of a banker, Emma was well versed in the world of finance and had listened to his tales of estate matters with interest, even offering her opinion from time to time.

The current seating was even more bizarre due to the fact that everyone else at the table, in fact at all the tables, seemed to be in the exact same position as the previous evening, except for Emma and his current dinner companion, Lady Amelia Gregory. Thomas knew little about Lady Gregory, except that she was the former Amelia Scott, a commoner, and the second wife of Frederic, Earl Gregory, twenty-five years her senior, who had passed away within the first year of their marriage. There were ruminations about the earl's untimely death, but nothing had been proven.

Lady Gregory had been linked to many men of import by way of illicit affairs since then, including Lord Daniel Farnsworth himself, before he became the Duke of Lybrook. Lady Gregory seemed pleasant enough and was very pretty. Thomas was chivalrous to a fault, so he filled her wine glass and saw to her other needs, despite the fact that he wished she were Emma.

"My lord," Lady Gregory said, "I must thank you for your attentiveness. I can't recall when I have been looked after so conscientiously."

"It's my pleasure, my lady."

"I had the delight of meeting your sister, Lady Lily, at the opening ball. And of course I'm acquainted with your parents. Frederic always said that Ashford had a unique head for estate matters. It's no secret that his is one of the most influential earldoms in England. I would love to know more about your family. Your dear mother, for instance. Where is she from?"

"My mother comes from London. She's the daughter of the Baron White."

"Really? How fascinating. How did she meet your father?"

"I'm not exactly sure, my lady. I've never asked."

"I bet it's a romantic story, my lord."

"Perhaps it is. My parents have always had an abundance of affection for each other."

"How nice. A love match, was it?"

"Whether it was at first, I don't know. It certainly is now." Thomas was beginning to find this conversation tedious, so he took a sip of wine, and then turned to Rose and Xavier.

"Oh, my goodness," Lady Gregory exclaimed. "My lovely new dinner gown, ruined!"

Thomas turned back to see that Lady Gregory had spilled her glass of red wine down the front of her dress.

"May I be of service, my lady?" the gentleman on her other side asked.

"Oh, no, I couldn't impose." Lady Gregory turned to Thomas. "My lord, I do hate to burden you, but it seems that I must excuse myself. Could I trouble you to escort me to my chamber?"

Thomas sighed. What could he do? "Of course, my lady." He rose, offered her his arm, and together they strode from the ornate dining room. Rose was engrossed in her conversation with Xavier, but both Lily and Emma saw him leave with Lady Gregory. Neither looked pleased.

★ ★ ★ ★

Later that evening Lily sat on the terrace with Rose, Alexandra, and Sophie.

"Have any of you seen Emma?"

"She took a walk with Thomas," Rose said. "Her mother went with them to chaperone."

"I need to talk to her when they return," Lily said.

"What about?" Sophie asked.

"I want to find out if that disgusting Lord Ludley tried anything uncouth during dinner. The poor thing was stuck between him and Wentworth this evening."

"Horrors!" Alexandra cried. "At least Wentworth couldn't stick his tongue into her mouth at the dinner table. He might have been able to reach her ear without anyone noticing, though."

"Goodness, Ally," Sophie said. "Where do you come up with such outlandish ideas?"

"It's not so outlandish. In a novel I read, the hero—"

Sophie clasped her hands over her ears. "I don't want to hear it! The thought of a tongue in my ear—how ghastly."

Lily smiled. Ghastly wasn't the term she would have chosen for that particular pleasure. "Wentworth and his tongue are the least of Emma's problems. His uncle is a complete lech. Rose and I have been dodging him for years."

"She's right, I'm afraid," Rose said. "He seems to know every trick in the book for stealing, shall we say, an impression of a woman's charms."

Sophie's hand flew to her mouth. "How horrid!"

"Yes, it is," Lily said. "I must talk to Emma. If he tried anything inappropriate, the duke will ask him to leave the estate. He told me so."

"You've gotten pretty chummy with His Grace, Lily." Alexandra smiled. "If there's anything going on..."

"There's nothing going on. I've been seated next to him at dinner twice, and we've gotten to know each other a bit. He's very charming."

"Charming and dashing," Alexandra said. "Too bad he's a renowned skirt chaser. But he's so handsome. And rich. I think that could be overlooked. Lily dear, how was your tour of the art collection last evening? You never returned."

"Didn't Rose tell you? I was feeling poorly."

"Yes, of course, Rose told us. She checked on you several times also." Alexandra winked. "That was quite the little coup you two devised."

"What on earth are you talking about, Ally?" Rose feigned innocence.

"Come now. You don't think we really believe that Lily was in her room resting after viewing the duke's art."

"Believe what you want," Lily said. "But that's exactly what—" She spied Emma and her mother returning to the terrace. "Emma!" She motioned. "Do come join us, please."

Emma approached them and sat down. "How are all of you this evening?"

"We're just fine, dear," Lily said. "How was your walk with Thomas?"

"Just lovely. He's heading back to the bachelor house now. There's a poker game tonight or something."

"Gambling? My goodness," Sophie said.

"It's probably just a friendly game, Sophie," Rose said. "Thomas enjoys gaming. Papa does too, actually."

"Emma," Lily said, "I'm so sorry about your unfortunate dinner companions this evening. If I had known you would be seated with Lord Ludley, I'd have warned you."

"Warned me about what?"

"About him. Tell me, did he try anything inappropriate?"

"He did seem to brush my thigh more than necessary, but I assumed it was because of his size. He is rather large."

"Large doesn't begin to describe him," Lily said. "And his thigh caressing was not an accident, I assure you."

"He also seemed to salivate a lot."

Lily laughed. "Yes, he's disgusting. Tell me, did he do anything that made you uncomfortable?"

"She'll have the duke kick him off the estate for you, you know," Alexandra said.

"No, no." Emma said. "I'm absolutely fine. There's no need... How can you get the duke to kick him off the estate, Lily?"

"Haven't you heard?" Alexandra held two fingers up side by side. "Lily and His Grace are like this."

"Ally, you're making that up," Lily said.

"I don't think so," she began, then, "My goodness, what time is it, anyway?"

"It was nearly ten when Lord Jameson and I parted," Emma said. "Why do you ask?"

"I have an engagement," Alexandra said, and then lowered her voice. "Mr. Landon and I are meeting on the back terrace."

"Ally!" Sophie exclaimed. "Without a chaperone?"

"Of course without a chaperone," Alexandra said. "What fun would it be otherwise?"

"I suppose I can't talk you out of this, can I?" Sophie shook her head. "Please use good sense though. Don't let him take any liberties."

"Oh, I wouldn't dream of it," Alexandra said, winking. "I plan to take the liberties myself. I'll see you all later. Will you be here for a while?"

"I'll only be here for a bit," Rose said. "I'm playing the grand piano in the conservatory for Lord Evan at eleven, and Lily is my chaperone. In fact, Lily, we should go. I'd like to warm up a bit. I haven't actually played the grand yet, and I need to get the feel of it. Would you two care to come along?"

She nodded to Sophie and Emma.

"Thank you just the same," Sophie said. "I think I'll stay out here. It's such a nice evening."

"I'll stay and chat with Sophie," Emma said. "But do have a lovely time."

"We will, dear," Lily said, linking arms with Rose and Alexandra. "Tomorrow evening there will be another formal ball. Won't that be fun?"

"Oh yes," Alexandra said. "I had a wonderful time at the first one. Except for Wentworth and his errant tongue, that is."

"Alexandra..." Sophie began.

"Sophie, darling, if you had been in my shoes, you would say the same thing. Do enjoy your evening, ladies." She broke away from Lily and hurried off.

Lily and Rose said goodbye and entered the house, making their way past the library to the conservatory. The chandelier had already been lit, and cast a luminous glow on the black lacquer grand piano in the center of the room. One wall of the large room was devoted entirely to bookshelves which housed written music of all kinds. In a corner stood a gilt-edged harp, and in another corner, several guitars and mandolins. The walls were filled with more paintings, and Lily slowly walked through the room, looking at each one with interest. She made a mental note to have Daniel explain them to her later and took a seat on a lush sofa covered in forest green satiny fabric.

"Start with the Mozart sonata, dear. It's my favorite," she said.

Rose sat down on the cushioned piano bench and sighed, lovingly running her fingers over the sleek ivory keys. "This is the most glorious instrument I have ever seen."

"It looks a lot like the one at our estate," Lily said.

Rose rolled her eyes. "Lily, this is at least two feet longer than ours, and the finish is far better quality. As for the sound, let's see." She played a few measures. "Can't you hear the difference?"

"Not really," Lily said.

"You are a goose. The tone is far superior." Rose began playing the Mozart. "It's almost as if the piano crescendos on its own. It knows exactly what to do."

"That's you, not the piano."

Rose blushed. "You put too much stock in my talent, Lily. I hope I don't embarrass myself."

"You play beautifully and you know it. When Daniel and Lord Evan get here, you should start with the Mozart. Then play your Bach. Then Handel's Water Music; that's lovely. And don't forget that cute little sonata by Scarlatti. I suppose you should play an English composer as well. How about Purcell? The music from the Fairy Queen is sweet."

"Goodness, Lily, this is just an informal little gathering. I'm not playing a full concert."

Lily ignored her. "Do you need me to go upstairs to the chamber and fetch your sheet music?"

"No, I can do it from memory. If only the Beethoven were ready."

"Try it now. I'll tell you if it's ready or not."

"I suppose I could, since the gentlemen aren't here yet." Rose began to play, her fingers dancing over the keys as the music soared from the piano.

"That's the Beethoven that isn't ready yet," Lily said to Daniel and Evan, who had entered while Rose was playing. "I thought it was tantalizing, Rose."

"Don't be absurd, Lily," Rose said, flushing. "I didn't even get through half of the concerto."

"You play beautifully," Evan said. "Which concerto is it?"

"Beethoven's *Fifth Piano Concerto in E Flat Minor*," Rose said. "He completed it in 1811. I've only been working on it a short time. I didn't mean for anyone but Lily to hear it."

"Nonsense, it was lovely," Evan said.

"Play the Mozart now, Rose." Lily turned to Daniel and Evan. "Mozart is my very favorite composer, ever since Papa took Rose and me to the opera to see *The Marriage of Figaro*. How old were we, Rose, about ten and eleven?"

"I was but nine, so you would have been ten," Rose said. "It was a wonderful performance." She laughed. "Thomas was seventeen. He escorted me and Papa escorted Lily. We had such fun playing grownup." Rose's face glowed. "All right, Lily, I'll play the Mozart for you." Her hands began dancing over the keys again, lightly bringing forth the delicate sonata.

Evan eventually went to sit beside her on the piano bench, watching her attentively. Daniel took Lily's hand in his and kissed her upturned palm. Lily smiled at him, enjoying the music and his attentions. Rose played for over an hour, ending with Scarlatti's sonata.

"You do play beautifully, my lady," Daniel said. "I don't know when I've enjoyed a concert more."

"You flatter me, Your Grace," Rose said. "But thank you for the compliment, and thank you also for allowing me to use the conservatory. It was a pleasure to play such a magnificent instrument."

"It's been a long time since anyone has played it so compellingly. Please feel free to use the conservatory anytime you wish during your stay at Laurel Ridge."

"Thank you, Your Grace."

"I must agree with His Grace, Rose," Evan said. "Your playing is compelling—more than just talent and technique. There is an emotional component to your music that is nearly indescribable. I'm not sure the composers themselves could have played their own pieces any better, or with more feeling."

"My lord, I do believe that is the nicest compliment I have ever received," Rose said, lowering her head. "I do thank you."

"It's quite late. May I see you to your chamber?" he asked her, standing and helping her to her feet.

"Yes, that would be fine. Lily can accompany us."

"Actually," Lily said. "I would like for Daniel to explain some of these lovely paintings to me. Would you care to wait a bit?"

"I'm frightfully tired," Rose said. "I-I suppose it's all right for us to go alone. It's just a walk to our chamber, after all. Shall we, my lord?" Rose took Evan's arm and he led her out of the conservatory.

"Alone at last," Daniel said to Lily, kissing her lightly on the lips. "Your sister is a splendid talent."

"I told you so," Lily said. "She has always considered herself a merely adequate musician. She's so blasted modest, it's annoying. But I think she's incredible."

"I agree, but you're even more incredible, in my humble opinion." He gathered her in his arms and kissed her, opening her lips with his tongue.

"Daniel, the paintings..."

"Can we talk about them tomorrow?" he asked softly, teasing her neck with warm, moist kisses.

"I suppose so. But Daniel, I can't go to your chamber again... I can't... Oh, bother."

Daniel led her out of the conservatory, down the hall and

up the servants' staircase to his chamber.

★ ★ ★ ★

Amelia stood in the dark outside the bachelor house. Jameson had come back from taking a walk with the skinny blond wench and then had gone inside and hadn't come out again. It was still early. What on earth was going on in there? Was she losing her touch? Jameson hadn't responded to any of her subtle advances when he escorted her to her chamber during dinner. She had ruined a perfectly good gown for nothing. She had never failed to attract any man of her choosing in the past, but just days ago the duke had rebuffed her. She would simply have to be more persuasive with Lord Jameson.

She may have lost the first battle, but she had every intention of winning the war.

CHAPTER TEN

In Daniel's chamber, a small feast awaited them again at the table in the sitting window. "What is that glorious smell?" Lily asked, inhaling.

"I'll show you in a minute. First..."

He turned her toward the wall facing the bed. In place of St. Praxedis hung Lily's two watercolors, framed in dark cherry.

"Oh!"

"Thank you for the paintings, Lily." He kissed the top of her head. "I hope you meant for me to keep them, because I'm going to anyway."

"Yes, of course, I want you to have them," Lily said. "But where is the Vermeer, Daniel?"

"I took it down."

"You can't possibly replace Vermeer with my work."

"It's my bedchamber. I'll do as I please. Now I'll think of you whenever I look up."

Lily turned around and kissed his cheek. "You are sweet. How on earth did you get them framed so quickly?"

"We keep a carpenter on the estate. When I returned from our ride and found the watercolors, I summoned him and asked if he could frame them by this evening, and he assured me he could. And there they are."

"But the Vermeer..."

"Don't worry about the Vermeer, Lily. It will be well

enjoyed."

"Where are you going to put it?"

"I haven't quite decided yet." His eyes sparkled. "But you'll be the first to know, I promise." He touched her cheek and smoothed his thumb over her bottom lip. "I wanted to thank you for the paintings when I saw you at dinner, but you went into a tirade about the seating, and then it slipped my mind. I'm sorry."

"Don't worry about that. You've thanked me more than enough by displaying them in such a touching way. But now that you mention it, what was going on with the seating?"

"I don't know. As I said, I told Aunt Lucy to keep the seating the same as it was last night."

"It's that Amelia Gregory." Lily seethed, her pulse jumping. "She wanted to sit next to Thomas so she changed her place card with Emma's. But when did she do it?"

"I don't know. Could we drop the subject now, Lily? I promise you it won't happen again, and I really don't want to talk about Lady Gregory and her—"

"I spoke to Emma," Lily interrupted. "She said Ludley did brush her thigh more often than she thought necessary."

"I'll see that he leaves on the morrow."

"No, you needn't. She said she was fine, and she didn't want him forced to leave. He is a lech, though."

"So you've told me." Daniel placed his hands on her shoulders. "Lily, if he so much as comes within ten feet of you, I want you to tell me."

"Don't worry about me. I can handle Ludley. I'm rather good at it, as I've had lots of practice."

"I'm serious. I want to know."

"Of course. My, do I have another protector now? As if my father and Thomas aren't enough."

"Your father and Thomas haven't been doing their job, if Ludley touched you when you were a child of fourteen."

"Good Lord, Daniel, I never told them, and neither did Rose. It's not something one talks about."

"You told me."

"Well, yes." Lily fidgeted with her skirt. Why had she told him? "I-I wanted you to understand the position Emma was in. She's an innocent girl."

"So were you, especially at fourteen. I really would like to strangle that man."

Lily smiled up at him, lacing her fingers through his gorgeous locks. "I can't say I wouldn't like to see him strangled myself. But I'm fine, really. He never got anywhere, I promise. No one ever touched me beneath my clothes...until you, that is. Besides, I don't want to see one little bruise on your beautiful body."

"I assure you, he would be the one bloodied and bruised."

"I don't doubt it." She pushed his velvet topcoat over his shoulders until it fell to the ground and slid her hands over his muscled arms. "I wouldn't want to be on your bad side."

"You never could be, love. But he is. He'll never get another invitation to Laurel Ridge as long as I'm the duke."

"Hush, now." Lily untied his cravat and unbuttoned the first few buttons of his shirt. She leaned up to kiss his throat. "Forget about Ludley. Everything is fine. Now, are you going to tell me what that magnificent aroma on the table is?"

Daniel led her to the table, sat down, and pulled her onto his lap. Two small pots on the table were heated by candles underneath them. A platter of cubed bread and a platter of fresh fruit accompanied them, along with two glasses of red wine.

"This is fondue. Have you ever had it?"

"No, actually, though I've heard of it. It's Swiss."

"Yes." He gestured to the pot nearer to them. "This one is made with Gruyère cheese and dry white wine, with just a touch of cherry brandy. You take a piece of bread, put it on the fondue fork, dip it in the cheese to coat it, and eat it off the fork. Go ahead."

Lily dipped the bread in the cheese mixture and swirled it around a bit, but when she pulled out the fork, the bread was gone. "I lost my bread."

"Poor angel," he said. "Now you have to pay the price. Anyone who loses his bread in the fondue pot has to kiss someone else at the table."

"But you're the only other person at the table," Lily said, giggling.

"I guess you'll have to kiss me then." His eyes gleamed at her. "I don't know how I shall tolerate it."

"I think you'll live." Lily bent her head to kiss his mouth lightly.

"That was no punishment." Daniel caught her lips with his, coaxing them open and devouring her mouth. "There," he said. "I hope you've learned your lesson. Now try again."

Lily placed another piece of bread on her fondue fork and swirled it in the cheese carefully.

"It's hot, so blow on it a bit first," Daniel said.

She obliged and then put it in her mouth. The tart creaminess of the cheese and the dry fruitiness of the wine exploded on her tongue. "My, that's wonderful." She put another cube of bread on her fork and dipped it in the cheese. "This one's for you." She blew on it and fed it to Daniel. "Good?"

"Excellent." He reached for a glass of wine. "Now take a

sip of this. It's the same wine we drank last night."

Lily took a drink, letting the berry flavors of the wine join the lingering tanginess of the cheese. "Oh, that's good."

Daniel took a sip. "I agree. Most culinary experts claim that one should drink a white wine with a cheese dish such as this, but I prefer red with just about everything."

"How dare you defy the conventions like that?" Lily said, smiling as she speared another chunk of bread and immersed it in the creamy mixture. "I'm going to be two stone heavier by the time I leave Laurel Ridge."

★ ★ ★ ★

The thought of Lily leaving Laurel Ridge jarred Daniel. He took her fork from her before she could eat, grabbed her cheeks, and drew her to his mouth, feasting. She tasted of the cheese and the wine, but mostly of the earthy, sensual flavor that he had come to know as her own. Intoxicating. They were both gasping when he ended the kiss.

"Don't you want any more to eat?" Lily rasped.

"No, I don't believe I do." He stood up with her in his arms and devoured her lips again. "I want to take you to bed. Now."

"But we haven't tried the fruit yet. Or the other pot—"

He silenced her with another ravening kiss, as he worked the fasteners on the back of her gown, his heart thundering so hard he thought it must be audible.

"Yet you make a very strong argument..." Lily sighed softly as he kissed her cheeks, her ears, her neck.

"I'm going to love you until dawn, Lily," he said huskily. "You're not going to get a wink of sleep tonight."

"Who needs sleep?" she replied in a low voice. "Take me

to bed, Daniel."

He set her on the bed and removed his own clothing quickly. His arousal sprang from his trousers. Lily's gaze burned into him.

"See something you like?" he asked.

She flushed, the redness meandering across her creamy skin. God, she was beautiful.

"Take me quickly, Daniel. I want you inside me."

"Anything you wish." He lay down beside her on the bed. He gently lowered his hand to stroke her. "You're already wet. My God, I can't get enough of you."

He entered her gently, finding a rhythm as she arched her hips to take in more of him. Sweet heaven, she fit him perfectly.

"Harder, Daniel. Faster!"

Daniel pulled himself up on his knees, lifting her bottom to meet him, and plunged into her. "You like it when I pound you, don't you, Lily? You like my cock deep inside your pussy." With one thumb, he massaged her peak in a counter rhythm to his thrusts.

"Daniel!" She shuddered in orgasm.

Her pleasure saturated every cell of his body, every recess of his soul, as if it were his own. He exploded with one last rush. "Lily!" A flood of emotion overtook him and his entire body shook with his release.

Gasping, he fell atop her, careful not to let his full weight crush her. "Lily, Lily," he whispered.

She rubbed his back in soothing patterns. When his breathing returned to normal, he moved to the side, his limp sex sliding out of her.

"Daniel, that was amazing," Lily said. "But I'm not done with you yet. You promised me a full night of love."

"You shall have it. I just need a few minutes." He sighed and laid one arm across his forehead.

"Very well." Lily sat up, left the bed, and came back with the platter of fruit. She pushed a grape between his lips. "You require sustenance. You'll need lots of energy for what I have in mind."

"God help me," Daniel said, swallowing the grape. "You drive me mad, do you know that?"

"I'll take that as a compliment."

"It's the highest compliment I've ever given." He smiled, and then sat up next to her and fed her a strawberry.

Lily left the bed again and came back with a glass of wine. She was so beautiful. He should have had flowers brought in for her. Lilies, of course.

"Where did your name come from?" he asked.

"Oh," Lily groaned. "Don't get me started. My mother's name is Flora, which is a Latin form of flower, and her sister's name is Iris. Mummy decided all of her daughters would have flower names also, hence Lily and Rose. Thank God Auntie Iris decided to forego the horrid tradition."

"So I suppose you won't be naming any daughters Begonia? Or Creeping Charlie?"

"Creeping Charlie isn't a flower, you silly." She laughed. "But no. I prefer more classic names."

"Like what?"

"I don't know. Caroline. Or Hilary. Or your mother's name, Morgana. It's a derivative of Morgaine, who was King Arthur's half sister, the sorceress. Her exotic beauty reminds me of a sorceress. It fits her."

"I think your name fits you."

"How so?"

"Well, calla lilies symbolize beauty, and yellow lilies symbolize gaiety, both of which you possess in abundance." He smiled, winking. "Of course, there are also white lilies."

"What do they symbolize?"

He pulled her to him and cupped her full breasts in his hands. "Virginity," he whispered in her ear, and then plunged his tongue into its depth.

Lily gave him a punch in the arm. "You are such a rogue! I'm afraid I'm not living up to my name." She pushed him back until he was lying on the bed and fell on top of him, straddling him. "Then again, what fun would that be?" She wiggled her hips, teased his cock with her wetness, and then moved aside.

"You're leaving now?"

"I'll be right back," she said, and she was, carrying a small plate on which she had placed several spoonfuls of the contents of the other fondue pot. "This looks amazingly like chocolate."

"It is. I had the cook melt some of the Belgian truffles with a little fresh cream. It's decadent."

"Is it now?" She swirled her finger into the creamy mass and licked it seductively.

God. His cock ached.

"Oh yes. Decadent. You must try it, Daniel."

He sat up, ready to dip his own finger into the chocolate, but she pushed him away.

"I think you'll try it another way." She circled her fingers in the dark mixture again. Slowly she spread the warm chocolate onto her erect nipples.

Daniel's arousal throbbed. "Dear Lord." He lowered his lips to her breasts and licked the sweet confection from her hard nubs, gently sucking.

She threaded her fingers through his hair. "Oh my. The

warmth of the chocolate, and then your tongue. Sucking. Yes, suck my nipple. Just like that. More. More."

Daniel's cock was ready to explode. He spread more chocolate onto her nipples and ravished them again, biting and nipping, twirling his tongue in intricate patterns around her rosy circles. The creaminess of the melted chocolate and the silky texture of her areolas combined in a sweet, fiery frenzy.

"Oh, Daniel. I feel that all the way down in my..."

He looked up and met her blazing cognac gaze. "In your pussy, love?"

"Yes, but I can't say that word." She blushed a rosy pink.

"What do you prefer, then? Cunny? Quim? *Boite aux lettres?*"

"None of—" She jerked her head. "*Boite aux lettres?*"

Daniel smiled. "It's French, for letterbox."

"I know what it means. Goodness, I've studied French. It's just— Why in the world would anyone call it a letterbox?"

"I haven't the slightest idea. I prefer pussy. Your pussy." He stroked her folds. "The tastiest, reddest, most beautiful pussy ever created."

"Perhaps I can make it even tastier." She swirled her fingers in the chocolate again and then liberally covered her cunt with chocolate.

"Oh my God." She was something, his Lily. So saucy and irreverent, yet so caring and lovely at the same time. Daniel lowered his head between her legs. "I'm going to eat you up, love. I swear I could live on your nectar alone." He savored the taste of her, the smell of her, growing harder by the second as he probed her moist pussy with his tongue.

She moaned and shuddered against his lips and cheeks. Before he could begin again, she pulled him forward and kissed him.

"I never imagined feeling the way I do with you," she said.

"I know. I feel it too," Daniel said hoarsely.

He kissed her again. Their tongues tangled deeply and intimately as they slowly made love with their mouths.

Lily broke the kiss, panting. "I want you to do something for me."

"Anything."

"Show me how to love a man."

"What?"

"I want to know how to please you. You've made love to me, given me pleasure. I want to do the same for you."

"You've already given me more pleasure than I've ever known."

She swatted his arm lightly. "I'm serious. I want to learn how to pleasure a man, and I want you to teach me."

"You don't need any teaching." Daniel smiled into her eyes. "But I will tell you one little secret."

"What's that?" she asked, lowering her head to his.

"Whatever I do to you, I would like you to do to me." He winked at her.

"But how could I—" Her eyes widened. "Oh..."

Daniel sensed her unease. "I don't want you to do anything that makes you uncomfortable, love."

"Don't be silly. I want to give you pleasure, and if you want...*that*, I shall do it." She smiled, her eyes so full of promise and desire that he thought his heart might burst open. "But I'm going to kiss every inch of your scrumptious body first."

"Sweet Lord," he groaned.

She spread tiny kisses along his jawline, rubbing her face against his. She kissed his neck and swirled her tongue in the hollow of his throat. She raised his arms over his head and brushed her fingers through the tufts of hair underneath. She kissed his shoulders and upper arms, tracing the lines of his muscles with her tongue. Sparks sizzled everywhere in her wake. Lord, he wouldn't survive this.

"You have the strongest arms, Daniel." She smoothed her fingers over his muscle. "I feel so safe when you hold me."

"You are safe in my arms, Lily." And he meant it.

Lily ran her fingers through the coarse curls on his chest and lightly touched his nipples. "How did you get this?" She touched a six inch scar below his right nipple.

"Fencing at school. I was trying to show off, but my opponent had more skill."

"Poor darling." Lily lowered her head and traced the scar with her tongue. She covered his chest with kisses, swirling her tongue through his hair, licking down to his navel and pushing her tongue inside it.

"Your touch, your kisses," he said. "I can't get enough."

She gave his cock a chaste kiss on the head. It jerked of its own accord.

She smiled up at him. "I'll be back," she said, and she ran her hands down the length of his legs, exploring every line of muscle. She kissed his thighs, his knees, his calves, his feet, and made her way back up, running her tongue along his inner thighs.

He shivered. "God, Lily, I feel like a lad."

"Is that good?"

"Yes, love, it's very good."

He closed his eyes as she came to his cock. She kissed the tip of it again and ran her tongue down its length.

"Tell me what to do, Daniel. I don't want to hurt you."

"Lord," he groaned. "You won't hurt me. Just do whatever feels right."

Slowly she ran her tongue over and around his balls and in the creases between them and his thighs. She moved upward, licking his swollen shaft, pressing her lips to it in tiny kisses. When she came to the head, she enfolded her mouth around it and sucked gently.

He gasped. Had anything ever felt so good? So right? Carefully she took more of it into her mouth, and then eased back. She licked down to his balls again, cupped them in her hand, and returned to his cock, sucking gently but firmly. Then she slid her mouth down as far as she could once again. He quivered, his whole body awash with sensation. Sweet Lord, he was going to come. His cock began to pulsate.

"Lily," he gasped. "Oh God!"

She looked up at his face, her dark eyes wide and her lips still enfolding him as he shuddered and spilled into her mouth.

Lily raised her head, and the viscous liquid slid down his shaft. She touched it, rubbing it between her fingers.

Daniel closed his eyes, embarrassed. "I'm so sorry." What was wrong with him? He had never spent himself in a woman's mouth before. Most prostitutes didn't allow it, and while some of his other lovers might have, he had always considered it too intimate for a casual sexual encounter.

"I don't know what happened. I just... It felt so good."

"It's all right. I don't mind." She cleared her throat. "At least I know I was doing an adequate job."

"Adequate? Sweet Jesus. Come here."

She climbed over him and lay on his chest. "I guess I don't need to worry about getting with child doing it that way."

With child.

Daniel's heart nearly stopped. He had promised Lily that he wouldn't impregnate her. He was supposed to pull out, or use a French letter, or do something. But he hadn't. He hadn't at all. *Ever*. She could very well be breeding. Although the thought of her lush body swelling with his child filled him with a primal joy, his stomach churned with guilt and remorse. It was a new feeling for someone who was used to thinking only of himself. He had completely violated her trust.

"Oh no," he said aloud.

"What is it?"

How could he tell her that he had been so blinded by desire for her that he hadn't bothered to take care of the one thing she had asked of him? She would hate him.

"Nothing, love. It's just that, I want to please you now."

"You don't have to."

He silenced her with his mouth, and then turned her over onto her back. He kissed her breasts and her belly, lifted her knees and dove into her, feasting on her taste, her scent, the feel of her. Soon she was shivering, moaning, as his fingers and tongue brought her to orgasm. He continued to lick her, plunder her, driving her to another climax, and then another, the sound of his name from her ruby lips fueling him to greater and greater passion. He pushed farther, even as the pleasure became too intense for her and she pleaded for him to stop. He forced her to the pinnacle again and again, until she was screaming in joyful agony.

When he finally released her, looking into her beautiful face tormented with ecstasy, savoring her spicy aroma, her sweet milky taste, a decision came to him quickly.

He could not let her go.

He *would* not let her go.

No other man would know her as he did. He would possess her body and mind. Her heart. Her soul. He would do whatever necessary to keep Lily at Laurel Ridge. With him. Forever.

He crawled atop her and thrust himself into her body, making her his the only way he knew how.

CHAPTER ELEVEN

A brisk knock on her chamber door startled Lily. She had fallen asleep almost as soon as she lay down after Daniel had returned her to her chamber early that morning. Rose had been sleeping soundly and hadn't stirred when Lily came in. Rose got up and went to the door. A housemaid stood there, feather duster in hand.

"Yes, what is it?" Rose asked.

"I beg your pardon, milady. Your parents want to see you and Lady Lily in the private sitting room of their chamber right away."

Rose yawned. "Why? What time is it anyway?"

"It's half past nine, milady, and I don't know what they want. They bid me to fetch you and your sister. A servant is fetching your brother at the bachelor house."

"What on earth?" Lily stumbled out of bed and joined Rose at the door.

"Mummy and Papa want to see us in their sitting room," Rose said. "I don't know why."

"Yes, I heard," Lily said. "But I'm too tired. I'm going back to bed."

"But milady," the maid pleaded. "I was bid to tell you to come quickly!"

"Why? Is something wrong?" Rose asked.

"No, milady. Your parents are well. But they said the matter was of utmost importance."

"We'd better go, Lily," Rose said. "They wouldn't send for us this early if it wasn't important."

"You go, and then you can come back and tell me what the devil is so urgent to wake me up at this hour."

"Lily..."

"Oh for God's sake, Rose, all right." She turned to the housemaid. "I require a bath. Could you send someone to attend me?"

"There's isn't time for that," the housemaid said. "But I'll bring you a basin of steaming water right away." She hurried off.

"No time for a bath?" Lily rolled her eyes and began to brush her long, thick hair. A maid returned with hot water for their two basins, and Lily and Rose washed quickly and helped each other dress in their best morning outfits. They braided each other's hair and pinned it, and when they were both satisfied with the results, they headed down the hall to their parents' chamber in the corner.

The Earl of Ashford was seated behind a mahogany desk, the spectacles that he used for reading perched on his nose. Before him were stacks of documents. The countess sat next to the desk, soft and pretty in her yellow morning garments. Thomas, dapper in a grey morning coat, stood next to her, nibbling on a croissant and drinking tea.

The earl looked up. "Lily, Rose, do have a seat. I trust you haven't broken your fast yet?"

"No, Papa," they answered in unison.

"See to my daughters," he said to the maid.

The maid prepared plates for them from a tray on a buffet table in the corner while Lily and Rose sat down with Thomas on the sofa. Lily looked at bread and fruit on the plate handed to her. Her stomach churned. She didn't feel the least bit hungry.

"Papa," she began, "what is going—"

"In a moment, Lily," Ashford said, glancing over some papers in his hands.

The maid brought Lily and Rose steaming cups of tea. Lily gnawed on a croissant but it tasted like saw dust. What on earth was wrong? They sat in silence, waiting for the earl to speak.

Finally, he cleared his throat. "I had a visitor this morning," he said. "A very important one."

"Who was it, Papa?" Rose asked.

"Well"—he cleared his throat again—"it seems that I have received a request for one of my daughters' hands in marriage."

My, Lord Evan certainly works fast. Lily turned to her sister. "Congratulations, Rose!"

"My goodness. I—" Rose began.

"The offer isn't for Rose, Lily," the earl interrupted. "It's for you."

Lily opened her eyes wide and she jumped off the couch. "For me? Who in the world would offer for me?"

Ashford cleared his throat one more time and adjusted his spectacles. "The Duke of Lybrook."

Daniel? *Daniel?* "The duke?" Lily gasped, grabbing for the arm of the sofa. What was going on?

"He came to me this morning with the proposal," the earl said. "It seems you've made quite an impression on him."

"I'd say so," Thomas said.

"Keep quiet, Thomas," Lily said. "Papa, I'm sorry. I don't wish to marry."

"That's quite irrelevant, Lily," the earl said. "I've already accepted his offer."

"Fine." Lily plunked her bottom back on the sofa. "Then you marry him."

"Lily!" the countess admonished.

"Be still, Flora," the earl said. Then, "Lily, you've made no secret of your feelings about the coming season. This arrangement will spare you being displayed like a pork chop, as you like to put it. Besides, you're a smart girl. I don't have to explain to you the advantages of an alliance between the Lybrook and Ashford houses."

"Alliance?" Lily's face heated. "If this is about money, why don't you put me on the auction block and sell me to the highest bidder?"

"Lily, my goodness," the countess said. "We've no need of Lybrook's fortune, and he has no need of ours."

"No, he doesn't," the earl continued. "He has already refused to take your dowry."

"Then what is the point of all of this nonsense? Why should I be forced to marry?"

"There are more important considerations than money, Lily. An alliance between our two families will have...political benefits."

"So you'll marry me off for the sake of politics? How charming."

"Lily"—the countess's voice was warm and soothing—"your father and I have always wanted what is best for you. The duke's offer is a generous one. He is a powerful man, and a kind one. You could do a lot worse."

"That is for me to decide, is it not?"

"No, it's not," the earl said. "Lybrook and I have already reached a betrothal agreement."

"What?" Lily screamed.

"Lower your voice, please," her father warned. "I'll not have our business aired like dirty laundry around this estate."

"Betrothal agreement?" Lily seethed, her pulse racing. "This is simply barbaric. Rose, Thomas, tell them."

Neither Rose nor Thomas spoke.

"Fat lot of help you two are," Lily said, scoffing. "Papa, you'll just have to break the agreement. I'm not getting married to anyone."

"You'll do as I tell you," the earl said. "Lybrook is a good man."

"He's a rake." Lily crossed her arms over her chest.

"A good man," the earl repeated. "He seems to have a genuine affection for you."

"Lily," her mother said, "you'll be a duchess, and the mother of the next duke."

"Yes, I'm sure he'll have me barefoot on my back in no time, pushing out his brats."

"Lily, please!"

"Let her get it off of her chest, Flora," the earl said. "She'll come to terms with the arrangement soon enough."

"I'll never come to terms with this. You and the duke seem to think you have the right to plan my whole life for me. Well, you don't! There are things I want to do. What about my art? My writing? I want to travel! Damn you! Damn all of you!" She clenched her fists tightly, her knuckles white with tension.

"This is ridiculous," the earl said. "I've allowed your silly infatuation with art and writing up to now because it seemed to amuse you, but you really didn't believe that I would tolerate a spinster artist for a daughter, did you? You have a duty to the Ashford name to marry and carry on our line."

"That is Thomas's duty, not mine!"

"Keep me out of this," her brother said.

"I...oh, bloody hell!" She unclenched her fists, and a trickle of blood ran down her left palm where a fingernail had dug into her fair skin.

"You have much to offer the duke," Lord Ashford said. "You are intelligent. Talented. Beautiful. And you have the Ashford name. But if you insist on talking like a sailor on shore leave—"

"Lily," Lady Ashford interrupted, "I've seen you with the duke at the evening meal. You and he share an ease together that... I don't know, you both seem to smile a lot. I guess it was my impression that you had affection for him as well."

"Enjoying his company at dinner is not sufficient reason to shackle myself to him for eternity," Lily said dully.

"If you'll just give this arrangement a chance, dear, I think it could benefit everyone."

"Everyone but me!" Lily cried. "I won't stand for it!"

"You will," the earl said. "You have no choice."

"Papa, please!" Then, "It just so happens that... Oh!" Lily's blood boiled. She wanted to throw in his face that she couldn't ever marry, that she was ruined, but that fact was irrelevant. It was the culprit who wanted to marry her.

"You need a husband," Lord Ashford continued. "Since you've made it clear that you have no intention of finding one on your own, this is a godsend, frankly. He's a well esteemed peer from a wealthy and respected house. He needs a wife of good lineage, and he wants you."

"I suppose I'll make an adequate broodmare," Lily said dryly. "My God, he has a lot of nerve."

"Do you have any idea how many women would love to be

in your shoes?" the countess said.

Lily took off her morning shoes and threw them across the room, one narrowly missing her father's ear. "They can all have my shoes!" she bellowed. "I won't be one of his strumpets, or his mistress!"

"I've had just about enough of this." Ashford strode toward her.

The countess waved him off. "Lily"—she sat down and took her daughter's hand in her own—"calm down. He's not asking you to be his mistress. Goodness, he's asking you to be his wife."

"While he keeps a dozen mistresses, no doubt." Lily's eyes filled with tears. "And he's not asking me. He and Papa are telling me."

"This is a very common way for marriages to be arranged." The countess rubbed the palm of Lily's hand with her thumb. "You know that."

"I don't give two figs about what is common, Mummy," Lily said, weeping. "I don't want to marry. Not now. Not ever."

"The agreement has been made," the earl said. He strode from the room briskly.

The countess continued to hold Lily's hand. "You'll come to accept this in time. The two of you will have a good and solid life together. He can give you everything you want."

"I already have everything I want."

"Rose, Thomas," Lady Ashford said, "take Lily back to her chamber. She needs to rest."

"Thank you both for your help," Lily said as they walked from their parents' suite. "Why, I don't know how I could have made it through this without your support."

"I'm sorry, Lily," Rose said. "I didn't know what to say. But you do like the duke, don't you?"

"Lybrook's a good man, Lily," Thomas said. "He was always a good man, even when he was a skirt chaser, but since his father and brother were killed, he's...different."

"How would you know? He's been on the continent for a year."

"There's been talk at the bachelor house. Don't get me wrong. Papa should have discussed this with you first. I wouldn't be any happier if it were me."

"But it will never be you, will it Thomas?" Lily said. "As a man, you can choose whom you will marry."

"Damn it, Lily, I didn't make the rules."

"You can both go to hell," Lily said. "I have business to attend to."

"Where are you going?" Rose asked.

"To see His Grace," Lily said, "and don't even think about trying to stop me."

"Dear God," Rose said.

"Dear God is right," Thomas agreed. "Poor Lybrook won't know what hit him."

★ ★ ★ ★

Daniel was relaxing in his leather chair wearing a dressing robe, his face half covered in shaving soap, when Lily barged into his suite without knocking. Putney stood before him holding a razor in his hand.

"My lady," he said. "This is highly—"

"Don't worry about it, Putney," Lily said sardonically. "Haven't you heard the good news? I am the duke's betrothed."

"Your Grace?"

"It's all right, Putney," Daniel said. "You can go."

"Here, I'll take that." Lily grabbed the razor out of Putney's hand. "Shaving is a wifely duty, is it not?" Then, when Putney had left, "Although I doubt you want me anywhere near your neck with a sharp object, Your Grace."

Daniel didn't think Lily would actually hurt him, but he didn't want her waving a razor around. She had worked up quite a head of steam and she might accidentally harm herself. He wiped the soap from his face with a towel and stood. "Give that to me, Lily."

"No."

"Come on." He took her hand and pried her fingers from the handle of the razor. "Let's talk about this like adults."

"Why should I talk about anything like an adult? I'm not being treated like one. Others are making my decisions for me. Decisions that should be mine alone to make."

"Lily—"

"Damn it, Daniel, we had an agreement."

"An agreement?"

"You know how I feel about marriage."

"I was hoping you might change your mind."

"Change my mind? Are you insane? You thought you could change my mind by forcing me into marriage? You don't know me at all."

Daniel sighed. He *did* know her. He would have talked to her, asked her to stay with him, had he not been afraid she might decline. Arranging a betrothal agreement with her father was the only way he could be certain of keeping her. "Maybe I should have talked to you first."

"Maybe? *Maybe?*" She raised her hands in the air. "I won't do it, Daniel. I won't be forced into some sham of a marriage for the sole purpose of carrying on your noble line!"

"Well, I do need an heir," Daniel said. "And your bloodline is excellent."

"Yes, I suppose I'm an acceptable purebred bitch, aren't I?" She stood, indignant, her fists clenched, her face flushed.

God, she was the most beautiful woman on earth.

"You sound like you're breeding horses or dogs. Why didn't you set your sights on Rose, then? She could have given you a gaggle of blond-haired babes. With me, half of them are likely to be dark."

Beautiful, yes. And headstrong. He had to have her. "I don't care what color of hair my heir has. Good God."

"Tell me, why are you so set on marrying me? Why would you want a wife like me? I'll make your life hell, and you know it."

Daniel reached for her hand.

She jerked away. "Don't touch me."

"All right." He gave her a moment. He didn't know how to tell her why he wanted to marry her. He wasn't exactly sure himself. All he knew was that he could not, *would* not, let her go. He was afraid of what he might become without her. She had changed him. He no longer wanted the same things out of life. He wanted more. He wanted her.

"Well?"

"Lily, I'm the duke now. I have responsibilities."

"And these responsibilities include forcing an unwilling woman into marriage?"

"No, of course not."

"Then you'll let me go?"

"No. Er, what I mean is, my responsibilities are..." He raked his fingers through his hair. "I told you, I need an heir."

"But why me, Daniel? Why does it have to be me?"

"I...hold you in high esteem."

"How touching."

Daniel winced. Was it possible that she didn't care for him at all? He could hardly believe it. Their lovemaking had been unlike anything he had ever experienced. They had shared so much else, too. She had to feel something for him, and he intended to find out exactly what. He cleared his throat. "Tell me, Lily. Why did you let me make love to you?"

"We're not talking about that," she said. "It has nothing to do with this subject."

"Maybe it does, and maybe it doesn't, but I want to know. Why did you stay with me? You were innocent. You knew who and what I was. You knew I would ruin you."

"Please don't say you're marrying me because of some false sense of honor."

"That isn't what I'm saying, damn it. I want to know why you let me make love to you."

"Education and experience," she said. "Nothing more."

"Education and experience?" A brick landed in his gut. Was that really all he was to her? "Well, I hope it was all you thought it should be."

"It was acceptable," she said, "but it was no reason to marry."

"All right, Lily. Then there's another reason." He set about to hurt her as she had hurt him. "You could be breeding."

Her beautiful eyes widened. "What?"

"You heard me."

"But you promised me you would take care of that." Her dark eyes shone with shock...and terror.

"I didn't," he said. "I forgot."

"You *forgot?*"

"Yes, it didn't seem important at the time. You didn't seem to care. At least, you never mentioned it."

"Oh!" She clenched her fists, briskly walking to the table where they had shared their small meal the previous evening. She picked up the nearly empty wine bottle and hurled it, barely missing one of her own watercolors. Burgundy liquid dripped down the elegantly papered walls as shards of green glass scattered across Daniel's Oriental rug.

"God forgive me for being so ignorant! I don't know how to prevent pregnancy. You told me you did. I trusted you!" Tears welled up in her eyes. "I should have broken that over your head!"

Daniel wanted to grab her and pull her to him. To kiss her and give her comfort. Seeing her tears nearly destroyed him.

"I can't do anything that I wanted to do now," she sobbed. "I can't go to the Louvre and paint the Mona Lisa like your mother did. I can't climb a mountain, I can't travel to the Orient, and I... Oh, I can't bear this!" She pulled at her braids, tugging strings of hair loose.

"You can still do all of that." He strode toward her hesitantly. "I'll take you anywhere you want to go. I always meant that."

"No," she cried quietly. "No, I can't. Not if I'm with child."

"You won't be with child forever."

"It doesn't matter. I still don't want to marry. I-I hereby release you from all responsibility for me and my child."

"*Our* child, Lily."

For a moment she seemed to soften, and he went toward her quickly. He put his arms around her and held her head to his shoulder. Her body relaxed, if only a bit, in his arms, one hand touching his hair, the other on his forearm. He held her gently, stroking her back, kissing her hair, saying nothing. After a few moments, she broke away.

"I'm not marrying you. You can't force me."

"Your father and I have reached an agreement."

"Yes, of course, the business agreement to make me your live-in whore. I don't think so. I won't be part of your band of strumpets, Daniel. I won't! You're nothing but a scoundrel."

Daniel had been called that name more times than he could remember, but never had it felt like an arrow in his heart. He went to her, held out his arms to her. Her skin was burning with fiery redness, her lips the color of the wine they had shared. God, how he wanted her. She was like a malady from which he couldn't recover. A drug that his body craved. He would take her, and he would love her until she screamed. He would make her want him.

But she cowered before him, refusing to come back into his embrace. "No. Once you force me into this marriage, I won't be able to stop you. But until then, you *will* maintain your distance."

Daniel's cock hardened under his dressing robe, aching for the sweet release that only she could give him. He rammed his fist into the wall, tearing the wallpaper and denting the panel underneath. Blood oozed from his knuckles, but in his angry passion he felt no pain. "For God's sake, Lily, do you have any idea how many women have tried to marry me over the years? I'm willing to give you what I've never even considered giving another!"

"Don't you dare include me in the troop of doxies who've tried to trap you. I'm not one of them. I never was. I will not marry you!"

"Oh yes, you will." She would be his, no matter what. "I will obtain a special license and we will be married at the end of next week, when the house party ends. Our betrothal will be announced at the ball tonight, after which we will share the first dance. Wear something appropriate. Now if you'll excuse me, I need to get dressed. I have business to attend to."

He guided her out the door and shut it in her face.

★ ★ ★ ★

Her fists still clenched, Lily strode toward her chamber. Appropriate? Ha! Appropriate attire to join his band of strumpets, no doubt. She would show him. She changed her route abruptly and went downstairs to find Crawford.

"I need a modiste brought in from Bath," she said to the butler. "Time is of the essence. I need a gown for the ball tonight."

"For tonight? I'm afraid that won't be possible."

"Make it possible, Crawford. Pay whatever is necessary to get her here and have the job done by tonight. Charge it to His Grace."

"Pardon?"

"You heard me. He'll pay for it. Trust me, he won't even flinch. I'll be in my chamber when she arrives."

Lily flew up the double staircase to her chamber. Thankfully Rose was out. Lily paced around the room, agitated, her teeth clenched and her nostrils flaring. Damn Daniel for forcing his will on her. If only she hadn't stayed with him that first time. If only she had never gone to his bedchamber to see the Vermeer.

But seeing the Vermeer...and sharing it with him—

someone who appreciated it as much as she did, enough to hang it in his bedchamber so he could gaze at it whenever he liked—had been a dream. Letting him love her had also been a dream. She had never imagined such passion and tenderness could exist between two people.

Of course she had no experience. Perhaps making love was like that for everyone.

Why did she still want him? Her heart still raced and her nipples still tightened when she thought of his hands caressing her body, his tongue tasting her, his cock penetrating her. She had refused him this morning to hurt him, but she had denied herself what she desired most.

She sat down on her bed and ran her fingers over her belly, wondering if Daniel's child slumbered inside. She had been a fool to trust him, and his actions, or rather his inactions, were unforgivable. Yet she had gone willingly. She should have been more prepared with knowledge before embarking on such an affair. She would never let ignorance get the best of her again.

Somehow, though, the thought of having Daniel's baby wasn't nearly as distasteful as she had told him it was. True, she didn't want to be with child. There was too much she wanted to do first. But a child. A little part of Daniel and a little part of her, linking them for all time. She smiled faintly as she stroked her belly, and for a moment she imagined a bright-eyed baby boy with silky blond hair and sparkling green eyes, bouncing on her knee and smiling up at her, loving her.

Yes, loving her.

Love.

Daniel didn't love her. He was only marrying her out of some misguided sense of responsibility for possibly getting her with child. She was an acceptable breeder for his heir.

Maybe, though, if Daniel loved their child, he could grow to love her as well. Maybe, someday, he wouldn't need his strumpets and mistresses.

But did she love Daniel? She cared deeply for him, more than she wanted to. And she certainly desired him. She had lied to him when she said she was only after education and experience. She had lied to herself as well. She had convinced herself at first that sleeping with him would be a valuable experience for her writing, but the truth was much more simple than that. She wanted him, and she had gone back to him because she wanted to be with him. She enjoyed his company. She liked talking with him, spending time with him, making love with him. She hadn't been able to stay away from him.

But was that love? Especially given the fact that they had spent all of three days together?

Even if it was love, she didn't want to marry him. He could never be faithful to one woman, given his reputation, and if she were going to marry at all, she at least deserved her husband's fidelity.

She rose from her bed, grabbed one of her empty canvases, set up her portable easel, and fetched the oil paint set. She took out the mixing palette, chose various tubes, and began mixing the paints with a small knife. She started with a bright green and added some blue. It made a nice turquoise, but that didn't suit her. She started with blue next, adding violet, and then went back to the green and mixed in a hint of black. Beautiful. Now a tiny smidgen of violet and dark blue. Gorgeous. She took a brush and stroked color onto the canvas, trying some of the different techniques she had read about. The hue was rich and lustrous, but it still wasn't quite right. She started again—

Drat! She was trying to recreate the color of Daniel's eyes.

Why couldn't she control her thoughts of him? Her desire for him?

She took the tube of black paint and squirted it on the canvas, annihilating the green, and then fell onto her bed, refusing to let the tears come.

CHAPTER TWELVE

Lily ordered a lunch tray in her chamber but barely touched it, unable to erase the memories of the morning.

Rose came in later. "I thought you would be with His Grace," she said.

"Why on earth would you think that?"

"You said you were going to see him when you left Thomas and me, and then you didn't come down for lunch, so I just assumed..."

Lily snorted. "You just assumed I jumped in his bed, didn't you?"

"Well, I don't mean to offend you..."

"No offense taken, dear. I've certainly done nothing in the past few days to indicate that I would have acted any differently." She sighed. "For God's sake, why didn't you stop me?"

"Lily..."

"No, don't answer that. You couldn't have stopped me. No one could have. Oh, if only I'd had more sense!"

"Lily, if there's anything you want to talk about—"

A knock on the door interrupted Rose, and Lily rose to answer it. Two footmen stood in the hallway, along with several packages.

"From His Grace, milady," one of them said. "Where should we put them?"

"Put them back wherever you found them," Lily said. "I

don't want them."

"Sorry, milady, we have our orders. We'll just stack them over there by the dressing room." They piled the packages neatly. "Do you require anything else, milady?"

"Yes." Lily stood with her hands on her hips. "Take them back out of here."

"Sorry, milady." He grinned, and the two left the room.

Lily eyed the pile before her.

"Aren't you going to open them?" Rose asked.

"Good heavens, no. I don't want his bribes."

"Come on. Your curiosity must be killing you. I know mine is."

"No."

"Just one?"

"You want to open them? Go ahead. I'll sit over here." She plopped down on her bed.

Rose giggled. "Maybe just one." She chose a box the size of a dinner plate and ripped off the brown wrapping. Inside was a leather case that snapped open. Rose lifted the lid and gasped. "Lily, look!" She hurried to her sister. Nestled on velvet was a diamond-and-ruby necklace with matching ear bobs, set in gold. "These are flawless. This must have cost a fortune!"

"They likely cost him nothing, Rose. They're probably part of the Lybrook collection." Lily shook her head, though she couldn't help admiring the jewels.

"They'll be lovely on you," Rose said. "Perfect for your coloring. I could never wear rubies. My blond hair and peachy pale skin would clash horrendously. But on you, why, they'll be exquisite." She sighed.

"I suppose they're...nice."

"Nice? They're amazing. May I open another one?"

"Open as many as you'd like."

Rose chose another small box in which she found a pearl choker with earrings to match. "How gorgeous!" She brought them to Lily.

Lily hated to admit it, but Daniel did have impeccable taste. "Oh, go ahead," she said to Rose. "Open the rest of them. You can start with that hat box. I detest hats. He doesn't know me at all."

Rose picked up the box and held it. "This hat box seems to be whimpering." She lifted the lid and squealed, holding up the small brown puppy from the day before. "Oh, she's adorable, and look, she has a leather strip around her neck with a tag. It says Brandy, Lily. He remembered that you said her color reminded you of Papa's brandy!"

Lily's heart began to melt. "Bring her here." She stroked Brandy's soft fur, while the small puppy nuzzled her breast. "Oh, you are a sweet thing."

"I'm going for the next one." Rose quickly tore open a small package and produced a book bound in rich red leather. "It's Mr. Dickens's *Oliver Twist*." She opened the front cover. "And it's signed!"

"Give that to me," Lily said. She ran her fingers over the soft leather, inhaling its robust scent. Inside was Mr. Dickens's signature in a crisp penmanship, dated 1839. "This is too much. I can't accept all of these gifts."

"He's going to be your husband, Lily. Of course you can accept them. I'm going to open this bigger one next." Rose removed the lid that had been loosened from a wooden crate and pulled out a bottle of wine. "Château Beychevelle, 1831. This must be from France."

"Yes, it's a Bordeaux. It's delicious, actually." Lily's eyes misted. "Daniel...that is, His Grace and I shared this wine. We... Oh, Rose, what am I going to do?"

"This is a whole case. Twelve bottles."

"Goodness."

"This wine has meaning for you?"

"I'm afraid so." Lily kissed Brandy's soft muzzle.

"Don't go getting all misty now. Remember, you don't want to get married." Rose smiled. "I'm going for the next wooden crate." She pulled out sketching paper and charcoal pencils. Pastels and water colors. Oil paints in more colors than her original set. Art books and a new journal. "Don't tell me this doesn't excite you."

Lily didn't answer. How could Daniel know her so well after only three days? So far every gift had gone straight to her heart, even the jewelry, because they had been chosen so expressly for her, to enhance her features.

Rose picked up a tin. "This is probably a confection of some sort." She lifted the lid. "I'm right, of course. It's bonbons." She brought them to Lily.

"They're truffles, dark chocolate from Belgium. Why is he doing this to me?"

"Yes, he is horrid, isn't he? Showering you with gifts that have meaning to you. Trying to make you happy. What a cad!" Rose laughed. "Lily, if you don't fall in love with him, I just might! Tell me the story of the chocolates."

"We shared them together, with the wine." She closed her eyes. "Then he kissed me and we shared the flavors. Dear Lord, what have I done?"

"You've fallen in love."

"No."

"Yes, it's obvious," Rose said. "Why can't you say it?"

"Because he doesn't love me, Rose. He's marrying me for all the wrong reasons. He feels an obligation because he compromised me."

"You don't know that."

"I'm fairly certain." Very certain, actually, but Rose didn't know about the possible pregnancy, and Lily didn't want to divulge that little tidbit quite yet. "But enough about that. Try one of the truffles. They're sinfully delicious."

Rose took a small bite. "That's the most incredible thing I've ever put in my mouth. Next to Evan's tongue, of course." Rose giggled.

Lily cracked a smile. "I can't believe you just said that. Here, let's open a bottle of the wine. You won't believe how wonderfully it goes with the chocolate."

"Lily, it's three in the afternoon."

"Who cares? I'm getting married. Don't you want to toast me?"

"Oh, all right," Rose relented. "Let's be a bit wicked this afternoon."

Lily opened the door to summon a servant to uncork one of the bottles and found a housemaid ready to knock. "The modiste is here, my lady."

"I forgot all about her," Lily said. "Set her up in an extra chamber, and come fetch me when she's ready, will you?"

"Yes, milady."

"I'm afraid we'll have to postpone our little celebration," she said to Rose. "I'm having a gown fitted for the ball."

"How wonderful!"

"Would you like a new gown? Come with me."

"I couldn't possibly."

"Of course you could. I'm almost a duchess, after all."

"No, Lily. I'll wait here for you, and we can drink wine and eat chocolate when you get back. But for now, there's one more gift to open."

Lily stared at the large gift covered in brown paper wrapping. "Don't let me stop you," she said.

Rose carefully removed the wrapping. Lily gasped, bringing one hand to her cheek and squeezing Brandy with the other until the puppy squealed.

"Lily, this isn't..."

Lily nodded.

"The Vermeer? Oh my," Rose said, staring. "It's wonderful, isn't it?"

"I can't accept it. It's too much. In fact, I can't accept any of this." Brandy squirmed in her arms. "I'll keep one." She stroked the puppy's sleek head. "I'll keep Brandy. Daniel said she's too little to be a hunting dog. What will become of her if I don't care for her?" She looked around at the gifts. "And I'm keeping the art supplies. But that's it. Well, the chocolates. They'll just go bad anyway." She fingered the diamond-and-ruby necklace, and then the Dickens novel. "Oh... But I can't. I'm just keeping Brandy."

Rose's lips curved upward. "It seems he knows you a little better than you think."

A knock on the door signaled that the modiste was ready. "I'll only be an hour or so," Lily said to Rose. "Would you keep an eye on Brandy for me?"

"I'd love to. May I take her outside?"

"Of course, she'll love that. Take her to visit her brothers and sisters. But be back here in an hour, and we'll have our wine and chocolates."

Lily left the room and followed a maid to the chamber

where the modiste had set up shop. "Good afternoon," she said to a pleasantly plump red-haired woman.

"Good afternoon, my lady," the modiste said in a clearly contrived French accent. "I am Madame LeRou. I understand you wish a gown for a ball this evening?"

"Yes. I'm terribly sorry for the short notice, but rest assured that my...intended will see that you are compensated at whatever rate you wish. Our betrothal is going to be announced tonight."

"How very wonderful for you, my dear. And your intended is?"

Lily cleared her throat. "The Duke of Lybrook."

"The duke? *Splendide!* How lucky you are. If I were twenty years younger, I would marry him myself. This calls for a special gown."

"Yes, I would like something...frivolous and compelling. Something that stands out in a crowd."

"With your beauty, *ma belle*, you already stand out. What are you thinking by way of *couleur?*"

"Something bright. Vivid, actually."

"For this time of year? *Non*, I do not think so."

"Yes. That is what I want. How about red? Or orange?"

"Orange would be dreadful with your skin tone, my lady. But perhaps red." She rustled through the garments she had brought with her and pulled out a red satin ball gown. "This color would be *magnifique*," she said, turning Lily around and unfastening her dress.

Lily stepped out of her dress and into the gown, turning to let Madame LeRou fasten her. The gown was beautiful, featuring a scalloped neckline and a high waist. It fit Lily's slender but voluptuous figure well, and she couldn't help thinking how perfect the diamond and ruby jewelry would complement it. Unfortunately, it wasn't quite what she had in mind.

"It's lovely, but I was thinking of something a little more...I don't know. Revealing?"

"Ah, so you would like to create a *petite scandale?*" Madame winked at her. "You are not the first well-bred lady to ask this of me. Let me take a look." She pulled out a gown of shocking red velvet.

The fabric stretched over every curve of Lily's body. The neckline was low, coming down in a curved V design that, between the shape of the bodice and of Lily's chest and waist, created the illusion of a large red heart. The short puffed sleeves were connected to the frock with only the tiniest clips set with pearls.

"Could we lower the neckline a little?" Lily asked.

"*Bien sur.* But with your ample bosom, my lady, I don't advise it."

"Do it," Lily said. "And I want the sleeves to be off the shoulder." She gestured to her bosom right above the neckline. "From here up, I want to appear naked."

"*Mon Dieu!* I cannot possibly recommend—"

"That is what I want. Cinch the waist in a bit also, and ruffle up the bustle a bit. I'll need dancing slippers to match. Can it be completed by the hour of ten? The ball starts at eleven."

"*Oui, oui,* my lady, but I must start right away. I will need you to come back here for a final fitting at, shall we say, eight?"

"Dinner is at eight."

"*D'accord.* Half past seven, but that is the best that I can do."

"I will be here. Do you require anything before then?"

"I suppose I will be hungry soon," Madame LeRou said.

"I'll have a tea tray sent up now, and I'll see that a dinner tray is delivered later."

"That is most kind of you, my lady."

Lily nodded and left the room briskly. If Daniel wanted to make her one of his many doxies, she should at least look the part. She returned to her chamber, but Rose was still gone, so she picked up the copy of *Oliver Twist* and began to read. Soon she was lost in the adventures of the young orphan.

★ ★ ★ ★

"We're here, Lily, wake up," Rose's voice said.

Lily opened her eyes to Brandy's adorable panting face. "Oh, you gorgeous little thing!"

Her sister and her cousins stood over her, giggling.

"Ally, Sophie, what are you doing here?"

"We came with Rose," Ally said. "She told us you two were having a little celebration, and we thought we'd join the fun. What is going on?"

"You mean you haven't heard?"

"No, Lily," Rose said. "Thomas and I found Mummy after we left you this morning, and she asked us not to say anything until tonight."

"Well, it's my life, and I want them to know." She turned to her cousins. "Apparently I am betrothed."

"What?" Sophie gasped.

"To whom?" Alexandra wanted to know.

"None other than the Duke of Lybrook himself."

"You're kidding!" Alexandra squealed. "How did this

happen?"

"Tell me and we'll both know," Lily replied cynically. "His Grace arranged everything with Papa. I didn't have a word to say about any of it."

"Who cares?" Ally shrieked. "You've just landed the most luscious man in England, Lily."

"Yes, he has a certain appeal," Lily admitted. "But you're forgetting one very important point. I don't want to be married."

"Lily, this is such an honor," Sophie said.

"An honor? Are you completely mad? To join his merry band of strumpets? I suppose there's some small consolation in the fact that at least I'll be his lawful wife, but that won't stop him from humping—"

"Lily!" Rose admonished.

"Well, it's true!"

"You don't know that," Rose said. "He may be faithful to you."

"He doesn't know the meaning of the word."

"Lily, dear," Sophie said, "if you're not happy about the betrothal, what are we celebrating?"

"We are celebrating my new arrival." Lily hugged Brandy. "Isn't she precious?"

"Yes, she is," Sophie agreed. "Where did she come from?"

"A gift from the duke," Rose said, "along with all of these other incredible offerings." She grabbed the leather case that held the diamond and ruby jewels. "Look at these."

"Oh my God," Ally said, her sandy eyes wide.

"And he gave her his Vermeer. Look." Rose gestured. "I can't even begin to imagine how much that painting is worth."

"That reminds me," Lily said, rising. "I'm going to move

it to the dressing room. Otherwise Brandy might chew on it." She lifted the painting. "I will miss looking at it though. My, he was inspired."

"You're the luckiest woman on earth, Lily." Alexandra fingered the pearl choker and earrings. "These are beautiful. And all these art supplies. He certainly knows you, doesn't he?"

"He doesn't know me at all, Ally. If he did, he wouldn't force me into this sham of a marriage. It's his father all over again, isn't it?'

"Not exactly," Alexandra said. "Her Grace hadn't even met the old duke when her marriage was arranged. You're acquainted with your duke, and you seem to get on well enough, not to mention he's handsome, rich, and titled."

"None of that matters, Ally," Sophie said. "Is he kind, Lily?"

"Well, he's forcing me to marry him. That can hardly be called kind."

"He is a kind man," Rose said. "Lily and I have spent some time with him. He's intelligent and articulate, and he has a pleasant personality."

"Traitor," Lily said.

"Lily, you are...fond of him. Admit it," Rose said.

"All right, damn it. I am fond of him. Are you happy?"

"Incredibly. Now, for our celebration."

Rose lifted a bottle of wine from the crate and summoned a servant to open it. It was returned quickly, along with four glasses.

"To our Lily." Rose lifted her glass.

They clinked their glasses and feasted on the wine and truffles. After her first glass of wine, Lily began to feel quite celebratory, and the girls rang for the servant to open another bottle.

"Do tell us, Ally," Lily said. "How was your tryst with Mr. Landon last evening?"

Alexandra giggled. "It was incredible, actually. We talked for a while, and then he put his arms around me and asked if I would grant him the honor of a kiss."

"He asked? How gentlemanly of him," Sophie said, "although I hardly approve of a man who requests that a lady meet him unchaperoned on a dark terrace."

"I approve of him, that's all that matters," Alexandra said. "He's incredibly wealthy, too. He has property in Scotland and America, and he owns a shipping company."

"Who cares about all that?" Rose said. "How was the kiss?"

"Much better than Wentworth."

"Well of course," Lily said. "Brandy here is better than Wentworth, aren't you, sweet?"

The puppy licked Lily's face.

"Are you going to see him again?" Rose asked.

"Yes, we're going on a carriage ride on the morrow. He's in Bath today, on business, but he told me he expected to be back in time for dinner. Now, Rose, do you have any news for us?"

"Lord Evan and I—" She reddened. "Well, he kissed me after our ride yesterday. It was lovely."

"How lucky you are!" Ally jumped up. "He's almost as handsome as the duke. What of the duke, Lily? Has he kissed you yet?"

Lily's skin heated all over, as memories of Daniel's seductive kisses flooded through her. "No," she said, glancing at Rose with a slight shake of her head. "But I expect him to be adequate, given his experience."

"No doubt," Alexandra agreed. "And I'm not sure I'd care one way or the other. Looking into that handsome face for a lifetime would be more than enough to keep me happy."

Lily rolled her eyes and poured the last of the second bottle of wine into her glass. "Let's open another bottle."

"Perhaps we've had enough," Rose said with a slur. "I'm feeling a bit lightheaded."

"I'm marrying the duke, and I want another bottle."

"The chocolates are almost gone," Sophie said, hiccoughing.

"We may as well finish them," Lily said, "and they go so sublimely with the wine, we simply have to open another bottle." She giggled uncontrollably.

"I agree with Lily." Alexandra rose to pull the cord.

Soon they were drinking again, laughing and chatting about their childhood, when a knock on the door interrupted them.

"The modiste needs to see you, milady," a housemaid said to Lily.

"What? Goodness, what time is it?"

"Half past seven, milady."

"All right, I'll be right there. I do hope I can walk," Lily said, her words coming out in a hazy slur. "One of you must acc...company me."

"Not me," Sophie said. "I'm beginning to feel wretched. Ally, take me to our chamber."

"Rose, it will have to be you," Lily said.

Rose lay on her bed. "In a moment." She let out a soft snore.

"For goodness' sake," Lily muttered. She walked against

the wall for support until she came to the chamber the modiste was using.

"*Ma belle,* do come in." Madame LeRou held up the red garment. "I think you will be pleased. I will do the final fitting and then bring the gown to your chamber by the hour of ten. Is that acceptable?"

Lily hiccoughed. "Yes."

Madame turned Lily so quickly that her head spun and she nearly lost her balance. Quickly the modiste unfastened her and had her step into the new gown. Lily stood quietly, her pulse racing, while Madame LeRou measured her and placed pins on the gown.

"*Bien,*" she said. "Now off with you. Madame has work to do."

Lily dressed with Madame's help, left the room, and walked back to her chamber slowly, blinking her eyes to keep them open. Rose was asleep on the bed. She would miss dinner. Lily decided not to wake her. Her afternoon dress was in decent shape, and it was one of her more glamorous ones. It would substitute nicely for a dinner gown. She took a deep breath and judged her appearance in the looking glass. Her reflection was blurry, but she was sure everything would be fine. She went to the door and grabbed the first servant she saw in the hallway and bade her to take care of Brandy until Rose woke up. Then she made her way to the double stairway, holding the railing for support.

★ ★ ★ ★

Daniel glanced up and saw Lily enter the spacious dining room. Something wasn't right. He rose and swiftly walked toward her, taking her arm.

"Lily, are you quite all right?"

"Of course, Your Grace." She enunciated her words slowly. "Why wouldn't I be?"

"Because your dress is rumpled and your hair is..." He inhaled. "Oh Christ. What have you been drinking?"

"The wine you gave me, my lord. That is, Your Grace. Who are you again?" She started to giggle.

"Come on." He briskly ushered her from the room.

"What will people think?" She hiccoughed. "Oops, sorry."

"Since when do you give—how do you like to put it?—two figs what people think?" He led her to the servants' stairway and up the two flights to his suite.

"Oh, no. I'm not going to bed with you." She hiccoughed again. "I'm not, I tell you."

"You must really think the worst of me." He shook his head. "Do you honestly believe I would take an inebriated woman to bed?"

"What?" Then, "Where's Brandy, Daniel? Oh, I left her with a maid in my chamber. I want her."

"Here, lie down." He led her gently to the bed.

"I want my puppy."

"I'll get her for you."

He pulled the bell cord and Putney appeared quickly. Daniel whispered to him for a few minutes and then went into his bath chamber. He returned, poured a glass of water from a pitcher on his dressing table, and went to Lily. "Here," he said, tearing open a small packet. "Put this on your tongue. It will ease your headache."

"My head doesn't ache."

"Call it a preemptive strike then. Stick out your tongue."

She obeyed, and he poured the powder on it.

"It's bitter!"

"Yes, I know." He held the water to her mouth. "Drink."

She gulped down a few swallows.

"Now, do you want to tell me why you were drinking wine this afternoon?"

"Not really."

"Indulge me anyway."

Lily hiccoughed again. "I'm not feeling very well, Daniel."

"Do you need a basin?"

Another hiccough. "No. I don't think so."

"Now, why were you drinking?"

"Oh, that. Rose, Ally, Sophie, and I were celebrating our betrothal. They're all terribly envious of me you know. Perhaps you should marry one of them."

"I don't want to marry one of them. I want to marry you."

"Oh. I think I'll take that basin now."

He brought it to her.

"Oh, never mind," she said. "It passed."

"Keep the basin here just in case." He went to answer a knock on the door, took a glass of brownish red liquid from Putney, and delivered it to Lily. "Drink this, and I'll get a cold compress for your head."

Lily shook her head at the thick liquid. "I'm not putting that in my mouth."

"Yes, you are, young lady. Come on, drink."

She took a quick sip. "Oh, it's disgusting!"

"Yes, I know, but it works. Come on, all of it."

Lily held her nose and swallowed the thick liquid until the glass was empty. "If I wasn't going to be sick before, I will be now."

"You'll be fine. In fact, within an hour you'll feel much better. The basin is here if you need it."

Another knock on the door delivered Brandy.

"Here's your puppy, Lily," Daniel said, placing Brandy in her arms.

"You adorable creature. I missed you." She yawned. "I'm sleepy, Daniel."

"Lie back now. Get some rest."

"What about Brandy?" she asked drowsily, snuggling into Daniel's pillow.

"Putney will take her to the kennels. They'll care for her until tomorrow."

"All right then." She closed her eyes.

Daniel pressed a damp cloth to her forehead.

"That feels nice," she murmured. "Come lie with me, Daniel."

"No, love, not while you're foxed."

She opened her eyes abruptly. "I am not foxed!"

He laughed softly. "Of course not. Now go to sleep, I'll wake you in a bit."

"I need to dress for the ball."

"I'll wake you in time. Close your eyes. I'll stay and watch over you."

"You're so sweet." She reached for him. "Hold me. I want to feel your arms around me." She closed her eyes.

What could it hurt? He lay down beside her and gathered her in his arms.

"That's nice," she murmured and then began to snore softly.

Daniel kissed her chastely on the forehead, smiling because she wanted him. Perhaps she did care for him.

In vino veritas, he thought. In wine, there's truth.

CHAPTER THIRTEEN

Lily awoke, naked, in Daniel's bed. He held her gently, making love to her, softly crooning her name. "Lily, Lily, Lily." She sighed, enjoying the feel of his hands on her skin. "Lily, Lily..."

Something cool and crisp fell from her eyes when she opened them to see Daniel sitting next to her, shaking her arm gently.

"Lily, Lily."

She was still fully clothed, lying on his bed. The lovemaking had been a dream... What had fallen from her eyes appeared to be thin slices of...cucumber?

"Daniel?"

"I'm here. How are you feeling?"

"Why was there cucumber on my face?"

"It's an old trick of my mother's. When her eyes are tired and puffy, she swears by slices of cucumber, so I had the kitchen send some up."

"Ugh. What is that awful taste in my mouth?"

"Just an after effect of your...indulgence."

"It's probably from that horrible glop you forced down my throat. What was in that stuff anyway?"

He chuckled. "You don't want to know. Does your head hurt?"

Lily shook her head. "I must look dreadful, though."

"You'll always be beautiful to me, love. Your face looks good, actually. I'll have to tell my mother that her old wives' tale has merit. But your hair needs a little work, and you need a bath and tooth brushing."

Lily twisted her face into a grimace. "You've seen me at my worst. Do you still want to marry me?"

"I'm sorry to tell you, but yes, I do."

"Good God." She stood, a little lightheaded, but remarkably sturdy on her feet.

"Lily, if you don't feel you can attend the ball tonight, we can announce our betrothal on the morrow."

"No, I feel...better. Surprising, but true. Perhaps Putney should market that concoction of his."

"I've often thought so myself."

She turned to face him. "Daniel, I..."

"What is it, love?"

"Thank you for looking after me."

"I would do anything for you. I had hoped that you knew that by now."

"I..."

"It's all right."

"No, it's... Your gifts were very generous, Daniel. They touched my heart, really. But I can't accept them, especially the Vermeer. It's too much."

"I want you to have the Vermeer. It will be half yours when we marry anyway."

"That's where you're wrong," Lily said. "When we marry, I cease to be. I'll have no ownership rights. Everything of mine will belong to you, and I shall be forced to obey you and yield to you in every way."

"Lily..."

"It's true, and you know it."

"I would never take away your identity."

"But you will exert your husbandly rights, won't you?"

"I'll have to exert some of them. It will be my duty to take care of you and see to your best interests," he said. "You'll be my responsibility."

"I don't want to be anyone's responsibility. Damn it all to hell!"

"Lily, please."

"I need to go to my chamber and dress for the ball. There isn't much time."

He strode toward her.

"No." She held up her arms. "Don't bother escorting me. Discretion is a moot point now, isn't it?" She walked out the door and shut it, not quietly, behind her.

Lily entered her chamber and found Rose bathing, looking pale and sickly.

"There you are, Lily. Lord, my head is throbbing."

"I can fix that," Lily said.

She rang for a maid. "I need a bath prepared for myself, and then I'll need my hair done. First, though, I need a headache powder for my sister, and find Mr. Putney and tell him I need a glass of whatever he made for me earlier."

"Milady?"

"He'll know what I mean. In fact, I need three glasses. Deliver two of them to Ladies Sophie and Alexandra next door. Now go."

"I would really like to die," Rose said. "I swear on Mother's life, I will never drink again!"

"Don't say that, dear, you'll miss out on the champagne tonight."

"My goodness, don't mention champagne."

"Come on." Lily held up a towel. "Out of the tub."

Lily helped Rose dry off and put on a dressing gown, and then brushed out her hair for her. The maid came back with the headache powder and Rose grimaced when the bitterness fell on her tongue.

"It will help," Lily said. "My bath is ready, and I need to hurry. When the maid comes with a glass of...disgusting liquid, I want you to drink it all, do you understand?"

Rose nodded. Lily bathed quickly, and then used double the amount of tooth powder and scrubbed her teeth thoroughly, trying desperately to remove the coating of invisible film that seemed to cover them. She brushed her hair briskly, noting that Rose was lying still on her bed. Lily responded to a knock on the door. Two maids stood in the hallway, one holding the concoction for Rose, the other her ball gown.

"Madame apologizes that the gown wasn't here earlier, milady."

"That's all right, no harm done." Lily took the gown and laid it carefully on her bed. "I'll need you to return in half an hour and see to my hair, and my sister's."

"Yes, my lady."

Lily carried the glass of liquid to Rose. "Drink up, dear."

Rose looked at the glass. "You can't be serious."

Lily nodded. "Every drop, or I shall have to use force. I won't lie to you. It's dreadful. But you'll feel much better in a half hour or so. Come on."

Rose held her nose and drank.

"You may feel a little bit sick, so I'll get a basin, but you probably won't need it. I want you to lie down and close your eyes, and I'll wake you in half an hour."

Rose nodded. Lily fetched a basin for her sister, wished for some cucumbers but knew there wasn't time, so she wet a cloth in cold water and placed it over Rose's forehead and eyes. She continued to brush her hair until it shone and rang for a maid to help her into her gown.

The gown was revealing, as she had planned, but it was also lovely and flattering. The color highlighted her rosy skin tone and her dark hair, and despite the fact that the low curved V neckline made her breasts look as though they were likely to tumble out, the bodice of the gown was remarkably secure. The ruffling about the bustle made Lily's narrow hips appear more luscious and curvy than they actually were, and the sleeves, which were off shoulder, draped seductively from the pearl-studded clips, showing Lily's well-shaped shoulders and arms.

"My lady, you are a vision," the maid said.

"Fetch my pearls from the dresser," Lily said.

Unfortunately, the rubies would clash with the vivid crimson of the gown, but the pearls would be exquisite. The maid returned and helped Lily clasp the choker and earrings.

"Now, what to do with my hair? I want something... shocking."

"Leave that to me," the maid said. "Come and sit."

"I need to wake my sister first." Lily hurried over to Rose's bed and gently nudged her. "Come on, Rose, it's time to wake up."

Rose yawned and opened her eyes. "Is it time for the ball?"

"Nearly, dear. Sit up now. How do you feel?"

"Much better, actually. How in the world?"

"Mr. Putney's secret." Lily rang for another maid to tend to Rose and then seated herself at a dressing table to have her hair done before Rose had a chance to scrutinize her gown.

By the time Lily's hair had been swept on top of her head,

Rose was seated next to her, dressed.

"My, Lily, that gown..."

"Lovely, isn't it?"

"Well, yes, of course, you're lovely in anything, but what will Papa say?"

"I don't give two figs what Papa says. He's marrying me off. I'm no longer his concern."

"Lily..."

"Everything will be fine, Rose. You look incredible, by the way."

"Thank you, but I'm afraid I can't hold a candle to you. I would never have the nerve to wear such a daring gown, but my, you are splendid in it."

"Thank you, dear."

The maid wove pearls through Lily's hair and curled the soft waves with a hot iron, creating a cascade of curls that just brushed the back of her neck.

"You've done a lovely job," Lily said to the maid.

"I'm glad you're pleased, milady. Do you have need of anything else?"

"No, not at the present. Thank you."

She dabbed clove oil on her wrists, behind each ear, and in her cleavage. She put on her white elbow-length gloves, sighed, and took them off again. "I'm going to use just a bit of rouge."

"Lily, you never paint your face," Rose said.

"I'm going to tonight."

Rose stood, nearly knocking over the maid just finishing her hair. "Your skin is beautiful, like a moonstone cabochon, and your cheeks have the natural flush of a sweet raspberry mousse. Please don't spoil it."

"Oh, never mind. I won't do it." She carefully put her

gloves back on.

"Thank God," Rose said under her breath.

"I heard that," Lily snapped. "Are you ready? We need to go."

"Yes, yes. I can't believe how much better I'm feeling."

"Amazing stuff, isn't it? Putney would be a rich man if he bottled it."

On the arms of their brother—who had scrutinized Lily's gown but said nothing—Lily and Rose were among the last to enter the magnificent ballroom. They found Sophie and Alexandra and sat down.

"My, Lily, you look radiant," Alexandra said. "Only you could pull off a gown like that."

"Don't be silly," Lily said. "You could do it in a heartbeat. Tell me, are you feeling quite well?"

"Yes, thanks to that concoction the maid brought us. What was it exactly? Goat's blood? Eye of newt?" Alexandra giggled.

"Could be. I don't actually know. His Grace's valet mixed it up. It's miraculous."

"I'll say," Sophie chimed in. "I wasn't sure I could make it to the ball, but I didn't want to miss the announcement of your betrothal."

"I'm so glad you're both here." Lily looked upstairs to the balcony. "Dear Lord," she said, her breath catching in her throat.

Daniel entered, descending the grand staircase. He was dressed formally, in a dark grey velvet coat and white shirt with a black silk cravat. His hair was pulled back in a queue, disappointing Lily slightly. She did so love the sight of his thick layered hair gleaming as it touched his broad shoulders. But pulling it back gave him a noble, no, *royal* look, as if he were the prince himself. He wore crisp white gloves and snug black trousers tucked into shiny black leather boots.

"Is your heart going pitter-patter yet, Lily?" Alexandra giggled, staring in the same direction.

"My, he is something," even Sophie admitted, fanning herself. "I know looks aren't paramount, but... Goodness!"

Lily stared at Daniel, barely hearing as the duchess strode with grace to the middle of the dance floor, silencing the room, and announcing the betrothal of her son, Daniel Farnsworth, the seventh Duke of Lybrook, to Lady Lily Jameson, daughter of the Earl and Countess of Ashford. The thunderous applause was muted in her ears, and she swallowed nervously as Daniel walked toward her, took her hand, and led her to the dance floor. She ogled him, his magnificence and gloriousness, as the orchestra began a waltz. Daniel took her in his arms, positioning her carefully, as her arms and legs seemed to hang limply, and started twirling her around the dance floor. She sighed audibly.

"You look stunning, Lily." He gazed into her eyes as if he couldn't stare at her hard enough.

She jolted back to reality. "For God's sake, I'm not trying to look stunning, I'm trying to look like—"

"A strumpet. Yes, I know. But you failed to take a few things into account, love."

She looked up at him, but said nothing.

"First of all, you have too much natural grace and class to ever be mistaken for a strumpet. You could have come out dressed in nothing but a feather boa, and it wouldn't have mattered."

"Perhaps I should have tried that," she said hotly.

Daniel's eyes narrowed, but he spoke smoothly. "Had

you done that, you would have no doubt earned the undying gratitude of every married woman here on the morrow."

Lily regarded him, confused by the comment.

"Secondly, you are the future Duchess of Lybrook. You make your own style. Within a fortnight, every woman here will be shamelessly imitating you."

"Oh, Lord..."

"So you see, your attempt to humiliate me and yourself has failed miserably. However, you have succeeded in convincing every man here that I am the luckiest bastard on the face of the earth."

"Daniel..."

"There isn't another woman here, not even your mother or your sister, who comes close to your beauty tonight. You were made for vivid colors. You were made to shock people. You were made for that gown, Lily. It works for you." He laughed softly, his breath caressing her cheek. "You will fill my life with surprises. Every day I shall wonder what you will do next. It will be a joy to be your husband. You haven't succeeded in driving me away."

"Will I ever drive you away?"

"I'm afraid not."

He twirled her in dance steps unfamiliar to her, but due to his superior skill she followed effortlessly, the momentum pushing her closer against his body, her skin tingling from his heat.

"You want to shock people?" He winked at her. "I'll show you how to shock people." He lowered his mouth to hers and kissed her.

"Daniel!" she gasped.

He winked again. "You bring out the beast in me, Lily."

"Oh my."

When the waltz ended, Daniel led her to the refreshment table. "You probably don't care for any champagne," he said.

"Punch will be fine, thank you."

Soon men were gathered around them, begging Lily for the honor of a dance.

"You can't keep her to yourself all night, Lybrook," Polk said, leading Lily to the floor.

She danced with Polk, her brother, Ally's Mr. Landon, Lord Evan, her father, one of Daniel's solicitors, his personal physician, and what seemed like a hundred other young men with whom she wasn't acquainted. Daniel also claimed her three more times. When her feet and legs could no longer bear the strain, she stole out to the terrace for some fresh air and found a private dark corner in which to regain her composure.

"That was quite a little exhibition you put on in there," a voice said from behind her.

She turned to face Lady Amelia Gregory.

"And may I say, that dress is quite...becoming."

"Oh, Amanda," Lily said, "how lovely to see you."

"It's Amelia, you fool, but you know that, don't you? Perhaps I should call you Lila?"

"Call me whatever you wish for now, but by the end of the house party, you'll be addressing me as *Your Grace*." Lily couldn't help smirking.

"I suppose so. Quite a *coup d'etat* for someone who wasn't the least bit interested in the duke a mere few days ago."

"I wasn't then."

"Of course you weren't. And I'm not the least bit interested in your brother. He's fascinating, by the way."

"Your threats won't work with me. My brother would

never lower himself to get involved with you."

"Why not? The duke did. He lowered himself many times actually."

Lily winced at the double entendre. "If you'll excuse me, there are many young men waiting for the honor of dancing with me."

"No, I don't think so," Amelia said tersely. "You and I need to have a little chat."

"I can't think of anything we need to chat about."

"You're going to step aside." Amelia looked Lily square in the eye. "You're not going to marry the duke."

"Ha! Fat lot you know. I've been trying to step aside. He won't let me."

"My God, do you ever tell the truth?"

"I tell nothing but the truth. I'm afraid he has his heart set on me, though. I know it must hurt to be the loser in our little game. Ta-ta." Lily pushed Amelia out of her way and headed back toward the ballroom.

Amelia grabbed her arm. "You will step aside, is that clear?"

"You have a lot of nerve. And if I don't?"

"You'll be sorry."

"I'm already sorry. Sorry that I gave more than two seconds to this conversation. Good evening."

Anger surged through Lily when she reentered the ballroom.

Daniel came to her. "Are you feeling well?"

"Yes, I'm fine," she said. "Aren't you going to dance with me again?"

"It's bad form for me to monopolize you."

"Thank God. My feet are killing me. Could we take a

walk?"

"Your feet are killing you, so you want to walk?" He gave her a lazy half smile.

"Just walk me to the library or the parlor, so I can sit down in peace."

"All right. Come on."

He led her to the dark library and lit a lamp on a small table. Lily collapsed on a sofa.

"What I wouldn't give for some warm water and Epsom salts right now. I've never danced that much in one evening. Never even half that much."

Daniel sat down next to her and pulled her legs onto his lap. He removed her slippers and gently massaged her feet.

Lily closed her eyes, leaning into the lush comfort of the cushion. "Oh, that's heavenly."

"Just relax."

Lily yawned and stretched her arms. "What's on the agenda for tomorrow?"

"I don't know what my mother and Aunt Lucy have planned for the guests, but I'll be in London."

"All day?"

"I'm afraid so. I'm leaving before dawn, and I won't be back in time for dinner. But I'll see you the next day."

"What is so important that will keep you in London all day?"

"Just business matters. You wouldn't be interested."

"Of course I'm interested," she snapped. "I'm more than just an empty-headed bauble for you to wear on your arm. May I go with you?"

"Not this time. I'll take you to London whenever you want after we're married."

"But why—" A disturbing thought jolted her mind. "You're not going to visit one of your— Oh, never mind." She drew her feet off of his lap and put her slippers back on. "I'm tired. I want to go to bed."

"It's early yet. You shouldn't leave the ball."

"I've had a trying day, Daniel, as you are well aware. I want to go to bed. You can walk me to my chamber, or I'll go myself."

"I'd rather take you to my chamber."

She didn't respond right away. She was exhausted, but she wanted him. Her body still sizzled at his every touch. Moreover, if she slept with him tonight, maybe he wouldn't go to London tomorrow to visit one of his mistresses. For that was the only possible reason for him to go. Any estate business could be conducted at Laurel Ridge. But if she went to bed with him solely for the purpose of keeping him from making love to someone else... Well, that wasn't a routine she wanted to set in motion. She deserved far better.

"I'll go to my own chamber."

"Very well then. I'll escort you. Come on."

He helped her up and took her up the back stairwell to her chamber on the second floor of the east wing. He leaned down, kissed her virtuously on the mouth, and opened the door for her.

Lily looked in quickly. Rose hadn't yet returned. She grabbed Daniel's arm and pulled him inside the room, flinging her arms around his neck. She kissed him as though it were her first taste of his maleness, exploring him with her tongue, tasting him, savoring him. She wanted him badly. One kiss wouldn't hurt, and maybe, on his way to London tomorrow, he might think of her.

He responded with a fiery passion. She pressed her breasts

against his hard chest and tugged his hair out of the queue so she could thread her fingers through it. He moved forward, their mouths clamped together, until her back was against the wall. Gently he separated her legs with his thigh. She rubbed her sex against him as his lips moved from her mouth to her ear, her neck, down between her breasts, which were swollen, tingling, and nearly bursting from her gown. He released one rosy globe from captivity and feasted on her nipple, covering it with wet kisses that landed like a flash of lightning between her legs. Her heart thumped against her chest, and moisture trickled in her drawers.

When Daniel returned to her mouth she fisted her hands in his hair, pulling him as close as she could as they kissed. They were both panting when Lily finally broke away. She hoped it was enough for him to forego his visit to his mistress on the morrow.

"Are you certain you don't want to come to bed with me?"

No, she wasn't certain at all. "Yes." Her voice cracked. "I-I just wanted a good night kiss."

"Dear God, Lily. Please. I'm aching for you." His voice was full of passion and smoke as he pressed his forehead to the wall, aligning his head with hers. His hard cock prodded against her belly.

Her eyes misted with tears. She had made a terrible mistake. Now he was aching for her, and he would ease his hunger elsewhere on the morrow.

"I can't. I'm sorry."

"Don't cry. Whatever it is, I'll fix it." He brushed a tear from the corner of her eye with his thumb.

"I'm just tired. Good night. I'll see you the day after tomorrow, I guess." She nudged him toward the door, gave his hand a squeeze, and closed the door silently. Then she threw herself onto her bed and wept into her pillow.

★ ★ ★ ★

Thomas walked to the bachelor house, having escorted Emma to her chamber. Amelia Gregory, several yards ahead, walked toward him.

"Good evening, my lord," she said when she crossed his path.

"My lady, what are you doing out at this hour unescorted?"

"Dear me," she said. "I'm afraid I shall never get used to this large estate. I seem to have taken a wrong turn. And you're right. It is late and I shouldn't be about alone. Could I trouble you to see me to my chamber?"

"Of course, it would be my pleasure." Thomas offered his arm.

Lady Gregory looked gorgeous in a pale tan ball gown that enhanced her shapely figure. Her dark hair had been swept up, braided, and fell in loops down her back. He took her to the door of her chamber and bid her good night.

"Won't you come in?" she said. "I have some wonderful Armagnac. It was a favorite of Frederic's, God rest his soul. I would so like to thank you for your chivalry."

A night cap sounded good, and Thomas did enjoy a good brandy. What would be the harm? "Thank you, my lady. I would be obliged."

She led him to a small table near the window of her chamber and bade him sit down. She brought a bottle and two snifters to the table.

"Allow me." Thomas poured the dark golden liquid into

the glasses and warmed one in his hand before giving it to her.

Amelia picked it up, swirling the fluid daintily, and brought it to her lips. "Shall we toast to your sister's impending nuptials?"

"By all means. Lily has done well for herself."

"I should say so. Landing the most eligible bachelor in England in a mere three days. One might think..."

"One might think what?"

"Oh, nothing," Amelia said. "I'd much rather talk about you." She took another sip of the Armagnac. "Why hasn't a handsome eligible bachelor like yourself settled down?"

"I'm not quite as old as Lybrook yet."

"Of course not. But your father no doubt has impressed upon you the importance of siring an Ashford heir, has he not?"

Thomas sighed. "Yes, I'm afraid he has. But he was two years older than I when he married my mother, so he can't get too excited about it yet." He took another sip. "My lady, this is excellent."

"Yes, my Frederic adored it," Amelia said. "Tell me, do you have anyone in mind for the position?"

"What position?"

"The position of mother to your heir, of course."

Thomas nearly choked on the brandy. "Well...I haven't given it a great deal of thought, to tell you the truth."

"Of course. A man like you doubtless enjoys his freedom."

Thomas grinned. "I won't deny it."

"I know exactly what you mean. Though I adored my dear Frederic—may he rest in peace—I, too, have become accustomed to a certain amount of freedom since his death. Being able to come and go as one pleases, without answering to another, is liberating." Amelia topped off their snifters. "May I speak frankly to you, my lord?"

"By all means."

"I'm a lonely widow. There have been rumors, I know, about various exploits that I have allegedly engaged in, but most of them are completely untrue. Not all, of course. A woman has needs, you know. But the majority are unfounded. It has been quite a long time since I have been...intimate with a man."

Thomas cleared his throat. He was no fool. She wanted to bed him.

Amelia lowered her voice to a husky rasp. "I find you very interesting and attractive, my lord."

"I'm flattered, my lady. However, you should know that my heart lies...elsewhere."

"It's not your heart I'm interested in." Amelia finished her brandy, stood, and moved behind Thomas's chair and began to massage his shoulders. "You're so tense, my lord. I've always thought it must be difficult for men of your station to balance all of your responsibilities. I know it was for my Frederic." She moved down to his upper arms, kneading his muscles tenderly, and leaned down to his ear. "I can help ease your tension."

Thomas fidgeted in his seat. The tickle of her breath on his neck aroused him, and his cock stiffened. She was nothing if not tempting. He placed his hands over hers and pulled her around to face him.

"What exactly is it that you're after, my lady?"

She sat down in his lap and entwined her arms around his neck. "A night of passion with you, my lord." She lowered her mouth to his.

CHAPTER FOURTEEN

Lily slept late the next morning, waking to Rose's gentle nudging at half past eleven. She opened her eyes to find herself on top of her covers, still in her ball gown from the previous evening with one breast precariously exposed. She hastily tucked it into her gown.

"Lily, you look terrible," Rose said. "Your eyes are puffy and streaked with tears. I didn't bother you when I came in last night, though you were sleeping fitfully. Can I do anything for you?"

"No. I'll be fine. I do hope I haven't ruined my gown."

"I'll call to have it laundered and pressed. Come on, let's get you out of it."

Rose helped Lily undress and rang for a bath for her. Lily sat in the tub limply, holding a cloth soaked in hot water to her face.

"Ask the kitchen to send up some cucumber slices, will you, Rose?"

"Whatever for?"

"My eyes. It's a trick the duchess uses. I'll show you when they get here."

"All right." Rose quickly rang for a servant and dispatched the order. "Now," she continued, "tell me what's going on."

Lily sighed. "The duke went to London today. He won't be back for dinner."

"Is that all? Don't tell me you miss him."

"Of course not." But she did. "It's just that, there's no reason for him to go to London except to..."

"To what?"

"Visit one of his mistresses." Tears welled up in Lily's eyes.

"Why would you think that?" Rose said. "He probably has business to attend to."

"Any business could be conducted here. All of his bankers, stock analysts, solicitors, and whomever else he needs are right here. Even his personal physician is here, for goodness' sake."

"That doesn't mean—"

"Of course it does. And it's my fault. I told him I wouldn't sleep with him again until we were married. I did it to punish him, and I've ended up punishing myself. Now he's going to find someone else to... Oh, I can't bear it!"

"You do love him. I knew it," Rose said, smiling.

"No, I don't."

"It doesn't matter whether you admit it. It's obvious to me. I'm the closest person in the world to you. I know your thoughts before you do sometimes, as you do mine."

"Rose..."

"The duke adores you, Lily. He may very well be in love with you. Why would he risk what the two of you share for an afternoon of physical pleasure?"

"It's no risk for him. He's forcing me to marry him anyway. I asked him to take me with him, and he refused. Besides, it's his way. You know his reputation as well as I do."

"We know only hearsay. We have no proof that he keeps mistresses or visits brothels."

"I have proof." Lily covered her eyes with the soft moist cloth. "I've met one of his mistresses."

"Dear Lord, who?"

"Lady Amelia Gregory. She's here at Laurel Ridge."

"Not that woman who sat next to Thomas at dinner?"

"That's the one." Lily dropped the cloth in the water and straightened her back. "Which reminds me, we must find Thomas. I have reason to believe that she has set her sights on him, now that the duke and I are betrothed."

"Why would you believe that?"

"Because she told me so. She's a horrible woman, and Thomas isn't known to be discerning." Lily reached for a towel and stepped out of the tub.

"You seem to be feeling a little better," Rose commented.

"Not really, but I can't sit here feeling sorry for myself when our dear brother may very well be in danger from that harpy."

"I suppose not. Let's get you dressed. We can go fetch him from the bachelor house and talk him into lunching with us."

"Splendid. But first I must lie with cucumbers on my eyes for about half an hour. You should try it too. Then we'll have just enough time to find Thomas. After lunch I'll get Brandy from the kennels and take her on a walk. Then maybe I'll paint."

"Sounds like you're trying to get your mind off something. Or someone."

"Perhaps."

"I know. Why don't you and I go riding?"

"I ride abhorrently, Rose."

"Only because you don't try. Wait. I know what will put a smile on your face. Let's go back to the hot pool!"

Lily couldn't help giggling. "Maybe... Although I did promise Daniel that I wouldn't go back without him. But he's not here, is he? He's with his strumpet in London. So why not?

Let's do it."

"I'm glad I thought to pack my bathing clothes. Did you bring yours?"

"Yes," Lily said. "I suppose that would be prudent, given that many are out and about on the estate today." Lily fetched the plate of cucumbers that a maid had left on one of the night tables. She handed two slices to Rose. "Lie down and put these over your eyes."

"If you say so."

★ ★ ★ ★

The girls found Thomas lazing on the front terrace of the bachelor house with half a dozen other young lords.

"Jameson, your sisters are among the most beautiful creatures on this estate," Lord Victor Polk said.

"Tuck your eyes back in their sockets before I bloody you," Thomas said. "This one's spoken for, as you well know." He kissed Lily's cheek. "I doubt Lybrook would appreciate your ogling. And this one"—he kissed Rose—"is under my complete protection. To what do I owe the pleasure of your visit?"

"We want to have lunch with you," Lily said.

"Where's Lybrook?"

"In London. All day. So Rose and I thought there was nothing we would rather do than take a meal with our charming brother."

"I was planning to take a leisurely lunch here at the house."

"You're mad, Jameson," Polk said. "Turning down lunch with two delightful women to stay here with a bunch of bachelors." Then, to the girls, "I'll have lunch with you two lovelies."

"So will I," another young lord said.

"No, you won't," Thomas said. "They invited me. All right then, I'll grace the two of you with my dashing presence. Although, knowing you as I do, I think there must be an ulterior motive at work here."

"Why would you think that?" Lily asked innocently.

"Because I'm familiar with your work, my dear."

Polk let out a snorting laugh.

"Nonsense." Lily took his arm. "We'll see you gentlemen later."

"I shall take not one breath until you return," Polk said, smiling as he bowed deeply.

"Then you'll be dead when we return, you fool." Thomas turned to his sisters. "My God, he thinks he's such a heartbreaker."

"He's quite engaging actually," Lily said. "As you recall, I spent some time with him our first night here. Ally was taken with him also."

"She seems to prefer young Mr. Landon," Thomas remarked.

"She prefers his fortune," Rose said dryly.

"You can hardly blame her, Rose," Lily said. "The earl left them penniless, and she doesn't want to be a burden to Papa and Mummy."

"She's no burden," Rose said.

"I know that, and you know that, but how would you feel if the situation were reversed? I wouldn't want to be dependent on someone else's good will either."

"I suppose you're right."

They chatted until they reached the side of the main manor. Thomas flagged a servant and requested that lunch be served to them on the side terrace.

"So, my lovely sisters," Thomas said, holding chairs for each of them, "what is it that you want to say to me?"

"Nothing Thomas," Lily said. "Tell me, how is Emma?"

"She's fine."

"Are the two of you getting serious?"

"Lily, I've known the girl for less than a week."

"The duke and I have only known each other that long."

"You make a good point. What about you and Xavier, Rose? What's going on there?"

"We're talking about you, not Rose," Lily said.

"He said he was going to ask Papa for permission to court me," Rose said. "To my knowledge, he hasn't yet."

"Let's get back on subject, shall we?" Lily snapped. "What are your feelings for Emma?"

"I'm fond of her. She's attractive and bright, and I enjoy her company. But that's it. I'm not looking for a wife. Now, tell me what you really want to know, will you?"

Lily sighed, rolling her eyes. "Fine. You really think you can read me like a book, don't you?"

"Yes. Go on."

"It's Lady Amelia Gregory, Thomas. I want you to stay away from her."

"What?"

"You heard me. I have reason to believe that she wishes to"—Lily lowered her voice—"seduce you."

Thomas shrugged. "Why would you believe that?"

"She told me so. She wants the duke, actually. She intimated that if she can't have him, she's going to take you."

"So I'm to be yesterday's leftovers if she can't have today's gourmet feast?" Thomas smiled lazily.

"That's not what I meant. I'm just saying that she may try to lure you into her bed."

"She already has."

"Oh, God." Lily groaned. "We're too late, Rose."

"Thomas, really," Rose said. "I should think you would have more sense."

"Holy hell," Thomas said. "Do the two of you really think I'm no more discriminating than a stag in rut?"

"You are a man after all," Lily said.

"I'm not Lybrook, damn it. I have no interest in the widow Gregory."

Lily widened her eyes. "You know about their affair?"

"It was never a secret."

"So you didn't sleep with her?"

"Not that it's any of your business, but no, I didn't, although she was quite persuasive."

"Thank goodness." Lily sighed, relieved. "She's bad news, Thomas."

"Yes," Thomas agreed. "There were rumors after her husband died. They weren't even married a year."

"How did he die?" Rose asked.

"I did some asking at the bachelor house. He fell down a flight of stairs in their London home six or seven years ago."

"How terrible!" Rose gasped.

"He was only forty-five years old, and Lady Gregory was twenty. She was a commoner, you know. The gossip was that she married Gregory for his fortune and did away with him. But nothing was ever proven."

"Oh Lord," Lily said.

"What is it, Lily?" Rose asked.

"It's just a little disconcerting to know that my intended

didn't have the sense to stay away from such a money-grubbing trollop. What has Papa gotten me into?"

"Lybrook is a good man, Lily," Thomas said. "I mean that. He's not the only man on earth to ever get blindsided by a seductress. In fact, he's in the majority."

"You men are all pigs," Lily said dryly.

"Men are simply men," Thomas replied. "On that note, may we please change the subject? This conversation has gone far beyond the limits of what I'm comfortable with. Why can't I have sisters who are loathe to mention body parts in the company of men?"

"You're not a man, Thomas, you're our brother," Lily said.

"Yes, but I agree with him," Rose said. "Let's change the subject. Discussion of Lady Gregory has become tedious."

"You don't have to convince me," Lily said. "I can't abide the little hussy."

★ ★ ★ ★

Amelia watched them from a distance—the two little Jameson shrews lunching with their devilishly handsome brother. He wouldn't be stupid enough to tell them about her failed seduction attempt. It irked her, though, that he hadn't wanted her. He was as attractive as Daniel, but in a different way—dark and classic as opposed to blond and exotic, the image of his father, the Earl of Ashford.

Hmm. Ashford himself was still an attractive man, and a wealthy one. Of course he was hopelessly devoted to his adoring wife. On the other hand, happily married men took mistresses all the time. He couldn't offer her a name, but he was likely to be an animal in bed. And wouldn't that just bunch

Lily's bustle, to find out that Amelia was fucking her father!

Alas, it likely wouldn't work. Amelia would only make a fool of herself, as she had with his son. She would refocus her efforts on Daniel. She would find him, seduce him, and show him exactly what he would miss by marrying his precious Lily.

★ ★ ★ ★

Lily and Rose never made it to the hot pool that afternoon. Miss Lucinda Landon approached them after Thomas had gone back to the bachelor house.

"My lady," she said to Lily, "the duchess is feeling poorly this afternoon, and today is our scheduled time to see to the tenants' needs. I was hoping you might accompany me."

"Of course, I would be happy to help," Lily said. "But aren't there some maids who would be better suited?"

"No, my dear. You're the future duchess, and this will be your responsibility before long. It's a good chance for you to see what will be required of you."

The future duchess. Responsibilities. Duties. Lord, help her. "Of course, Miss Landon." She turned to her sister, "I'm sorry, Rose. I won't be able to spend the afternoon with you."

"Nonsense," Rose said. "I'll come along with you. I'm sure an extra hand would be helpful."

Lily and Rose rode with Miss Landon in the duchess's private carriage, followed by several wagons full of food, clothing, and other necessities for the Lybrook tenants.

"Twice a month, the servants pack up leftover food, old clothing, medication, whatever else we have in abundance that the tenants might need," Miss Landon explained. "Maggie and I bring it out to them, visit with them, and then return and let the duke know how they are getting on and if they have need of anything from us. Most of them are quite nice folk, as you shall see."

"This will all be my responsibility after I'm married?" Lily asked nervously.

"Yes, my dear, but Maggie and I will still be here to help you." Miss Landon took Lily's hand. "I'm sure you and your sister have helped your own dear mother see to the Ashford tenants."

"Yes, of course."

"This won't be completely new to you. I've no doubt that Flora has prepared you well for the responsibilities you will face as the duke's wife. You will be a splendid duchess, my lady. My nephew adores you. It's plain to see. I'm not sure I've ever seen him as happy as he has been since you arrived at Laurel Ridge."

Lily's neck warmed. The thought that Daniel adored her filled her with elation soaked in despair. After all, at this moment he was no doubt warming another's bed.

The tenants welcomed them and accepted the offerings with gratitude. Miss Landon had an affectionate and humble way of giving, making it seem like the tenants were doing the Lybrooks a favor by taking the extra food and supplies. She knew them all by name and asked after those she didn't see. The women and children were thrilled to meet Lily and Rose when Miss Landon introduced them and explained that Lily would be marrying the duke.

"You're both so pretty!" one adorable little girl with dark brown hair exclaimed. She carried a basket and was accompanied by an older girl of about fourteen or fifteen.

Lily picked the small child up and gave her a kiss on the

cheek. "What is your name, little one?"

"Katrina, my lady."

"And how old are you, Katrina?" Rose asked.

"Six, my lady. How old are you?"

"You shouldn't ask that question, Katrina," Lily said. "You'll understand when you're older. My, but you are precious."

"Will you come back to see us again?"

"Of course, we both will," Lily said.

"This is my sister, Patricia," the little girl said, introducing her companion. "Would you like to come home with me to meet my mum and brother?"

"No, Kat," the older girl said. "I'm sure the ladies don't have the time."

"We'd be delighted," Lily said. "Is it all right with you, Miss Landon?"

"Of course, dear. I'll come along. I haven't had the chance to chat with the widow Price the last couple of visits. It will be nice to see her."

Katrina and Patricia hopped into the coach and led them to a small brick house surrounded by several gardens and plowed fields. A young man sat on the large front porch, playing a guitar. Even from a distance he was striking, with hair the color of coal in unfashionably long wavy layers, clear silver-grey eyes, and a strong jaw covered in the beginning of night beard.

"Cam!" Katrina shouted. "I brought some ladies to meet you. This is Lady Lily." Katrina gestured. "She's marrying the duke. And this is her sister, Lady Rose. My brother, Cameron."

"It's a pleasure." Cameron bowed slightly, his gaze focused on Rose.

"Mr. Price," Miss Landon said. "It's very nice to see you. Is your mother at home?"

"Yes. Go on inside. She'll be happy to see you."

"Thank you." Miss Landon entered the humble dwelling, leaving Lily and Rose on the porch with Cameron and the girls.

"So, Kat," Cameron said to his sister, "how did you talk these nice young ladies into following you home?"

"How do you know it wasn't Tricia?"

Cameron winked at his little sister. "Because I know you, Kitty-Kat." He turned to Lily and Rose. "I'm sorry if she caused you any trouble, my ladies."

"Oh, not at all. She's adorable," Lily said.

"Yes," Rose agreed. "I think we would have followed her anywhere."

"She has that effect on people." Cameron began to strum his guitar again, bringing forth a haunting melody.

"That's lovely," Rose said. "I can't quite place the tune. What is it?"

"I wrote it myself."

"Cam has sold two songs in London!" Katrina beamed.

"Really?" Rose said. "Which songs?"

"I'm sure you've never heard of them, my lady," Cameron said. "Neither had a very large distribution. They were only popular among us common folk."

Rose reddened, and Lily seethed. How dare this man speak to her sister so rudely? But his silver gaze, as he looked upon Rose, was not rude. It was very nearly...intimate.

Lily gritted her teeth and said, "Rose is quite the musician also. She plays the pianoforte beautifully."

"I'm no composer," Rose said shyly. "I've always admired those who could string notes together into melody and harmony. I've never quite had the aptitude for it."

"I'm afraid my work would probably disappoint a highbred lady such as yourself." Cameron laid down his guitar. "If you'll excuse me, I've loafed long enough on the porch. I need to get back to the fields. Kat, take them in to meet Mum, will you?"

"Yes, Cam."

Miss Landon sat on a davenport next to a striking woman with silvery streaked black hair.

"There they are now," Miss Landon said. "Come, my ladies. I want you to meet Mrs. Clementine Price. Mrs. Price, this is Lady Lily Jameson, the duke's betrothed, and her sister, Lady Rose."

"Congratulations on your betrothal, my lady," Mrs. Price said.

"Thank you, Mrs. Price."

"I think Cam likes the other one," Katrina said, an impish grin on her adorable face. "He couldn't take his eyes off her!"

Rose blushed and fidgeted with her handkerchief.

"Kat, do be quiet," Mrs. Price said.

"It was wonderful to see you," Miss Landon said, rising. "I so enjoyed our chat. However, the girls and I have many more families to visit this afternoon, so we must be going."

"Yes, of course," Mrs. Price said. "We do thank you for the provisions."

"It's our pleasure. Good day to you all."

As they walked back toward their carriage and wagons, Lily nudged Rose and whispered, "That young man was rude and impudent, but a wonderful musician. And he fancies you."

"It doesn't matter," Rose said, flushing. "Lord Evan wants to court me, and Mr. Price is a commoner."

"Yes, I know," Lily said. "But for a commoner, he strikes

me as quite...uncommon."

Rose didn't reply. They both knew it didn't matter whether he fancied her, or she him. Uncommon or not, Mr. Price was not for her.

★ ★ ★ ★

Lily chose to take dinner alone in her chamber that evening, unable to bear sitting next to Daniel's empty space at his table. When she had finished her meal, she took Brandy on a walk about the estate. After strolling for over an hour, she dropped Brandy back at the kennels to be cared for overnight and went to her chamber. Rose came in later and asked her to come down to the terrace and visit with her and Sophie and Alexandra, but Lily declined. She would be terrible company anyway.

Visions of Daniel plagued her, as she imagined him embracing another woman, kissing her, touching her, loving her the way he had loved Lily. As hard as she tried to shoo the images from her mind, she could not escape them. Touching her belly, she again wondered if Daniel had given her his babe—and whether he had sired any bastards during his last decade of exploits.

"Oh, Daniel," she whispered aloud. "Why do you torment me so?"

CHAPTER FIFTEEN

Because Lily had gone to bed so early, she awoke at dawn the next day and could not fall back to sleep. Finally giving up, she quietly summoned a maid to ready a bath for her, trying not to disturb Rose. When she had dressed in a morning outfit, she descended to the first floor, lugging her oil paints and a large canvas. She took a light breakfast in the ladies' sitting room and then summoned a servant to help carry her supplies to the library.

"Could you unlock the art gallery for me please?"

"I'm sorry, milady," the servant said. "That room can only be opened at the request of the duke or the duchess."

"I'll be the duchess in little over a week," Lily said. "I only want to look at the art for inspiration."

"I'm sorry, milady," the servant said again.

"Where is the duke?"

"In his chamber. He returned very late last night."

"Well, go get him."

"I cannot. He asked not to be bothered."

Lily's heart lurched as a wave of nausea enveloped her. "He's...alone, is he not?" she asked timidly.

"I'm afraid I wouldn't know, my lady."

"Well then, what about the duchess? She'll let me in the gallery."

"I'm sorry. She was feeling poorly yesterday and asked not to be disturbed this morning."

"Fine. Set my supplies up in the library then, please. Make sure you drop an oilcloth about...four by four feet at least, I'd say. I'll be back in a moment."

"Right away, milady."

Lily hurried though the kitchen and up the back stairwell to Daniel's suite. If he was with another woman, she would damn well catch him in the act. How dare he bring one of his strumpets to her home! Granted, it wasn't her home yet, but no doxy chasing would occur at Laurel Ridge once she was its mistress. On that she would not compromise. She opened the door without knocking and walked briskly through the sitting area and into the bedchamber itself.

"Daniel!"

He was in bed, naked, at least as far as she could see, as he was covered from the waist down. She gasped slightly at the sight of his muscular chest and beautiful face softened in sleep. He appeared to be alone. *Thank God.*

"Daniel!" she said again.

He stirred, rubbed his eyes, and looked up at her. "Lily?"

"Yes, it's me. I want to go to the art gallery, and no one will let me in."

"What the devil time is it?"

"Half past seven. Now, about the art room—"

"What are you doing up at this hour?" He sat up in bed, a lock of wavy gold falling over his brow.

"I want to paint, and I want to see the paintings in the gallery for inspiration."

"Dear God. You are a handful, you know that?"

He got out of bed, and as Lily had surmised, he was wearing nothing. Not a stitch. She sighed at the sight of his well formed legs and buttocks as he put on a dressing robe.

"I wouldn't do this for anyone but you."

Her heart nearly leaped through her mouth as he smiled at her and rang for a servant.

"Lady Lily would like to use the art gallery. Please see that it's opened for her, and let all the staff know that she is allowed to use it whenever she chooses. In fact, give her full run of the estate. I'm going back to bed."

"Yes, Your Grace." The servant bowed.

"There you are. Satisfied?"

"You didn't have to give me full run of the estate."

"You'll have it in little more than a week anyway." He flung the dressing robe on a chair and climbed back into bed.

Lily looked at the floor, suddenly sorry for her actions. "I apologize. You must think I'm nothing but a spoiled brat."

"I know who you are, Lily Jameson. You're not spoiled and you're not a brat. But you are impulsive." He chuckled, shaking his head. "There is not another person on this estate, including my mother, who would dare to barge into my chamber without knocking."

"I just wanted—" She stopped. "There's no excuse. You're absolutely right. I do act on impulse. I'm sorry."

"Apology accepted. Now if you'll excuse me, I'm exhausted and I'm going back to bed." He winked seductively, eyeing her from head to toe. "Feel free to join me if you'd like."

"I couldn't..."

"At least come give me a kiss." He held out his arms to her. "I missed you yesterday."

He beckoned to her like a magnet. She went to him, and he pulled her down beside him, positioning her head in the crook of his arm, and kissed her tenderly. Moving on top of her, straddling her and using his knees for support, he held her arms over her head and kissed her again, exploring her slowly but hungrily.

Lily welcomed the honeyed spiciness of his mouth. The velvety caress of his tongue. The sweet pressure of his lips on hers. The kiss catapulted her into a frenzy, and the hardness of his naked body over her while she was fully clothed was almost too much to bear. Arousal tickled between her legs. She was dangerously close to surrendering to him.

She broke the kiss and gulped for air. "I have to go."

"Stay. Please."

"I...can't."

"Tell me you don't want me," Daniel said, his voice a gruff rumble. He forced her gaze to his. "Look into my eyes and tell me you don't want me to make love to you."

"I don't..." She looked away, burying her face in his satin pillow.

He cupped her cheeks and compelled her to look into his eyes again. "You can't say it," he said. "I can feel how much you want me. You want my kisses, my cock. Why are you punishing both of us?"

"I'm sorry." She pushed him off of her. "Please don't be angry with me."

He sighed. "I'm not angry. A little dog drawn, but not angry."

"Dog drawn?"

"I've a terrible cockstand, Lily. Lord, you're beautiful when you blush like that." He covered his eyes with one hand. "Go on and work on your painting. I'll fetch you in a few hours. I want to take you on a carriage ride."

"We'll need a chaperone."

"I'll take care of everything." He breathed rapidly, his eyes still covered. "Don't have lunch. We'll eat while we're out."

★ ★ ★ ★

"Where's our chaperone?" Lily asked as Daniel helped her into his carriage. "You said you'd take care of everything."

"I did," he said. "I decided we didn't need a chaperone."

"You decided?"

"Yes, we're betrothed. It's an open carriage. Everything is fine."

Lily couldn't be too angry. The thought of being alone with him filled her with joy. And sorrow, remembering where he had been the previous day. "If you think best. Where are we going?"

He took her hand and entwined their fingers together. "I'm taking you to the outer vineyards. It's beautiful, and the vines are beginning to bloom."

"That sounds lovely," Lily said. His hand felt perfect in hers. "What did you do in London?"

"Nothing that would interest you."

"Damn it, Daniel, I *am* interested."

"All right, Lily, calm down. I'll tell you all about it after we eat lunch. In the meantime, what did you do yesterday?"

Lily told him about accompanying Miss Landon to see the tenants. He asked a lot of questions, clearly concerned about the tenants and their needs. Lily smiled as she chatted, glad that her involvement with the tenants pleased him.

"I'm sure you charmed them all to pieces," he said.

"All but one, I'm afraid. There was a Mr. Cameron Price who seemed to think Rose and I were a couple of uppity snobs."

"Yes, I know of him. A talented musician actually. You

can't blame him. It's the luck of the draw, who's born where and to whom. The poor fellow will have to work his whole life to make ends meet, while you and I live like kings."

Lily nodded. "Not that I'm complaining, but it doesn't seem fair." She continued, "I think he was a bit taken with Rose."

"I'm not surprised. But he'll get over it and find a girl of his own station."

"How old is he, do you suppose?"

"A few years younger than I am," Daniel said. "I think he's twenty-seven or twenty-eight. His father died when he was barely out of his teens, so he stayed with his mother to run the farm."

"But what of his music?"

"He has responsibilities, Lily."

"I suppose you're right."

The carriage jolted to a stop.

"Here we are." He helped her down. "Come with me."

They walked through the rows of vineyards, inhaling the sweet fragrance of the grape blossoms. In a small clearing, a blanket and picnic lunch awaited them.

"Come on, let's have our lunch." Daniel filled Lily's plate with cold cuts and cheese, bread and fruit, and poured her a goblet of wine.

"Now are you going to tell me what kept you in London all day yesterday?"

He smiled lazily. "Did you miss me, love?"

God, yes, she had. "That's not what I said."

"I missed you," he said, pulling her close to him, "and I know you missed me. You can deny it all you want, but you missed me." He sprinkled wet kisses over her cheeks and her neck. "Tell me you missed me."

His lips scorched her skin. A lie teased her lips, but couldn't emerge. "I missed you."

"Good girl." He lifted his head from hers. "Since you missed me, I'll tell you what you want to know. I went to London for you, Lily."

"For me?"

"To find this." He pulled out a small velvet box from his coat pocket and handed it to her.

Inside lay a gold ring adorned with a large striking green gem sparkling in the sun's rays.

"It's beautiful," she said, her eyes shimmering.

"It's your betrothal ring." He took the box from her and slipped the ring on the fourth finger of her left hand.

She held her hand out, moving it slightly, the glint of the sun catching in the facets of the stone. It was the most incredible piece of jewelry she had ever seen.

"It took you all day to find me a ring?" she asked, unable to tear her gaze away from the beauty of it.

"I was looking for a particular color."

"My, it is beautiful. It's like nothing I've ever seen before. It's the most amazing shade of green I've—" She looked up at him, her eyes misting. "Daniel, it's the color of your eyes!"

His lips curled into a smile that illumined his entire face. "You wouldn't believe the looks I got from the jewelers I visited when I told them what I wanted. There's probably a rumor in all of London by now that the Duke of Lybrook is a complete narcissist."

"It's perfect. Just perfect. I'm so glad you—" She quickly willed back the tears that threatened to fall. "It's not an emerald is it? The color isn't quite right."

"It's a sapphire."

"But sapphires are blue."

"Not this one. They actually come in many colors. Do you like it?"

"I love it, Daniel. I really do. To think I was worried..."

"What is it, love?"

"Oh, it's nothing."

"Tell me."

"It's just...when you wouldn't tell me why you were going to London, and then you wouldn't let me go with you, I just assumed..."

"What?"

"I thought you were going to see one of your mistresses." She bent her head, unable to meet his gaze.

Daniel drew her chin up, forcing her to look at him. "Lily," he said. "I don't have any mistresses."

"But Lady Gregory—"

"Was never my mistress. We had an affair. It went on and off for several years. But I never kept her. I never kept any woman. I never even wanted to."

"But I thought..."

"It's all right. I know my reputation precedes me. I'm not particularly proud of my exploits, and if I could erase them all for you, I would. But I can't. I know I'm not worthy of you. But I've never wanted anyone like I want you. I'll do anything to make you happy." He kissed her lightly on the mouth and cupped her face in his hands, gently caressing her cheeks. "Lily, would it really be so terrible to be my wife?"

Lily attempted a smile as tears slowly trickled down her cheeks. "I never wanted to marry anyone," she said. "But you... You..."

Daniel wiped her tears away with his thumbs. "Don't cry, love. I'll do anything for you. Just tell me what you want. A castle in France? A yacht on the Mediterranean Sea? I'd buy the whole Louvre for you if I could."

"I've no need for more fluff, Daniel," she said, sniffling. "There are only two things I want from you, and neither will cost you a shilling."

"Anything. I swear it." His green eyes penetrated her. "Just tell me."

Her entire body trembled. Such feelings! They overwhelmed her, and she feared he wouldn't be able to offer her the two things she desired most—his love, and his fidelity. She couldn't bring herself to admit what she needed from him. "Just kiss me. Please."

He complied, pushing aside the remains of their lunch and lowering her onto the blanket. He kissed her mouth tenderly, licking and stroking, whispering her name. She pulled him close, seeking the answers to all her questions. When he held her like this, kissed her, whispered her name as if in prayer, she imagined that he loved her.

And it came to her, as if she had known it all along, that she loved him. Somehow, she knew that she would never have gone to bed with anyone but him. She loved his passion for art and horses, his sense of humor that threw her into fits of giggles. She loved the way he made her body and her heart sing. She wanted to be wherever he was, beside him, helping him. She wanted to bear his children, grow old with him, share everything that she was with him. She wanted him at her side when she strolled through the Louvre, dined in Paris, climbed a mountain in Switzerland.

Somewhere along the way she had given him her heart,

and everything had changed.

She loved him more than she had ever loved anyone, yet her heart ached. Could he return her love? And if he wasn't satisfied with her alone, could she live with that?

He had lavished her with generous gifts, gifts he had known would touch her heart. He had treated her kindly, taking her virginity with great care and affection. Whether they were riding, looking at art, talking, laughing, or making love, a closeness existed between them. Did he feel it too?

"Please let me love you, Lily," Daniel whispered. "I need you so much."

"We can't." Lily breathed sharply. "Out here. Someone will see." She sought his mouth with her own.

"It will be all right. No one will come out this way. I promise you."

"How can you make such a promise?"

His eyes twinkled at her. "Because I have servants on the perimeters of the vineyards, standing guard."

"I see. So it was your intent to bring me out here and seduce me," she said coyly. "And now I suppose you expect to get what you want."

"I don't expect anything, my love," he said, kissing her neck and fumbling with her bodice. "I only wish. I want nothing more than to make love to you right now."

How she wanted him! If she couldn't have his love, she would take whatever he could offer. Soon she would be his wife, and she would not be able to deny him then.

"Yes, Daniel. Make love to me. I want to feel your body against mine. I want to feel your arms around me. I want to feel you inside me. Please make love to me."

"God, Lily. I've missed you so much." He opened her

bodice and freed her breasts, lavishing them with kisses and caresses. "You're so beautiful."

He tugged at one nipple and then the other, her body shuddering. She grasped his cravat, untied it quickly, and began to unbutton his shirt. When she could get no farther, she clutched his jacket at his shoulders, trying to remove it.

"I want you naked, Daniel. Naked on me, while I'm still clothed. Like this morning."

He smiled naughtily. "You liked that, did you?"

"Yes, I liked that a lot. You said you'd do anything for me."

"I did, at that." He pulled away from her, removed his shoes, his trousers, his jacket and shirt, and came back to her. "Is this what you wanted?"

"Oh yes." She sighed, running her fingers across his rippling back, down along the smooth contours of his buttocks. He gasped. "Your body is a work of art," she said. "I love to touch you." She reached under him, found his hard arousal, and grasped it.

Daniel sucked in his breath.

"Did I hurt you?"

"God, no," he said. "But I'm aching so badly for you that I'm liable to spend myself like a lad if you keep doing that." He pulled her hand upward and kissed it. "I don't know how long I can hold out, Lily. I need you to be naked under me. I want to feel every part of you. I want nothing between us. Nothing ever."

He gently undressed her and threw her clothes into a heap next to his.

"Open your legs for me, love." He kissed down to her opening. "So sweet, so wet." He slid his fingers into her, stroking and teasing. "You feel amazing."

He licked and probed until the familiar jolts rippled through her body, crashing her into euphoria. She wept his name, arching into him, and kissed him when he came back up to her.

"Have you missed me, Lily?"

"Yes," she said breathlessly.

"My God," he said, "you're so much to me. Not just a fuck. Tell me you know that. Tell me."

"Yes, Daniel. Yes."

He rolled over so she was on top of him. He positioned her over his cock.

"What are you doing?"

He lifted her gently over his shaft, nudging her open, and slid her down, impaling her.

"Oh!"

"Ride me." He gently moved her body up and down over him, until she caught the rhythm and took over. "Yes, love. You're so beautiful, so tight." He took her hand and led it to her clitoris, showing her how to stimulate herself. "Touch yourself there. Yes, that's it."

Lily warmed with embarrassment, but she wanted to please him, so she touched herself, finding the spot that made her convulse. "Oh my. That's so...oh my!" Another orgasm struck her.

Daniel reached behind her and rubbed a finger over her most private place. She widened her eyes, but allowed it, as she had previously. His touch made her sizzle, and the sensitivity of her anus still surprised her.

"Did you know, love, that I can take you there?" Daniel said, massaging her lightly as she continued to ride his cock.

"I never..."

"For another time, of course."

He removed his finger and grasped her breasts, squeezing her nipples. Her pussy pulsed, on the edge of another orgasm, when suddenly he released her breasts and grabbed her hips. He thundered into her, pulling her down onto him until she could swear he nudged the edge of her womb.

"I'm going to come, Lily. I'm coming for you. Only you." He plunged upwards, his eyes squeezed shut, his abdominal muscles tense and taut.

Lily collapsed on top of him, kissing his face, his neck, his lips. Inside her head she shouted, *I love you! I love you!*

But she didn't say it aloud. She was afraid.

★ ★ ★ ★

Lily found Rose, Sophie, and Alexandra on the terrace with some of the other women when she returned, and she couldn't resist showing them her amazing engagement ring.

"You look very happy." Rose smiled. "Have you resigned yourself to this marriage yet?"

"Almost," Lily said. If only she could be sure Daniel loved her and would be faithful to her. "I'm done fighting it, at least."

"I would trade places with you in an instant," Ally said. "If only a man would look at me the way the duke looks at you."

"Someone will," Sophie consoled her sister. "Someone will for all of us, someday."

They chatted until Crawford interrupted them. "My lady," he said to Lily. "Please pardon my intrusion. Her Grace would like to see you in her private sitting room."

"Her Grace? Whatever for?"

"I don't know, my lady. But please come at once."

"All right. I'll see you all later."

She followed Crawford into the house. He led her up the double staircase to the third floor, to the duchess's suite of rooms in the west wing.

"My dear Lily, do come in," the duchess said.

Lily curtsied politely. "I do hope you're feeling better, Your Grace."

"Quite a bit, thank you, dear." The duchess motioned for Lily to be seated. "What do you take in your tea?"

"Nothing, thank you."

"Like my Daniel." She smiled. "Here you are."

"Thank you."

"I'd like you to accept my gratitude for accompanying Lucy on our errands yesterday. It was a great help to me."

"It was my pleasure. I enjoyed it."

"I'm very glad." The duchess set her teacup down on the tray, a serious expression on her graceful face. "Now, tell me, why don't you want to marry my Daniel?"

"Pardon?"

"My dear, I know a girl who's being forced into marriage when I see one. I was that girl myself once. Don't you care for Daniel?"

"Yes, I care for him, but... Well, he didn't ask me what I wanted. He arranged everything with my father."

"Yes, I'm aware of that. I thought he would know better than to mimic his own father in that regard." She sighed. "But you should know, Lily, that the duke and I had a happy and successful marriage. We grew to love each other very much. I can't imagine having married any other."

"But it doesn't always work out that way."

"No, it doesn't. But Daniel cares for you, and you care for

him. I can tell by the way you interact with each other. Lucy and I both agree we've never seen Daniel happier. You have that advantage over my marriage."

"Your Grace, if you don't mind my asking, how long did it take you to grow to love the duke?" Perhaps it wouldn't take Daniel long to grow to love her.

"Not long. He was kind to me, and he was interested in my opinions. I became pregnant soon after we married, and he insisted on naming our first son after me. He was named after both of us, Morgan Charles. Lord, how I miss them."

"I'm so very sorry for your loss."

"Thank you, dear. I appreciate that. It's been harder on Daniel than on me, I'm afraid."

Lily nodded. "He told me he wasn't close to either of them." Then, "Your Grace, may I speak frankly?"

"Of course."

"I don't believe that Daniel has ever allowed himself to grieve for his father and brother. I believe he keeps his emotions locked inside himself. I...worry about him."

"You are very perceptive, Lily. And you are correct. I don't believe he has grieved. And it isn't true that he wasn't close to them. He no doubt told you that to convince himself, so he could hide his hurt at their passing. But it isn't easy to be a second son."

"How so?"

"Morgan and Daniel were not quite a whole year apart. They were the very best of friends. I think they knew each other better than they knew themselves."

Lily nodded. "I understand what you mean. Rose and I are less than a year apart also. We are close in that same way."

"Then imagine, dear, if Rose had been snatched away

from you when you were not but seven years old. That is what happened to Daniel."

Lily raised her eyebrows. "What?"

"Morgan was Charles's heir, Lily. When the boys were small, Charles was devoted to both of them. He played ball with them, took them fishing and hunting, taught them how to ride. But when Morgan turned eight, Charles decided it was time to start grooming him into the next Duke of Lybrook. He was no longer allowed to play with Daniel. Charles monopolized him, taking him to business meetings, estate affairs, the like."

"But what of Daniel?" Lily's heart ached for the sad little boy. "Surely it would have benefited him to learn about the affairs of the estate, especially considering how things turned out."

"Yes, hindsight is always clear, isn't it? With Charles, everything was either black or white. Morgan was the heir, and Daniel was not, so Daniel was left to flounder. He lost not only his father's time and devotion, but also his best friend in the world. Charles and I decided to send Daniel away to school, while Morgan stayed on the estate and studied with private tutors. We hoped being with other boys his own age would ease his loneliness for Morgan."

Lily gasped. "You sent a seven-year-old boy away?"

"Don't judge us too harshly, dear. Had I the chance to do it over again, I would not allow it. When you have your own child, you'll know a love like no other. It tore my heart out to lose Daniel. But Charles insisted, and I'm afraid I wasn't strong enough to fight for my son. I live with that to this day. Not only did Daniel lose his father and brother to the dukedom, he lost Lucy and me as well when we sent him away."

"I'm sorry. I didn't mean to sound judgmental."

"It's all right. And Daniel did enjoy school. He made some lifelong friends, and he excelled in his studies. He especially loved the arts, and he was also quite gifted in the sciences. He's very bright, my Daniel."

"Yes, I know. I think he'll be a fine duke."

"I know he will, especially with you by his side. He is learning, and he is trying. But he has been thrust into this position with no preparation whatsoever. Charles put everything into Morgan."

The duchess paused, stirring more honey into her tea. "Daniel eventually made peace with Charles, although they were never as close as they once were, but I believe he loved his father, and I know he loved Morgan. And I believe he loves me and Lucy. But he never allowed himself to love anyone else. After he finished his schooling, he had nothing to do. He could have been a huge help to Charles and Morgan, running the estate. I tried to talk to Charles about it, but his response was that Morgan was the heir, and it was his responsibility." The duchess cleared her throat. "My Charles was a great man and a loving husband, but as I said, everything was either black or white with him. Consequently, Daniel, with nothing to occupy his appreciable intelligence, and a great fear of loving, embarked on a decade of indiscriminate affairs, of which I'm sure you've heard."

Lily nodded. "He's quite well known."

"I know. Not my proudest moment as a mother, of course. But I do adore my Daniel. He has so much to offer, and now, for the first time, I believe he is trying to open his heart."

"To me?"

"Yes, my dear, to you." The duchess smiled. "You see, I know that the two of you have been...seeing each other."

Lily's face warmed. She wanted to disappear into the plush rug under her feet.

"I couldn't be happier with Daniel's choice," the duchess said. "I hold both your parents in the highest esteem. I've known your mother since she was a babe."

"Yes, I know. She told me that your sister and my Auntie Iris were best friends as girls."

"All four of us were close, actually. I've tried to get Flora to use my Christian name over the years, but she won't hear of it, insisting upon calling me 'Your Grace.'"

"That's just Mummy," Lily said.

"Yes, I know. She's a fine woman. We lost touch over the years. But I had a good life with Charles. It wasn't easy to watch Daniel engage in so many meaningless dalliances."

"I understand."

"When Charles and Morgan passed on, Daniel became the seventh Duke of Lybrook."

The duchess's eyes shimmered with tears, and Lily offered her handkerchief.

"Thank you, dear. Imagine, for a moment, what it was like to lose a father and a brother, and then be plagued with new responsibilities for which you were completely unprepared. So what did Daniel do? He ran."

"To the continent," Lily said.

"Yes. I didn't try to stop him. I don't think I could have anyway. I understood his need for escape. I let him go. Luckily, our solicitors and bankers took care of the estate while he was gone, and our holdings are secure. Then, a few months ago, I received a letter from Daniel, telling me he was returning to resume his responsibilities. He apologized for leaving me when I needed him, and he vowed to do better in the future as a son, as a duke, and as a man. Lucy and I planned this house party to come out of mourning, but I had an ulterior motive. I wanted you and Daniel to meet again."

"Did you know that we had actually met before?"

"Yes. He told me the day he found you in my little alcove. He mentioned your talent and what a pretty child you were."

Lily's heart jumped and her lips curved into a smile.

"I couldn't think of a better match for my son than one of Flora and Crispin's daughters. I intended to formally introduce the two of you, but somehow that took care of itself. I was elated when Daniel arranged for you to sit with him at dinner. I don't know how the two of you managed to get together, but I thank God for it." The duchess laid her hand on Lily's forearm, squeezing gently. "You are Daniel's savior, Lily. Please don't abandon him."

"I don't want to leave him, it's just..."

"What, dear?"

"I have reason to believe that he's only marrying me because... This is difficult to say."

"You're going to be my daughter, Lily. You can tell me."

Lily concentrated on a small wrinkle in her skirt. "He believes I might be with child."

The duchess lifted her eyebrows. "With child? But Daniel ought to know how to prevent that."

"He does. He told me he would. But he didn't. I was...quite angry with him."

"Oh my."

"I'm sorry, Your Grace. I assure you that I never meant to... That is, if it had been anyone but him, I wouldn't have... He and I seem to... We're drawn together, or something." Lily sighed. "This isn't coming out right at all."

"My dear, I don't think any less of you. But don't you see what this means?"

"No, I'm sorry."

"He didn't try to prevent you from conceiving his child. Lily, Daniel is in love with you."

A tear slid down Lily's cheek. "He's never said that. He's said other things. I suppose one might be able to construe..." She shook her head. "No, I need to hear the words."

"I understand, but he's afraid to love. The only people he ever allowed himself to love were ripped from him as a young boy." The duchess wiped a tear from her cheek. "You must tell him how you feel first."

"But that's not the way..." Lily shrugged. "I'm afraid to."

The duchess took both of Lily's hands in hers, smiling into her eyes. "My darling girl, sometimes we women have to be the brave ones. You'll find out for yourself once you're married. Go to him. Admit your feelings to him. Show him he can love again."

Lily gulped, apprehension flooding her. But the duchess was right. Poor Daniel had lost everyone.

"May I ask a favor, Your Grace?"

"Yes."

"Would you keep this conversation in confidence?"

"Of course."

"Thank you. I've enjoyed talking with you. It's been enlightening." She gathered her courage and rose. "I shall go to Daniel."

CHAPTER SIXTEEN

Daniel rose from his giant tub and toweled himself dry, smiling as he remembered his afternoon with Lily. He swathed himself in a velvet dressing robe, ready to ring for Putney to assist him, when a knock came on his outer chamber door. No one but Lily would come to see him at this time during the day. His heart leaped in anticipation of seeing her face, hearing her voice. He walked through his bedchamber to the sitting room.

"Come in, love," he said, loudly enough to penetrate the closed door. "You're not going to start knocking now, are you?" He went back into the bedchamber, grabbed a towel, and began to wring the moisture from his hair.

"How very kind you are, to say that I don't need to knock."

Daniel turned. Amelia Gregory stood in the door of his bedchamber.

"I thought you were someone else."

"Your lovely Lily, no doubt?"

"I'm busy, as you can see. Please leave at once."

"No. I want to talk to you."

"We have nothing to say to each other."

"I disagree, Daniel. I have much to say." She walked toward him. "I have missed you so very much. I can't sleep at night for want of you."

"I'm sorry. As I've told you before, it's over between us."

"No, it can't be."

"It is."

"But why? We shared so much together."

"We shared a bed, Amelia, that's all. I'm going to be married, and I have every intention of—"

"Don't tell me that you have feelings for that little whore."

Rage boiled in Daniel's gut. "Do not ever refer to her like that again, do you understand? Leave her out of this. Your quarrel is with me."

"Does she make you feel like I do? Do you remember our fun? Our escapades?"

Daniel remembered, though he wished he didn't. "You need to leave now, Amelia."

"You're mine, Daniel. She can't have you!"

"She already has me. I'm hers."

"What does she have that I don't?"

A smile teased his lips. "She has my heart. She's had it from the beginning. I love her." The words lifted a great burden from his shoulders. "I love her," he said again, more to himself than to Amelia.

"You don't know the meaning of the word." Amelia lunged forward and tackled him to the ground. She straddled him, clamping her mouth down upon his, seeking entrance with her tongue. She wrenched the dressing robe from his chest. "Here's what you'll be missing with her, Daniel. Look what I can give you."

God, Polk had been right about Amelia. She was bad news. He tossed her aside him and closed his robe. "I have reconsidered allowing you to stay here, Amelia. I want you gone by the morrow."

"You won't get rid of me that easily, Your Grace." Amelia smoothed her rumpled dress and stood. "I was invited here. What would the duchess think of you throwing me out?"

"I don't righteously care what the duchess thinks."

"Perhaps Her Grace and I should have a little chat. She might like to know what her baby boy has been up to in my bedchamber."

"You leave my mother alone, damn it." Daniel closed his robe and rose. "She's been through hell, losing her husband and son, and I won't tolerate your interference with her. Have your bags packed. You'll leave after dinner."

Amelia turned and flounced toward the door. "You know," she said, looking back at him, "your intended isn't interested in you. She told me so."

Daniel winced. "When did you speak to her?"

"We've had several chats, the future duchess and I. The first night of the house party, I found her in the ladies' sitting room after you molested her outside. I enlightened her as to why you grabbed her. You had mistaken her for me, of course. She told me she wasn't the least bit interested in you. Then the other night, after you announced your betrothal, she told me she didn't wish to marry you."

Daniel's stomach churned, and he swallowed. "You stay the hell away from her. I mean it. I want you off this estate."

"Why do you wish to marry someone who doesn't want you? She'll never be able to satisfy you. I know your sexual appetites. You can have me, Daniel. I want you. I need you. Let me be your duchess. I'll make you proud."

"For the last time, Amelia, leave this chamber at once, or I will physically remove you!"

Amelia smiled seductively. "I'd like to see you try. Once you put your hands on me, you'll be mine. You won't be able to resist."

"I assure you, I will. Now go."

"Fine, I'll go, but I'm afraid I'm not leaving the estate."

"Yes, you are, damn it."

"Daniel, I will stay and enjoy the rest of the house party. I was invited. If you force me to leave, I swear I will make sure all of England knows of our exploits. And the first two people who hear about them will be your sweet Lily and your dear devoted mother."

"Both Lily and my mother are aware of our affair."

"Perhaps. But do they know all the juicy details? Like the time my young housemaid joined us in bed? Two pairs of lips on your hard cock? But that was nothing compared to the cockstand you had when she and I sucked each other. And what about that handsome gardener?" Amelia lifted her skirts and slid a hand into her drawers. "One cock in my cunny and one in my arse... Heavens, I still burn from time to time thinking about it."

Daniel grimaced. How had he ever been so young and foolish? He couldn't risk Amelia poisoning Lily against him. "Do as you please," he said through clenched teeth, "but stay away from my mother, stay away from Lily, and stay the hell out of my sight!"

He pushed her out the door and slammed it.

★ ★ ★ ★

Amelia blazed with temper as she walked down the hallway to the back stairwell. She wasn't finished yet, not by a long shot. "Oh, no," she groaned aloud as she spied the very bane of her life, Lady Lily Jameson, coming up the back stairwell.

"Lila, dear," Amelia said, approaching. "How lovely to see you."

"Good afternoon."

"Going to see your intended, I presume?"

"It's none of your business where I'm going. If you'll excuse me."

"I was just in his chamber. I'm afraid he's a bit...indisposed at the moment."

"What were you doing in his chamber?" Lily demanded.

"I'm sure you can guess." Amelia straightened her wrinkled gown and smoothed her hair.

"I don't believe you."

But Lily wrung her hands nervously, fumbling with a handkerchief. No, she wasn't nearly as confident as she wanted Amelia to believe.

"You don't? Surely you're not such an innocent that you thought Daniel would stop his affairs just because he's getting married."

"What?"

"I must thank you," Amelia said. "You've obviously been a marvelous influence on him. Daniel has never been quite so, shall we say, *prurient*, in his lovemaking."

"Daniel would never..."

"He told me that it's only a matter of time before he gets his heir on you, and then he'll ship you off to Scotland and make me his live-in mistress." She spied the green engagement ring on Lily's hand. "You may as well give that to me now. Daniel said I could have it."

Tears glistened in Lily's eyes. "No, he wouldn't do that."

"Are you going to cry, my dear? How dreadful." Amelia grabbed Lily's hand. "Now, give me that ring!"

"Daniel chose it for me. He went to London, he... You can't have it!" Lily backed toward the stairwell.

"It's mine!" Amelia screamed, yanking the ring from Lily's finger.

Lily toppled a bit, losing her balance.

"And Daniel's mine! He'll never be yours! Never!"

Amelia shoved Lily hard, closing her ears to the screaming sobs as Lily rolled down the stairs and fell with a thud on the landing below. Quickly Amelia looked around. No servants appeared to have witnessed the exchange. Breathing a sigh of relief, she strode to the front stairwell, descended smoothly, and made her way to her chamber.

★ ★ ★ ★

Daniel understood only about every third word the flustered servant said. All that mattered was that something had happened to Lily. Buttoning his trousers, he ran to the stairwell. Dear Lord, she was on the landing, Crawford and a few others attending her. He leaped down the stairs taking them three at a time.

"What the hell happened?" He knelt beside Lily, her body crumpled, her face streaked from tears, her eyes locked in unconsciousness. His heart pounded and anguish enveloped him. "Lily, my God, Lily. Don't leave me. Please don't leave me." He gathered her in his arms.

"You shouldn't move her, Your Grace," Crawford said. "She could be bleeding inside, and she probably has broken bones. I've sent for your physician."

"I can't leave her here, damn it! She's everything to me." He lifted her gently.

"Please, Your Grace, it's best—"

"Send the physician to my chamber, Crawford. Oh dear

God. Just send him to my chamber."

Daniel carried Lily up the stairwell, as gently as if she were a babe, took her into his chamber, and laid her on his bed. He kissed her forehead, her cheeks, her lips, as tears streamed from his eyes.

"Lily, Lily, please wake up. It's Daniel, Lily. I love you. I love you. Oh, why didn't I tell you?"

He knelt down beside her, begging God to bring her back, and then sat down next to her and gently touched her face. Her eyes fluttered for an instant.

"Daniel?" Her voice was hoarse and raspy.

"Lily, yes, I'm here, my love. Tell me what happened."

"It was...Amelia." Her eyes closed into unawareness again.

Amelia? Had she pushed Lily down the stairs? He would send that bitch to hell! He got up to ring for a servant when Lord and Lady Ashford burst in.

"Your Grace, what happened?" The countess turned to see Lily on the bed. She crossed herself. "Crispin, she's—"

"What happened, Lybrook?" the earl asked calmly, taking his wife's hand.

"I-I don't know," Daniel stammered. "Crawford found her at the bottom of the back stairwell. She—" He swallowed. "I believe she was pushed."

"By whom?" the countess asked. "Why would anyone want to harm her?"

"She...she said it was..."

Daniel turned toward the sound of a clearing throat. Dr. Michael Blake stood in the doorway.

"Blake, thank God. She fell down the stairs. You've got to help her. Please."

"Stand back. Let me to her." The doctor sat down on the

bed next to her and began palpating her arms and legs.

Thomas strode into the room. "What happened? I heard that Lily was hurt."

"She's unconscious, Thomas," Lord Ashford said. "The doctor is looking at her now."

"I don't think any bones are broken," Blake said. "That's good news, and surprising, considering her fall." He opened his bag, pulled out an instrument, and slit Lily's gown down the front. He eased her arms out of the sleeves, loosened her corset, and listened to her heart with a stethoscope. "Her heartbeat is strong, and she seems to be breathing normally. She most likely has a concussion." He moved his hands down her body, gently kneading her stomach and abdomen, and then lifted her petticoat and gasped.

"What is it, doctor?" the countess asked.

"I'm sorry to say this," Blake said. "She appears to be bleeding from her womb."

"No," Daniel said. "No, no."

"I'll have to stop the bleeding."

"Of course, do what you must," the earl said.

"Crispin." The countess turned her head into her husband's shoulder, choking back sobs.

"I'm sorry," Dr. Blake said, "but I have to ask. Is there any chance she might be breeding?"

"Of course not," Lord Ashford said.

Daniel looked down at his feet and raked his fingers through his thick hair. "Yes," he said, barely audibly, "there is."

Thomas started forward. "Lybrook, I'll throttle you!"

"Not before I do," the earl said, holding his son back with his arm.

"Stop it, the both of you," Lady Ashford said, motioning to

Daniel. "Can't you see this is killing him?"

"Flora, he took our daughter into his bed!" The earl said, his hands clenched into fists.

"Stop being such a barbarian," the countess said quietly, but harshly. "You know as well as I do that Lily never would have done anything that she didn't want to do. And have you forgotten our own courtship? We weren't saints, as you should well recall, and by the time I was her age I was married and had a child." She turned to her son. "As for you, I know more about your dalliances than I wish to, so just keep your mouth shut from here on. None of this is helping Lily."

"I know this is difficult," the doctor interjected. "But I need all the facts. How far along would she be if she were breeding?"

Silence.

"Your Grace?" the doctor said again.

"I'm sorry," Daniel said. "Days. Only days."

"I must try to stop the bleeding. There is no other way. The method I need to use will terminate the pregnancy if there is one. However, it is likely that she has already lost the babe."

"Just save her, damn it!" Daniel said.

"There is something else."

"What?" Daniel yelled. "What is it?"

"If I'm unable to stop the bleeding, I'll have no choice but to remove the womb."

Lady Ashford gasped. "Then she won't be able to—"

"No," the doctor said. "She won't be able to bear children. I'm sorry."

"I don't care," Daniel said. "I don't care. Just do what you have to do to save her life. I can't live without her."

"I'm sorry, Your Grace, but that decision is not yours to

make. You're not her husband yet." He turned to the earl. "My lord, may I have your permission for the procedure?"

"Give him permission. Please," Daniel begged. "I need her. I need her."

"Of course, do what you must," the earl agreed.

Lady Ashford turned to a housemaid. "Fetch the duchess at once. Tell her that her son needs her." She went to Daniel and guided him to his leather chair. "Sit," she said. "Come on. It will be all right." She took his hand in hers. "She is strong, so very strong. She will be all right."

"I can't live without her. I can't."

Daniel sat, his mind numb, as Lily's mother held his hand, massaging it lightly. Several moments later, his mother and Aunt Lucy entered.

"My God, Flora, I'm so sorry," the duchess said.

"It's all right, Maggie," Lady Ashford said. "I'll take care of my child. You take care of yours. He needs you."

"Daniel, my darling, I'm so sorry." His mother took his hand from Lady Ashford. "Come with me."

"I can't leave her," he said, his voice cracking. "I can't."

"Come. The doctor must be able to do his work."

"Her Grace is correct," Blake said. "I'm sorry, but you must all leave. I'll need a few maids to attend me."

"I shall stay," Lucy said. "I've attended many of the tenants in my day."

"Lucy will be of great assistance to you," the duchess said. "She's had some training in nursing."

"Thank you. That will be fine. Miss Landon, I'll need some clean towels and sheets, and have the kitchen send up some boiling water." He turned to a maid. "Light a fire in the grate, so we can keep water boiling in here while I operate."

"I don't want to leave her, Mother," Daniel said, as the duchess gently pulled him up from the chair. "She needs me. I need her."

"I know, darling, but you must come with me. You must let the doctor help her."

His mother nudged him forward, out the door.

Moments later, Daniel sat in his mother's suite of rooms on the third floor of the west wing. She helped him sit down on a comfortable sofa and rang for some tea.

"My darling boy," she said. "Can you tell me what happened?'

Daniel raked his fingers through his hair again, disheveling it further. "She fell down the back stairwell, from the third to the second floor. My God, she was probably coming to see me."

The duchess nodded. "This isn't your fault, Daniel."

"It is," he said. "I believe she was pushed."

"What? Why would you think that?"

"She regained consciousness for a few moments in my chamber. She said... My God, she said it was Lady Gregory."

"She actually said that Lady Gregory pushed her?"

"No. Not exactly. She just said 'It was Amelia.'"

"Why on earth would Lady Gregory push Lily down the stairs?"

"I told you this is all my fault. Damn it all to hell!" He stood and started pacing, his heart thundering.

"Please, my darling, sit." The duchess patted the sofa beside her. "None of this is your fault."

"It is. Lady Gregory wants me for herself. She told me so."

"Surely she wouldn't..."

"She would. Remember how her husband died?"

"Nothing was ever proven."

"It doesn't matter. She pushed him, and now she pushed Lily. And if Lily dies, it will be all my fault. I can't bear this. I can't! Just when I thought I had everything." He sat down and buried his face in his hands.

The duchess put her arms around him. "Daniel, if this is true, we need to summon the authorities."

"Yes, yes. I want her off this estate. I want to see her rot in Newgate. The hangman's noose is too good for her!"

"Do sit still for a moment." The duchess rose and rang for a servant, whispered to him for a few minutes, and returned. "Crawford will summon the authorities, and Lady Gregory will be escorted from the premises."

"Thank you, Mother."

"I'm going to take care of you, Daniel, the way I should have taken care of you when you were a boy. There are so many things I'm sorry about. So many things..."

"None of that matters now," Daniel said, resisting his mother's embrace. "All that matters is Lily. I don't know what I'll do without her."

"You will go on, of course. But you're putting the cart before the horse, darling. Lily is young and strong. There is every chance that she will come through this."

"She changed everything for me. She made me feel alive again. She showed me kindness and tenderness when I needed her. I love her, Mother. I love her."

"I know you do. I know," the duchess said, trying again to embrace him. "She will be all right, Daniel, and the two of you will have a long and happy life together."

A maid brought in a tea tray, and the duchess poured a cup. She held it out to Daniel.

"Drink this. Come on."

He pushed her hand away.

"Just one sip."

He obliged her.

"Good boy." She took a sip of her own tea. "She's going to come back to you. Just wait and see."

"It doesn't matter whether she comes back to me. I just want her to live. She has so much vigor and passion. I love her more than I ever thought I could love anyone. Christ, I never told her." He shook his head. "I'm going to let her go."

"What do you mean?"

"I'm not going to force her to marry me."

"Daniel..."

"I'll beg her to. I'll tell her how much I love her and I'll give her anything she wants. But in the end, I won't force her. I was wrong to go behind her back and talk to Ashford. I just couldn't bear the thought of her refusing me. But I was being selfish. Her happiness means more to me than my own. If, in the end, she wants to leave, I will let her go."

"She won't leave you, my darling. She loves you."

"I don't know that she does."

"Of course she does. How could she not?"

"I never dared to hope that she could love me. I've made so many mistakes. So many years of wandering aimlessly, engaging in affairs." He looked at his mother in wonder, his heart full, yet breaking. "But it all led me to her, didn't it?"

"Yes, it did."

"I'll do anything for her. Even if she can't give me an heir. All I want is her."

"She will stay with you."

"God, I hope you're right." Daniel rubbed the nape of his neck. "If I lose her, I don't think I can go on. She seems to know me better than I know myself. I don't know how, but she can read me like no other. She told me I hadn't mourned for father and Morgan. How did she know? She offered to help me, to talk to me. I turned her down. If I could take that back I would tell her everything. I would..."

"Come here, my darling." His mother pulled him close. "It will be all right. It will be all right."

Daniel resisted at first, but then let his mother cradle his head as if he were a babe. His stomach ached as he trembled, his mother's caresses doing little to soothe him. His breath came in rapid pants as daggers sliced into his marrow. His stomach churned and his bowels cramped. Fear. Gut-wrenching terror. Sorrow ripping out his soul.

Slowly he breathed. In and out. In and out. Then he did something he hadn't done in over two decades.

He cried in his mother's arms.

★ ★ ★ ★

Thomas walked around the estate looking for Rose, his heart pounding. If only he had kept a better eye on Lily, kept her out of Lybrook's bed. But he had failed her. How in the world had Lily managed to fall down the stairs? He spied Rose at the stables, walking with Lord Evan. He ran toward them.

"Rose!" he shouted. "Rose, you need to come quickly!" Thomas caught his breath. "It's Lily. She's had an accident."

Rose gasped. "What happened?"

"She fell down a flight of stairs. She's...she's bleeding from her womb. Lybrook's physician is with her now."

Rose nearly lost her balance.

Evan steadied her. "Easy, Rose," he said. "It's all right."

"I must go to her at once," Rose said. "I'm sorry, my lord."

"Don't be," Evan said. "I'll come as well. Jameson, what is the prognosis?"

"The doctor says he has to stop the bleeding. If he cannot, he'll remove her womb."

"No!" Rose cried. "What about the duke's heir?"

"There won't be one," Thomas said. "At least not by Lily."

Tears formed in Rose's eyes. "No, no. That's too horrible to contemplate. Oh, Thomas. What are we going to do?"

"Pray," Thomas said. "Come on. We'll go to the manor and wait for word."

They walked quickly toward the mansion. A constable's carriage stood out front. Two constables from Bath escorted Lady Gregory out of the house.

"What is going on here?" Thomas demanded.

"We have a warrant for this woman's arrest," one of the constables said. "We have reason to believe that she pushed the duke's betrothed down a flight of stairs."

"You!" Thomas bellowed at Amelia. "I should have known you were behind this, you conniving little bitch."

"Thomas!" Rose admonished.

"She pushed Lily, Rose," Thomas said. Then, to Amelia, "My sister could be dead because of you. She may never be able to bear children!"

"Good riddance, my lord," Amelia said. "The little fool isn't fit to be a duchess, much less to bear the next duke."

"You take that back," Rose said.

Evan tried to calm her. "It's all right, Rose."

"No, it's not all right." Rose cocked her head. "Why, that's Lily's ring!"

"It's mine," Amelia said.

"Thomas, it's Lily's," Rose said. "She showed it to me earlier. The duke gave it to her for their betrothal."

"Are you sure?"

"Yes, I swear it. I'd recognize it anywhere. It's a sapphire, not an emerald. It's a very unique shade of green."

"Constable," Thomas said, "you can add theft to your charges. It appears Lady Gregory has stolen my sister's ring."

"Give it to me. Now." Rose held out her hand.

"I'll do no such thing." Amelia seethed. "It belongs to me."

Rage surged through Thomas. "Give that ring to my sister right now, or I swear to you by all I hold dear, I'll break my cardinal rule of never striking a woman!" He moved toward Amelia, the constables doing little to stop him.

"Are you going to stand there and let him threaten me?"

"You'd best give the ring back, my lady," one of the men said.

"Now, Amelia," Rose said. "Lily's ring, please."

Amelia took the ring from her finger and dropped it in Rose's hand. "Take the damn thing. It's a silly bauble."

Rose stepped forward and punched Amelia square in the nose.

"You little bitch!" Amelia screamed, tears streaking her face as blood gushed from her nostrils. "You broke my nose!"

"I don't share your sentiment about never striking a woman, Thomas," Rose said. "This one had it coming."

"I don't disagree," Thomas said.

"Nice right hook," Evan added. "When did you learn that?"

"Today," Rose replied.

★ ★ ★ ★

Daniel sat on a bench in the chapel, his head buried in his hands. *Please, God, save her. Please, I'll do anything.*

"Your Grace?"

Daniel looked up. "Lady Rose," he said hoarsely. "Is there any news?"

"No, Your Grace. Not yet. I'm sorry."

"Oh." He stood. "Is there something you need?"

"No, Your Grace. I came to...give you this." She held out the green engagement ring.

"Lily's ring." He took it and fingered the green stone. "Where did you find it?"

"It was on Lady Gregory's finger. Thomas and I saw her as the constables were escorting her out of the house."

"The ring I found especially for Lily?" He clutched at his hair. "Dear God, what must she have said to her?"

"I'm sorry. I didn't mean to upset you. I thought...that you'd like to have the ring."

"Yes, yes, of course." Daniel sat back down, his anger at Amelia giving away to fear and grief. "How did you get it back?"

"I made her give it to me," Rose said. She gave a light smile. "I punched her in the nose."

"You did?"

"Yes, I did. She had it coming." Rose sat down beside him. "Your Grace, Lily cares for you very much. I want you to know that."

Daniel closed his eyes, trembling. How he hoped Lily's sister was right. "Thank you."

Rose sat beside him, and he continued to pray silently, until Evan entered.

"Lady Lily's out of surgery," he said. "The doctor wants to talk to all of you."

CHAPTER SEVENTEEN

"Good, you're here," Blake said, when Daniel and Rose entered. "Everything went well. I have stopped the bleeding. It wasn't necessary to remove the womb."

"Oh thank God!" Lady Ashford said.

"I want to see her," Daniel said.

"Of course, in a moment," Blake said. "I need to explain a few things. She has a concussion. She will drift in and out of consciousness for the next day or two. I have her sedated right now and on morphine for the pain. She may develop a fever. It's quite common after a surgical procedure."

"Oh dear," the countess said.

"She's young and healthy. We'll keep her cool as best we can."

"Is there any risk at this point?" Daniel asked.

"There is always risk after any invasive procedure, Your Grace, but I have every reason to believe that she will recover nicely. May I speak privately to you for a moment?"

"Yes, yes, of course." Daniel sighed with relief as he moved with Blake to the other end of the room. "What is it?"

"You'll need to stay away from her, Your Grace. She can't engage in...intimate relations for about six weeks. She needs time to heal."

"Will she be able to have children?"

"Assuming everything heals as it should, yes."

Daniel sighed again. "I want to see her."

"You may sit with her, but she'll be unresponsive."

"I don't care. I need to be with her."

"Of course. I will go rest at the bachelor house. I'll check in on her later. Meanwhile, have a servant fetch me if I'm needed. I won't venture off the estate."

"I'd prefer you stay here in the main house, if you don't mind. I'll have a chamber made up for you on this floor and your personals brought over."

"That's fine. Just direct me to wherever I'm staying. I'm exhausted."

Once the others all left, Daniel sat by his bed, Lily's hand in his. She slept soundly, though a bit fitfully, breathing irregularly with small beads of sweat forming on her forehead. He had dismissed the maids and the housekeeper, preferring to tend to her himself. He rose, dipped a cloth in a basin of cool water, wrung it out, returned, and placed it on Lily's head. Exhausted, he lay down next to her, clasping her other hand in his, and drifted off.

He awoke to someone nudging him. "Daniel, Daniel."

Wiping the sleep from his eyes, he recognized his Aunt Lucy.

"It's time for her morphine."

"What time is it?" Daniel sat up abruptly.

"It's one in the morning, dear."

"I didn't mean to fall asleep. I need to watch over her."

"No one expects you to stay up all night after what you've been through. She needs her morphine every six hours. Dr. Blake says the pain will be excruciating for the first day.

Daniel hugged Lily's hand to his chest. "I can't stand the thought of her being in pain."

"She's strong. She'll be all right. Here, I'll show you how

to give her the medicine, and you can give her another dose in six hours." Lucy sat down beside Lily and felt on her forehead. "She's warm. I'm afraid the fever is starting. Let's give her the medication, and then I'll show you how to cool her."

Lucy took a packet of powdered morphine and lifted Lily's head from the pillow. With her other hand, she opened Lily's mouth, poured the powder on her tongue, and held a glass of water to her lips. "Come on, sweetheart, take a drink," she said. Lily's head shook slightly and her eyes remained closed, but Lucy managed to pour some water down her throat. "Daniel, call for some ice. We need to cool her."

"Shouldn't we get Blake?"

"I think we can handle this. But if you'd feel better, I'll summon him."

"No, I'm sure he's exhausted. I'll get the ice." He quickly rang for a servant and dispatched the order. When the ice arrived, Lucy crushed some in a cup and gave it to Daniel.

"Hold her head up and feed her some ice chips, one by one. They'll melt quickly in her mouth because she's so hot."

Daniel did as he was told, while Lucy dropped some ice in a basin of cool water. She dipped a cloth in, wrung it out, and placed it on Lily's forehead.

"Daniel, I need to undress her. We need to cool her body." Lucy uncovered Lily and began to unbutton the nightdress that covered her. "If you'd rather…"

"No, I'll stay. I want to take care of her."

"What would the earl say?"

"I don't care. I'm the one who will care for her. I want to. I need to."

"All right, dear. It's the middle of the night anyway. Who will know?"

Lucy removed the nightgown. Lily's naked body was covered in a soft gleam of perspiration. Daniel frowned at the purple-and-blue bruises marring her beautiful arms and legs.

"The contusions are quite normal considering the fall she took," Lucy said. "She's lucky she didn't break any bones."

Her comment did little to ease Daniel's worry. Lucy brought another cloth soaked in ice water and smoothed it over Lily's parched body.

"The fever will go up and down, Daniel. That's the course of it. When she's hot like this, she needs to be cooled. When she shivers with fever chills, you need to cover her and warm her."

"Yes. All right. Let me." He took the cloth from Lucy, moistened it with the ice water once more, and continued moving it over Lily's body in long strokes. He rewet the cloth frequently, as her body seemed to heat the cloth all the way to his hand in no time at all.

Lucy touched her lips to Lily's forehead. "She's a bit cooler now. Give her a few more ice pieces. If you'd like to get some sleep, I'll sit with her for the rest of the night."

"No. I'm not leaving her."

"All right, if you're sure."

"I'm sure."

"You know where I am if you need me. She's likely to go into chills soon. Wrap her in blankets, hold her, anything that seems to comfort her, all right?"

"Yes."

"Good night."

"Good night, Aunt Lucy. Thank you."

Daniel didn't sleep for the rest of the night. As Lucy had predicted, Lily began to shiver within a couple of hours. Daniel wrapped her in blankets and held her in his arms, speaking soothing words to her, hoping she could hear him.

"I love you," he said softly. "I love you, Lily."

Her body trembled against his, her eyes closed. He held her as close as he could, trying to transfer his body heat to her, kissing her temples, loving her, willing her to come back to him. When the chills finally subsided, he laid her back on the bed and tried to feed her some water, most of which dribbled down her chin. "Come on, love, just a little," he said, "for me."

In another hour she was burning again, so he fed her pieces of ice and cooled her as Lucy had shown him. Dawn broke, and at the hour of seven, he gave her another dose of morphine. Soon after, Dr. Blake came in.

"How is she?" he asked.

"Feverish," Daniel said. "My aunt showed me what to do."

"Have you been up all night, Your Grace?"

"I slept a little."

Blake shook his head. "Let me examine her." The doctor removed the covers and gazed upon Lily, clad only in a dressing robe that Daniel had draped over her. He held his hand to her forehead. "She's a little warm, but not burning. You've taken good care of her." He looked between her legs. "No residual bleeding. That's good. When was her last dose of morphine?"

"Just a little while ago, at seven."

"Good. Let's continue it every six hours for the next full day. We should be able to cut back after that. She may wake up for a few minutes today, but that remains to be seen. Her concussion may keep her unconscious for another twenty-four hours. I'd like for her to take some broth if she wakes up. I'll have some sent up. You'll need to keep it warm on the grate since we don't know when or if she'll wake up today. Has she taken any water?"

"A little. It mostly drips down her chin."

"How about ice?"

"When she's burning, I let it melt in her mouth. It seems to go down."

"Try ice for now, then. It will be easier to get into her than water. Keep feeding it to her."

"Yes, all right."

"Also, I'd like her bed linens changed. She'll be more comfortable if they're changed every day. More frequently if possible. The sweat from her body soils the linens and will irritate her skin."

"I'll see to it."

"Good. Have her parents been in yet?"

"I'm here now," the Countess of Ashford said, entering the room carrying a wicker basket. "How is my daughter?"

"She's doing well, my lady. She's feverish, but His Grace has taken excellent care of her. He's hardly slept."

"You should go, Your Grace. I'll sit with her."

"She needs her bed linens changed," Daniel said.

"I'll call for a maid," the countess said.

"No, I want to do it."

"Your Grace, that's silly. There are servants—"

"I want to take care of her."

Dr. Blake bowed. "If you'll excuse me, I'll leave you two to fight this out. I'll be back in to check on her in a few hours." As he walked out, he turned to look at Daniel. "Your Grace, Lady Ashford is right. You need to rest. Have the servants change the linens, and let her mother sit with her for a while. She's in good hands." He shut the door behind him.

"You really do love her, don't you?" Lady Ashford said.

Daniel sat down in his leather chair which had been

moved to Lily's side of the bed. "More than my own life."

The countess sat down next to Lily, facing Daniel, and took one of her daughter's hands in her own. "She's not an easy one to love, you know. She's stubborn as a mule, impatient, impulsive, quick to anger. She has little respect for authority or convention. She gave her father and me more trouble than Thomas and Rose combined."

The countess laughed softly, smiling, drawing her daughter's hand to her lips and kissing it lightly. "Oh, but she's worth it. She's so very intelligent and strong, so avidly curious. She has a passion and excitement for life that I've always envied. She finds joy and beauty in the simplest things." She looked up at Daniel. "When she was younger, she used to share her journals with me. She wrote about everything, sometimes about the most mundane things, a cricket chirping, or a clump of weed growing in one of the gardens. Yet her descriptions made me feel as though I were experiencing something amazing for the first time. She has a manner of wriggling her way into one's heart."

She took one of Daniel's hands and joined it to hers and Lily's. "She has a big heart, you know. There's room for you. Just be patient with her. She'll come around."

Daniel nodded numbly.

"Come now," the countess continued. "You need to take care of yourself. You need a bath, a decent meal, and some sleep. Go to your father's old chamber. I'll send Putney to attend you."

Daniel shook his head. "I can't leave her."

"You're no good to her in this condition."

Daniel stood up. Lily's mother was right. "If anything changes..."

"I'll send for you. Now go."

"But—"

"Goodness, let me be her mother a little while longer. You'll take care of her for the rest of her life."

"I hope so." Daniel raked his fingers through his disheveled hair moist with sweat and oil. "I want nothing more than to be her husband. But I won't force her to marry me. I was wrong to go behind her back and arrange it with the earl."

Lady Ashford rose from the bed and fetched the basket she had brought with her. "Some of Lily's things," she said. "To make her feel more comfortable when she wakes up." She pulled out the Dickens novel. "From you?"

"Yes."

She pulled out another book. "This is Lily's journal. I couldn't resist sneaking a quick peek. Her writing used to give me so much pleasure. I'd like to show you something." She opened the book and leafed through the pages until she found the entry she sought. "I want you to read this."

"I couldn't," Daniel said. "It's too personal."

"Under the circumstances, I don't think she would mind."

Daniel took the journal and began to read.

Daniel has the most remarkable green eyes I've ever seen. He no doubt inherited them from his mother, whose vivid eyes are striking, but Daniel's are unique. On the surface, the color is like a flawless emerald, but beneath is a darker green, and then a layer of light violet, which is especially apparent around the edge of his irises. Beneath the violet is a sea of midnight blue, adding depth. When I stare into his eyes, I'm almost positive that I can see the very innermost chambers of his soul.

Were I a musician, I would compose a symphony for his

eyes. *The violins and violas would be the emerald green, floating over everything else, giving the music its structure, with the cello and bass viols providing the darker forest color that lies just under the surface. A trio of flutes, joined by a clarinet and oboe, would be the flutter of violet beneath the green, and the brass and percussion would be the ocean of midnight blue, thundering under all the rest, giving the orchestration its profound depth and meaning.*

As an artist, I don't think I could ever do justice to his beautiful eyes. How could I? The angels themselves must have come to earth to paint them in his mother's womb. They have a celestial quality, as if I can see heaven when I look into them. Yet they're reflective as well, like a looking glass wherein I can see not only his soul but my own. I feel defenseless, looking at him and knowing that my hidden thoughts and emotions, the very recesses of my heart, are visible to him. But I can't look away. I don't want to. My greatest desire is to lose myself in his eyes forever. It frightens me.

Daniel looked up at the countess, tears misting in the corners of his fatigued eyes.

"You should be proud, you know." Lady Ashford smiled. "The chirping crickets didn't merit half that much detail."

Daniel began to smile. The countess was so different from Lily, but she shared a strength with her daughter. Lily's strength was like a bolt of lightning, cascading down when she needed it, while her mother's was like the soft glow of a candle in the fog, with quiet and patient determination. The countess had a sense of humor as well, so much like her daughter's.

"There's an ode to your hair on the next page," Lady Ashford continued, "but we'll save that for another time." She took the journal from him, replaced it in the basket, and patted his hand lightly. "Dear boy, do you truly think my daughter could write about your eyes like that if she didn't love you?"

"She writes that way about everything," Daniel said. "About crickets chirping, you said so yourself. It's who she is."

"I don't want to rain on your parade," the countess said, smiling, "because your eyes are quite nice. But they're green, Your Grace. Simply green. What she sees in them comes from her feelings for you."

"I would give anything for her to love me."

"She does." Lady Ashford squeezed his hand lightly. "And she will realize it eventually. Now go on, out with you. I'll tend to Lily."

"I don't want—"

"We've been through this. I'll send for you if she wakes up. Please, take care of yourself. Do it for Lily. She needs you."

Daniel nodded. Those were the words he needed to hear. "She needs another dose of morphine at one, but surely I'll be back by then. Also, the doctor sent for some broth. She needs to try to take some if she wakes up. Of course, if she wakes up, you'll come for me."

"Yes, I promise."

"All right."

Daniel reluctantly left the room, negotiating his way to his father's chamber in the west wing. Putney was waiting for him and started to speak, but Daniel silenced him with a gesture.

"Wake me in two hours, Putney," he said, and fell on his father's bed.

★ ★ ★ ★

Two hours later Daniel bathed and shaved. He ordered a lunch tray but couldn't eat more than a couple of bites. He went back to his chamber and found Rose and Thomas tending to her.

"How is she?"

"The same," Rose said. "She had a bout of the chills about an hour ago, but she's better now."

Daniel went to her side. "Where's the countess?"

"She went down to the kitchen to instruct the cooks on how to prepare some special broth for Lily," Rose said. "She'll be back in a few minutes."

"You two can go," Daniel said. "I'll care for her."

"You look like hell, Lybrook," Thomas said.

"Thank you. I just had a bath."

"I didn't say you weren't clean. But have you slept at all?"

"Only for two hours. I wanted to get back to Lily."

"Goodness, you need your rest," Rose said. "Have you eaten anything?"

"Just a few bites."

"That's ridiculous. I'm ordering a tray for you. You can eat in here while you sit with her." Rose stood.

"I don't want—"

"Nonsense, you'll do as I say."

Daniel turned to Thomas. "She and your mother are just like Lily, aren't they?"

Thomas smiled. "I'm afraid so. Lily's a bit noisier than they are, but all three of them manage to get their way no matter what."

"Do be quiet, Thomas," Rose said.

"My father and I pretty much let them do as they please,"

Thomas continued. "They will anyway. You may as well eat. She'll hover over you until you do."

Daniel shook his head, a trace of amusement touching his lips. "Has my mother been in?"

"Yes, she was here about an hour ago. She visited with my mother and Rose, and left about the same time I came."

"And the doctor?"

"He was here a half hour ago. Said things were looking good. Miss Landon came and checked her also, and my aunt and cousins were here."

Daniel sat down on the bed and took Lily's hand. "Damn it, why won't she wake up?"

"Blake said she may not," Thomas said. "He said not to expect it for sure until tomorrow."

Daniel touched his lips to Lily's forehead. "She seems a little cooler."

Rose got up as a maid entered with a tray. "Just set that on my sister's night table," she commanded. Then, to Daniel, "Eat every bit, Your Grace."

"I need a little fresh air," Thomas said. "I'll be back to check on her later."

"Jameson, don't leave me alone with her," Daniel pleaded.

Thomas chuckled as he walked out the door. "It'll be good practice for when you're married to Lily."

"Come on," Rose said, "or I shall have to summon my mother, and yours."

"That's hitting below the belt." Daniel took a bite of a scone, which tasted like sawdust. He noticed a quick flutter of Lily's eyelids. "Lily?"

"What happened?" Rose asked.

"Her eyes moved just a little." He shook Lily gently. "Lily, can you hear me?" Another flutter. "I think she's responding."

Rose came quickly. "She may just be dreaming."

"Yes, I suppose you could be right."

"I'm going to go get her puppy from the kennels," Rose said. "I'll be back in a little while."

"All right. Thank you for taking care of her."

"I would do anything for her. She's the closest person to me in the world." Rose left the room briskly.

Daniel leaned down and kissed Lily's parched lips. "Please wake up, my love. There are so many people who love you and need you. Especially me."

Lily's eyes fluttered again. "Daniel?"

Daniel's heart thumped. "Lily, Lily. I'm here."

"Where am I?"

"You're in my chamber. You fell down the stairs. Do you remember?"

"I-I think..."

"Don't try to talk, love. I'll take care of you. I'm going to get you some broth."

"Don't want..."

"Shh." Daniel brought the broth and helped her lift her head. "Come on, love." He spooned some into her mouth. "That's a good girl." Lily took two more spoonfuls before she fell back into unconsciousness.

"Damn it, Lily, don't leave me again!" He laid her head down on the pillow as she started shivering. Daniel wrapped her in blankets and held her close.

CHAPTER EIGHTEEN

Lily awoke in darkness, drenched in sweat, her body wrapped in a dank chemise. Cold and clammy bed linens clung to her bare skin. As her eyes slowly adjusted to the darkness, she attempted to move her body, but dull aches overwhelmed her. She groaned softly and tried to sit up, bracing her hands beside her, startled to feel another body next to hers. Daniel was on top of the covers, dressed in a shirt and trousers.

"Daniel?" she whispered. When there was no response, she gathered all the strength she could muster and nudged his arm gently. "Daniel?"

His eyes flashed open. "Lily? My God, Lily!" He sat up quickly. "My love, how are you feeling?"

"I hurt."

"I know. I'm so sorry. Don't try to move."

"I'm all wet. The linens are soaked. I don't know why."

"Your fever must have broken." He touched his lips to her forehead. "Thank God!"

Daniel tumbled out of bed, fumbled for a lamp, and lit it. He looked out his window. "Dawn will break soon." He brought her a glass of water. "You need to drink. Come on."

"Daniel..."

"You're probably dehydrated, especially after all that sweating. Please, love, for me."

Lily nodded and downed the entire glass. The cool liquid tasted like ambrosia.

"What am I doing here?" she asked.

"You fell down the stairs. Don't you remember?"

Confused, Lily willed her jumbled thoughts to clear. "Yes, yes. I ache all over."

"I know. I'll get you some morphine."

"Morphine? No, I don't want that."

"You've been taking it for nearly two days."

"Two days? What?"

"Closer to a day and a half, actually. It won't hurt you."

"I don't want any. Please, Daniel. I don't. It will make me groggy." Her mind was already muddled. She couldn't bear the idea of a drug creating further cloudiness.

"All right, love. Whatever you want. Thank God you're all right."

"I hurt between my legs, and my head aches, and my arms and legs, they're all... Ow!"

"Take it easy, love. I'll tell you everything. First I need to change your bed linens. The perspiration will irritate your beautiful skin. Then, if you're feeling up to it, we'll talk."

He moved her gently from one side of the bed to the other as he discarded the soiled linens and replaced them with new ones. "There you are. I'm going to get you a nightdress." He fumbled in the wicker basket until he found one. "Here, let me help you."

Daniel discarded the soaked chemise and helped Lily ease into the gown. "Now, do you need to rest, or do you want to talk?"

"I want to talk." Her tone was edgy, but she couldn't help it. "What am I doing here?"

"I brought you here after you fell. Your head aches from a concussion, and the pain you're feeling between your legs is from a surgical procedure. You were bleeding from the womb. Dr. Blake had to stop it."

Chills coursed through Lily's veins. "My God, he didn't..."

"No, he saved your womb."

"Thank God." Lily breathed heavily, until a wave of panic struck her. "Our child?"

Daniel stroked her cheek. "Not this time, love."

Lily's eyes filled with tears, and her heart lurched. "No! Oh Daniel, I'm so sorry."

"Hush now." Daniel brushed her tears away. "We don't even know if there was a child. It was too early to tell."

She reached for him. "I didn't know how much I wanted it. Oh, this is too horrible for words. I feel so...empty."

"Lily, don't upset yourself. It's not good for you in your condition. You're still very weak." He gently held her. "I want you to rest. I need to fetch the doctor and let him know your fever has broken and that you're awake."

She clung to him, the warm hardness of his body an anchor in a sea of haziness and uncertainty. "Don't leave me."

"Never, I promise. He's just down the hall. I'll be back in an instant."

Blake was happy with Lily's progress and ordered a small meal for her, with orders to eat every bite. He also suggested a warm bath once she felt up to it, to help assuage the discomfort from the surgery and to ease the pain from the bruising.

By the time he left, the sun was edging over the horizon, signifying the dawn of a bright new day. Daniel fed Lily small pieces of dry toast and fruit and helped her sip some tea.

"I want you to rest now," he said, when she had finished most of the food on her tray.

"I can't. I want to stay with you."

"I'm not going anywhere."

"I don't want to go back to sleep yet."

Daniel smiled and brushed his lips over hers. "All right. I want to talk to you anyway."

"What about?"

"Lots of things. Are you up to it?"

"I suppose so. Is anything wrong?"

"No, love, everything is right, now that you're back."

"What do you want to tell me?"

He took both of her hands in his and kissed them. "I love you, Lily. I should have told you a thousand times before now. I love you."

A glowing warmth spread through her upon hearing those cherished words. "Oh, Daniel..."

"Shh. I'm not finished yet."

She needed to hear nothing more, but clearly he needed to speak. "All right."

"I'm so sorry for going behind your back to arrange our marriage with your father. I was desperate. I couldn't bear the thought of losing you, of another man touching you. Knowing how you felt about marriage, I thought it was my only chance to keep you. I wanted to ask you, to talk to you about it, to try to convince you to stay with me, but in the back of my mind I was afraid you might refuse me. Going to your father seemed like the only option. I was selfish."

She swallowed a lump in her parched throat and squeezed his arm.

"And what I did to you before that—not taking precautions when I promised you that I would—it was unforgivable."

"I forgive you." And she did. She would forgive him anything.

"Thank you." He shook his head, his eyes sunken and sad. "I don't deserve it."

"I'll decide what you deserve."

"Please believe me. I honestly *did* forget. My desire for you was so great that I didn't think, and I should have. Again, I was selfish. I've spent so many years being selfish, I just... There's no excuse. I'm sorry."

"It's all right." She longed to stroke his flesh, to give him comfort, but she didn't have the strength to move.

"Please." He quieted her. "Let me finish. You changed everything for me. I felt joy with you like I had never known. We had such fun together. You made me laugh, and you showed me tenderness when I didn't deserve it." He touched her hair. "The way your eyes lit up when you saw the Vermeer, and the way your cute little nose wrinkled when you smelled the wine, the way you laughed when your puppy licked your face, the way you couldn't choose between painting and writing, so you did both. I could go on forever. Then there was making love to you. It was like nothing I've ever known. I felt like I had found the other half of my soul."

"It felt that way for me too," Lily said, smiling as much as she could. "Having nothing to compare it to, I just assumed it was always like that."

Daniel chuckled and pressed his lips to her palm. "No. It was special with us." He rubbed her hand against his jawline. "You touched me like no one ever has. I promise you'll want for naught if you marry me. I'll do anything you ask. Anything at all."

"Daniel..."

"But I won't force you. I was wrong to try. If you don't think you can be happy as my wife, I will let you go."

Lily brought his hand to her lips and gently kissed it. Her head hurt and her mind was still hazy, but she needed to be honest. "I don't want to go."

Daniel's handsome face lit up like a candelabra. "Then you'll stay with me and be my wife?"

Lily longed to reach for him, to tangle her fingers in his silky hair. "Do you remember when I said I only needed two things from you?"

"Yes, but you never told me what they were."

She sighed. "You've given me one. Your love."

"You'll have that until the end of time. What is the other? If it's within my power to grant, I will do it."

"First, I know I'm impulsive, but I...I never would have gone to bed with anyone but you. I need you to know that. If it had been anyone else I wouldn't have."

He brushed a dewy lock of hair from her brow. "I'm glad."

"I'm not sure what it was about you that called to me that first time. I was frightened beyond measure, and I had no desire to bed any man, or so I thought. Perhaps it was the fact that you had a Vermeer, and enough appreciation for it to keep it in your bedchamber. Or that you kept kissing me that first night, even after you saw who I was. Or maybe it was because you remembered me and my painting from all those years ago. Whatever it was, I couldn't stop myself from wanting you, so I told myself that sleeping with you would be a good experience. I never planned to marry, so I didn't care about my virtue. But all the time we were together, I couldn't imagine leaving you at the end of two weeks. I vowed to be careful, not to lose my heart. Every time I went to you, I told myself it was the last time, that the longer I let it go on the harder it would be to leave. But I couldn't stop myself from going back for more, even though Amelia told me she was going to bed my brother if I pursued you."

"Amelia told you what?"

"That's another story, but yes, Amelia and I have had words. It doesn't matter. Well, in a way it does. I knew your reputation, Daniel. Everything you said to me—I wanted desperately to believe it all, but knowing what I did of your past... Well, frankly, I figured you were just really good with lines."

"I meant everything I said to you."

"I know, and I'm sorry I reacted so harshly to the idea of marrying you and having your child. I was angry that you hadn't come to me first, and I was angry at myself for finding out I wasn't who I always thought I was, if that makes any sense. I feared I was to be one of many, and that you wanted me only for my bloodline and the heir I might be carrying."

"I'm so sorry I made you feel that way. I love you so much. I can't imagine life without you."

"I... I love you too, Daniel." How wonderful to finally say the words! "Somehow I think I always have."

Daniel sighed and looked straight into her eyes. "I never felt worthy of your love."

"That's not for you to say, is it?" she said with a half smile. "My love is mine alone to give, and I choose to give it to you. I think you're very worthy."

He brushed his lips over her hair. "You have my love, Lily. Now what is the other thing you want?"

Her heart lurched. Would he be able to give it to her? "I want your fidelity, Daniel. I want to be your only woman."

He laughed softly. "You are. Do you really think I could ever go to another woman after what we've shared?"

His laughter irritated her. "There's nothing funny about it. Given your past, I wasn't sure."

His lips brushed her temple, her brow, her nose. "I promise you. I'll never touch another woman. I'll never even want to."

A tear fell from the corner of her eye. "Oh, Daniel, I never dared to hope."

"It's an easy wish for me to grant, Lily."

"I knew Amelia was lying, the little tramp. She told me you had been in bed with her, and that you were going to ship me off to Scotland once you got me pregnant. Then she took my ring, said you told her she could have it...and then, she pushed me." Lily wept quietly.

Daniel embraced her, wiping away her tears with his fingers. "Don't cry. Amelia's in custody now, and she will never harm you again, I promise. I never made love to her, and I never said any of those horrible things. Please tell me you believe me."

Lily sniffed. "I believe you. I just wish she hadn't taken my beautiful ring. I loved it."

Daniel smiled into her eyes as he knelt down on the floor beside her. He took Lily's left hand in his, drew a ring out of his pocket, and placed it on her fourth finger. "Lily Jameson, will you do me the honor of becoming my wife?"

Lily widened her tired eyes, joy coursing through her. "Daniel, where did you find it?"

"Rose saw it on Amelia's finger when she was being taken away by the constables. She punched Amelia in the nose and made her give her the ring."

"My sweet Rose?"

"Yes, your sweet Rose. Now you didn't answer my

question. Will you be my wife?"

"Yes, Daniel, yes!" With all her strength, she held her hand toward the window, admiring the facets of her gem sparkling in the morning sun. "This is so beautiful, and every time I look at it I see your marvelous eyes."

"I promise I'll make you happy, Lily."

"You are wonderful. "I wish we could make love right now."

Daniel groaned low in his throat. "God, you have no idea."

"Maybe later we can. I'm feeling all right, I guess."

"No, love. We can't. You're clearly exhausted and still quite weak. Besides, you have to heal. Blake says I can't touch you for six weeks."

"Six weeks?"

"It won't be so bad," Daniel said, smiling. "I'd wait six years for you if I had to."

"If you can wait, I suppose I can." Lily warmed all over. Then a yawn nearly cracked her parched face. "I'm growing tired, and I want to have a bath before I go to sleep again. I feel all greasy and slimy, and my hair is pasted to my head."

"I'll call for a maid to bathe you. Or would you rather have your mother?"

"Neither. I want you to bathe me."

"I can't. What would your father say?"

"I wasn't planning to ask his opinion." She smiled weakly. "Lock the door."

"Lily..."

"You said you'd do anything for me."

"God help me. All right." Daniel rose and locked the door to his bedchamber. He strolled into the bath chamber and readied a bath. Then he fetched Lily from the bed, removed her nightgown, and carried her to the tub.

"You get in with me," she urged.

"No, love. You're too weak. Maybe in a few days." He lathered her body and her hair with soap and gently cleansed her.

"That feels nice," she said, closing her eyes.

"Let me know if anything hurts."

"Everything's fine. I love the feel of your hands on my body. It's soothing."

"It's soothing for me too. I live for the day that I can hold you and make love to you again. You're so beautiful, Lily." Daniel held her and rinsed her hair. "I want you to sit in here and soak for a while. It will help the pain."

"Mmm. I wish I had my clove oil."

"Hold on a minute." Daniel left the bath chamber and returned a few moments later holding the small amber vial. "Here it is."

"Just a few drops in the water."

Daniel obliged and then brought in a chair and sat beside the tub. When Lily started yawning, he lifted her out of the tub, dried her gently with a soft towel, and dressed her in a clean nightdress. He helped her brush her teeth, he combed her hair, and placed her back in bed.

"Daniel..."

"Hmm?"

"I'm sorry about...the red dress."

Daniel pressed his lips to her cheek. "I love the red dress. But from now on you'll wear it only for me. Promise?"

"I promise."

"Good. I love you, my beautiful Lily," he said, and kissed her gently on the mouth.

"I love you too, Daniel. Always."

CHAPTER NINETEEN

Cameron Price wasn't sure whether he should be honored or angered when the Duke of Lybrook demanded his presence at Laurel Ridge Estate in the middle of the afternoon. He couldn't afford to waste the precious hours of daylight that were better spent tending his farm, preparing the ground for planting, which would begin within a fortnight. Yet here he was, being led by a stiff butler to the private study of the duke himself.

"Mr. Cameron Price, Your Grace," the butler said.

"Thank you, Crawford. Please come in, Price."

The duke sat behind an ornately carved mahogany desk. He gestured to a pair of lush leather chairs. "Have a seat."

"Thank you, Your Grace." Cameron sat, inhaling the zesty aroma of the fine grain cowhide. This had to be the most comfortable chair he had ever sat in. "I'm a bit confused as to why you summoned me."

"I can imagine. First, how is your family?"

"They're fine. Thank you for asking."

"I understand you met my future wife several days ago."

"Yes. We were all quite sorry to hear about her accident and very glad to know that she's on the mend."

"No more so than I, Price, which brings me to why I have asked you here. I would like to hire you."

Cameron jerked in his seat. "For what purpose?"

"I would like to commission a waltz for Lily, for our first dance as man and wife."

"I'm flattered, Your Grace, but I hardly think I am qualified."

"You're a published composer, are you not?"

"Well, yes, but, my work is more... That is, I'm not sure..."

"I'll be the judge. I happen to have copies of both of your pieces here, one of which, I believe, is a waltz?"

"Yes."

"It has a haunting quality that I like."

"For a wedding waltz, though, you'll want something more joyful?"

"Yes, of course. I want it written for Lily." The duke let out a breath. "This is difficult for me to say, since you and I don't know each other very well, but I need you to know the circumstances so that you can compose the right type of music. Lily came into my life and taught me how to love again. She showed me beauty and kindness and laughter. I want the music to portray those feelings. It will be my wedding gift to her."

"That's a tall order, Your Grace."

"Which I'm sure you'll be able to fill. Now, what is the going rate for commissioning a piece of music? One hundred pounds?"

"Your Grace, I don't think..."

"Two hundred then."

"That's too much."

"Nonsense. I'll pay you a hundred now, and the rest upon completion."

Cameron paused. Two hundred pounds was a huge amount of money, more than any composition of his could possibly be worth. But with it he could hire someone to care for the farm, and he could devote himself to his music. Better yet, he could leave the farm and take his family to Bath, or even to London. He could find work composing, or at least doing something other than hard farm labor. Perhaps he could eventually send Tricia and Kat to school and buy his family a town home.

"How long do I have?" he asked.

"The wedding will be in five or six weeks. I'll let you know the exact date as soon as possible. I would like to hear the music before then. Is four weeks enough time?"

"Not for a full orchestration, I'm afraid. That will take months, and I'm really not qualified for the task."

"I'm sorry, I should have mentioned this earlier. I want the waltz arranged for the pianoforte, not for a full orchestra. I would like for Lily's sister to play it. She has a remarkable talent, and I think it would mean a lot to Lily."

"Her sister?"

"Yes, Lady Rose Jameson. You met her when you met Lily, didn't you?"

"Yes." Cameron cleared his throat. Lady Rose's blond beauty had haunted him since that day. "I'll do my best, Your Grace. I appreciate your confidence in me."

"Not at all, Price. Thank you for coming."

As Cameron rose to leave, a gentle knock on the door startled him.

"Come in," Daniel called.

Rose entered. "You wanted to see me, Your Grace?"

"Yes, Lady Rose. You know Mr. Price, do you not?"

"Of course," Rose said. "It's nice to see you, Mr. Price."

"My lady." Cameron bowed politely. She was a vision, honey-colored hair plaited and coiled around her head, with wispy golden curls framing her face. Blue eyes the color of sapphires, lips as pink as the roses in his mother's garden, and skin like pale peach velvet.

"Mr. Price has agreed to write a waltz for Lily's and my first dance together as husband and wife," Daniel explained. "It will be written for the pianoforte, and I was hoping you would do Lily and me the honor of playing it."

"I'm flattered," Rose said. "But surely the orchestra would do it more justice."

"I think not," Daniel said. "It would mean a great deal to Lily, and to me, if you would do it."

Rose blushed. "I would need time to prepare the piece for public recital."

"Mr. Price will have the piece ready in four weeks. That will give you a week or so. Is that enough time?"

"I-I'm a decent sight reader," Rose stammered, "but I'll need more time than that, especially depending on the complexity of the piece."

"Then you'll need to work closely with Mr. Price." Daniel turned to Cameron. "Make sure that Rose has access to your work in progress."

Cameron cleared his throat. "That's not how I normally work."

"I'll be happy to compensate you for the extra effort," Daniel said. "How much more do you require?"

"No, I didn't mean... You've been more than generous already, Your Grace."

"Then surely it wouldn't be too much of an imposition to work with my charming future sister-in-law, would it?" Daniel smiled.

"Of course not, Your Grace." He bowed and turned to Rose. "I will be in touch, my lady." He walked briskly out of the study.

★ ★ ★ ★

Lily let Rose help her bathe and dress in one of her best dinner gowns, and then she waited patiently for Daniel to arrive. Lily had been on the mend for over a week, and Daniel had arranged for them to take a private meal together. He strode in a few minutes later, dressed formally in his burgundy velvet coat, a dark grey cravat, and snug black trousers. His hair was freshly washed and hung in gleaming waves at his shoulders. Lily's breathing became shallow and hurried as she stared at him. He took her breath away.

He walked toward her, his green eyes full of smoke, took her hand, and kissed her upturned palm. He drew her to her feet and captured her lips with his. They hadn't shared a kiss—a real, honest to goodness kiss—since before her accident. How she had missed it! She let her tongue wander into his mouth, tasting his masculine sweetness.

"I've missed you." Her voice was a breathy rasp.

"I've missed you, too," he said, "and I love you." He slid his tongue down her neck, between her breasts. "God how I love you." He caught her face in his hands and took her mouth again, until several servants interrupted them, ready to serve their dinner.

They started with Swiss potato soup and olive-and-oyster canapés, and then feasted on vegetable marrow stuffed with shrimp, French stewed quail, and spinach Alsace. Lily was stuffed but forced down a few bites of cheese and fruit. She asked Daniel if they could save their lemon cream cake for later.

"I couldn't eat another bite. Really, I don't think I've consumed this much since I've been here."

"That's fine, love. Would you like some more wine?"

Lily giggled. "Maybe just a little. I feel lighter than air tonight, Daniel, despite the amount of food I just put away. I'm so happy to be here with you."

"You read my mind, as usual," he said, as he poured her wine. "Tell me, what would you like to do with the duchess's suite? My mother has several decorators in Bath whom she uses. I could bring them out for you to meet if you'd like."

"I feel terrible kicking your mother out of her rooms," Lily said.

"You're going to be the duchess. She understands that."

"Still, you and I could be perfectly comfortable here." She looked around the sitting room. "This suite has grown to mean a great deal to me."

"My mother wouldn't hear of it. She wanted to move out of her suite right after my father died, but I told her to stay. I didn't want to move into the duke's suite then, but now I do. I want to be the duke, Lily, and I want you to be my duchess. It all seems within the realm of possibility with you. It never did before."

"That's sweet of you to say."

"It's the truth. I want you to stay in this suite until we're married. I'll move into the duke's suite. But I'll continue to spend my nights here with you, if that's all right."

"I'd love that. But shouldn't I return to Hampshire with my family prior to the wedding?"

"No, I've already arranged for you, your mother, and Rose to stay here after the house party ends, to help plan the wedding. Your aunt and cousins also."

"Really? That sounds wonderful. But couldn't we..."

"Yes?"

Lily fidgeted. "Would you mind terribly if we...postpone the wedding for several weeks? I...I want a real wedding night, Daniel. I don't want to be cheated out of it."

He smiled. "It's already arranged, my love."

Her heart hammered and she grasped his hand. "That's wonderful. Thank you."

"I thought you would be pleased. I hope you don't mind being married here. Since my title is above your father's socially, he and I both thought it would be best."

"Goodness. I don't think I've considered that before."

"What?"

"That I will be above my parents socially. I'm not sure I find that at all comfortable."

"I find titles as a rule uncomfortable, but I possess a powerful one. One I never thought I'd have, that's for certain. Your discomfort won't keep you from marrying me, will it?" He winked at her.

"Of course not," Lily said. "Tell me, though, how do the titles work in your family? Will our children have titles?"

"Our first son will carry the lesser title of Marquess of Gordonshire. That was Morgan's title. Personally, I hope we have many daughters and only one son. Being a second son is difficult."

"Your mother told me a little about you and Morgan as boys. I'm sorry it was so hard for you."

"My mother talks too much." Daniel smiled lazily.

"Perhaps. Before my accident, she told me you were in love with me."

"She was right about that." He laughed, but turned serious.

"If you and I have more than one son, I plan to do things a lot differently than my parents did."

"We're not shipping any seven-year-old boys off to school, that is for certain," Lily stated.

"My, she did bend your ear, didn't she?" Daniel rubbed his thumb in the palm of her hand. "I wholeheartedly agree with you. All my sons will learn about the estate, as will you, Lily. I expect full cooperation from my duchess. I plan to put your intelligence to good use."

"That's the highest compliment you've ever paid me," Lily said. "I am very interested in being a true partner to you in this marriage."

"Another reason why I'm marrying you." His eyes gleamed. "Aside from your amazing kindness and tenderness, your incomparable beauty, and your"—he lowered his voice to a smoldering whisper—"unbelievable prowess in bed."

Heat crept up her neck. "Any prowess I possess comes from your lead." She rose from her seat and curled into his lap. "You taught me everything I know." She wrapped her arms around his neck and gave him a light kiss on the mouth.

"My beautiful Lily," he said, nuzzling her cleavage. "How am I going to wait five more weeks for you?"

"We'll wait together," she said. "I miss you as much as you miss me."

"I love you so much." Daniel kissed her hand. "There's something I want you to know."

"What?" She kissed his neck.

"I want to tell you why I was waiting for Amelia that night."

Lily sighed. "Daniel, it doesn't matter. In fact, I'd rather forget the little harpy even exists."

"Please, Lily. I don't want any secrets between us."

His beautiful green eyes held remorse, and her heart melted. She threaded her fingers through his luscious hair. "All right. Tell me."

Daniel inhaled sharply and let out his breath slowly. "I met Amelia about six years ago at a house party, not long after her husband had died. She came on strong, as you can imagine, and I didn't try to resist her. We began an affair that went on and off for the next five years, until my father and Morgan died. The encounters worked for me because she wasn't interested in a commitment, and neither was I. We never had any meaningful conversation. I couldn't tell you what her interests are to this day. I didn't care then and I don't now. I'm not proud of my past."

"It's all right. I love you just as you are."

"You'll never know how much that means to me." He sighed, closing his eyes for a moment, and then opening them again. "I bedded many women during the last decade or so, and my affair with Amelia lasted the longest of all of them. It wasn't that I cared for her more than the others. I didn't care for any of them, at least not in the way I care for you. But she and I seemed to run into each other a lot. I wonder now if she planned it that way."

"Of course she did," Lily snapped. "For a man with your experience, you don't know two figs about women, do you?"

"I know a few things." He smiled slyly.

"I'm not talking about that. Women like Amelia are conniving and sneaky. They'll do anything, say anything, to get what they want. Believe me, I know. I've seen many of them wrap my sweet brother around their little fingers. It's sickening."

"You're not like that."

"Of course not. But there are many out there who are, and with your looks and background, you no doubt attracted them all."

"I won't deny it. At any rate, my affair with Amelia continued until my father and Morgan died. Suddenly, I was the duke, with no preparation at all. Frankly, Lily, I was scared to death. So I went to the continent."

"No one blames you for running."

"I do. I blame myself. It was cowardly and stupid. But it's done, and I can't undo it. I can try to make up for it though."

"You will. I'll help you."

"I know. I can do anything as long as I have you." He pressed his lips to her chin. "But I want to tell you what I did on the continent."

"You don't—" The distress on his face stopped her. "All right."

"I don't remember much about the first two months. I was drunk most of the time, and I spent my nights in an expensive Paris brothel. Not my finest hour." He took a few deep breaths. "One day I woke up and decided to go to the Louvre. Walking around, looking at the works of the great masters, I decided I wanted more from my life. The next day I traveled to the Orient and spent three months at a Buddhist temple studying and praying. I thought about my father and Morgan, and what they would think if they could see what a mess I had made of everything. But you were right, Lily. I didn't mourn for them. I couldn't. I turned off my feelings for them long ago, when I was sent away from Laurel Ridge as a boy, to keep from pining for them. No matter how hard I tried, I couldn't get those feelings back."

Lily kissed his cheek and rubbed his shoulders. "Have you mourned for them yet, Daniel?"

"Yes, I've started to, love. They both meant a great deal to me, especially Morgan. He and I were very close as lads."

"I'll help you if you need me."

"I always need you. This is helping me right now, talking to you." He cleared his throat. "When I left the temple, I traveled to Florence to see more art, and then I spent several months on the beaches of Nice, reading philosophy, sketching, and thinking. Around that time, I sent my mother a letter, apologizing to her for leaving and vowing to be a better person and a better duke. Then I made my way home."

Lily kissed his mouth chastely, urging him to continue.

"I got home and found my mother and Aunt Lucy planning this house party. Suddenly I was overwhelmed again, unable to bear the thought of being the Duke of Lybrook. I would be the host of the house party, in charge of everything. I would have to make small talk and make everyone feel welcome. My father and Morgan were good at that sort of thing, but not me. Never me. I was still ignorant in the affairs of the estate as well. I wanted an escape, just for a little while. So I sent Amelia an invitation to the house party."

Lily sighed. None of this mattered now, but she couldn't help a little jolt of jealousy.

"Are you all right, love?"

"Yes, yes," she said. "I just can't abide the mention of her. But do go on."

"I'm sorry. I'm not proud of my association with her, but I don't want to have any secrets from you, Lily. I don't."

"I know. Go ahead."

"Amelia came to the house party and I made arrangements

to meet her clandestinely on the side of the main house the night of the ball. You'll never know how glad I am that I caught you instead of her. You changed everything for me. You made me want to be the duke, the best duke I can be. I want to make my father and Morgan proud."

"You will, Daniel, you will."

"Amelia came to my chamber that night, but I couldn't make love to her. I told her to go. All I could think about was you. Your innocent sharpness, the way you felt in my arms when I kissed you, when I danced with you. I felt as though my arms were created to hold you, Lily. I couldn't sleep that night or eat breakfast the next morning. I was consumed with thoughts of you. No woman had ever affected me like that before."

"So you and Amelia never..."

"Not since before my father and Morgan died. In fact, after my two months of debauchery in Paris, I was celibate until you."

Lily choked back a sob.

"No one ever mattered until you. It wasn't the most romantic way for us to meet, and I never should have taken you to my bed the next day, but it worked out, thank God." He caressed her cheek. "I'm sorry you had to deal with Amelia. You'll never know how sorry. I don't know what she said to you, but if I could make it all go away, I would."

"It's all right." Lily threaded her fingers through his hair and massaged his scalp lightly. "She told me bunches of lies and said if I didn't back away from you, she'd seduce Thomas. She did try to bed him, he told me, but he resisted her, thank God."

"He's a better man than I." Daniel sighed.

"No, just one who knows what his future holds. You never felt you had a future, did you? I don't mean to be disrespectful, but I can't help but blame your father for doing that to you."

"My father was a good man, Lily, and a great duke. He just made a few mistakes in parenting along the way."

"A few mistakes? You're very forgiving. We'll do better by our children, I promise." Lily touched her abdomen, her insides aching with loss. "I'm so sorry about our child. I wish he were still growing in me."

"We don't know if there ever was a child, love." Daniel closed his large hand over Lily's. "But not to worry. We'll have more, as few or as many as you want."

"All I want is a little boy with blond hair and incredible green eyes like his papa."

He reached up and stroked her cheek with his thumb. "We'll have to have two then, because I want a little girl with dark hair and piercing cognac eyes that can heal a person's heart." He moaned softly, kissing the silky skin above her breasts. "I do wish we could start on them now."

"So do I," Lily said, "but in the meantime..." She fumbled with the buttons on his trousers and slid off his lap to kneel before him.

"Lily, you're still weak. You don't have to..."

"Hush," was all she said, before her lips were otherwise engaged.

CHAPTER TWENTY

Six Weeks Later

After she changed into her new sheer green nightdress and brushed her long dark hair until it shone, Lily waited in her bedchamber for Daniel to come to her. He appeared in a silk dressing robe, his hair glittering around his shoulders, his green eyes filled with smoke.

"Good evening, wife," he said huskily.

"What took you so long, husband?" she asked innocently.

"In a hurry are you?"

"Not so much," she said coyly. "We have a lifetime."

Daniel removed his dressing robe and lay down next to her on the bed. "I think you're even more beautiful now that you're my wife." He eased the sheer gown off her shoulders. "I wouldn't have thought it possible."

"I want you to do something for me," Lily said, as he cupped her full breasts, massaging them and teasing her nipples with his thumbs.

"Anything."

"Put your babe in me tonight, Daniel. I want to have your child."

He looked up at her, his eyes blazing. He opened his mouth to speak, but she placed her fingers on his soft lips.

"And after that, I'd like to try the...*other* entrance."

"God, are you sure?"

"Very sure. I want to experience everything with you."

Daniel moaned softly as he took her mouth, his capable hands ridding the rest of her body of the gown. He showered her face and neck with light fluttery pecks, pausing at her ears to suck on her lobes and tease her ear canals with his tongue. Lily shivered, running her fingers through his blond locks and moaning his name softly. Daniel made his way down to her breasts and ravished them, tugging on her nipples until she arched off the bed, her fingernails digging into the hard muscle of his shoulders.

"God, how I've missed you, Lily," he rasped, kissing and biting her inner thighs.

He pushed his tongue into her pussy and tugged on her swollen flesh, sucking it into his mouth. Lily grabbed his head and laced her fingers through his silky hair, grinding into his face harder and harder.

"Daniel," she moaned. "Now, Daniel, I need you!"

He kissed her belly, her breasts, her mouth. She reached down and clutched his cock, his breath blowing short puffs against her neck. She led him to her opening, which was warm and wet, ready to receive him.

From the wall opposite the bed, the serene face of St. Praxedis watched over them.

THE END

Continue The Sex and the Season Series
with Book Two

ROSE IN BLOOM
THE STORY OF ROSE AND CAMERON

AVAILABLE NOW

AUTHOR'S NOTE

Johannes or Jan Vermeer van Delft, born in 1632, was a Dutch genre painter. His most famous painting is *Girl with a Pearl Earring.*

When Vermeer married Catharina Bolnes in 1653, he converted to Catholicism, which might explain his interest in the subject of *St. Praxedis.* The painting may be Vermeer's earliest surviving work. It was only recently conclusively attributed to Vermeer.

The Duke of Lybrook is a fictional character, so of course he never owned *St. Praxedis.* It was discovered in 1943 in a small New York auction room and was most recently sold in 2014 at Christie's in London on behalf of the Barbara Piasecka Johnson Collection Foundation. Who knows where it was in 1853? Perhaps it was hanging in a ducal residence near Bath.

After his death in 1675, Vermeer was overlooked by most art collectors for nearly two hundred years, until a French critic re-discovered him in 1866. However, I like to think that a young lord might have purchased one of his works around 1850, and that a young lady, enamored with art, might have discovered his talents and become fascinated with his life and work.

MESSAGE FROM HELEN

Dear Reader,

Thank you for reading *Lily and the Duke*. If you want to find out about my current backlist and future releases, please like my Facebook page: **www.facebook.com/HelenHardt** and join my mailing list: **www.helenhardt.com/signup/**. I often do giveaways. If you're a fan and would like to join my street team to help spread the word about my books, you can do so here: **www.facebook.com/groups/hardtandsoul/**. I regularly do awesome giveaways for my street team members.

If you enjoyed the story, please take the time to leave a review on a site like Amazon or Goodreads. I welcome all feedback.

I wish you all the best!

Helen

ALSO BY HELEN HARDT

The Sex and the Season Series:
Lily and the Duke
Rose in Bloom
Lady Alexandra's Lover
Sophie's Voice
The Perils of Patricia (Coming Soon)

The Temptation Saga:
Tempting Dusty
Teasing Annie
Taking Catie
Taming Angelina
Treasuring Amber
Trusting Sydney
Tantalizing Maria

The Steel Brothers Saga:
Craving
Obsession
Possession
Melt (Coming December 20th, 2016)
Burn (Coming February 14th, 2017)
Surrender (Coming May 16th, 2017)

Daughters of the Prairie:
The Outlaw's Angel
Lessons of the Heart
Song of the Raven

DISCUSSION QUESTIONS

1. The theme of a story is its central idea or ideas. To put it more simply, it's what the story *means*. How would you characterize the theme of *Lily and the Duke?*

2. Discuss the relationship between Lily and Rose, and compare and contrast it with what you know about the relationship between Daniel and Morgan.

3. How do you suppose Daniel's life would have differed had his father and Morgan lived? Do you think he and Lily would have found each other and married? Why or why not?

4. Discuss Lily's personality. Why do you think she finds such magic in the mundane? Discuss what she might have found fascinating about a cricket chirping and a weed in the garden. And what about Daniel's hair and eyes? Do you think they're truly as amazing as Lily suggests? Or is she looking through the eyes of love?

5. Helen Hardt calls this series of novels *Sex and the Season*, a Victorian version of *Sex and the City*. Draw parallels between Lily, Rose, Alexandra, and Sophie and Carrie, Samantha, Charlotte, and Miranda of *Sex and the City*. Which characters are similar and in what ways?

6. Get online and pull up an image of Vermeer's *St. Praxedis*. What do you think Lily sees in this painting? Knowing her, why does she enjoy Vermeer's work so much? Why do you think Daniel purchased the painting?

7. Who defies convention and authority more, Lily or Alexandra? How so?

8. What did you think of Lily's decision to sleep with Daniel? When did you first realize that Lily had feelings for Daniel? And vice versa?

9. How did you feel when Lord Ashford told Lily she was marrying the duke? What did you think of Lily's reaction at a time when most young ladies of the peerage would have been thrilled with such a match? Discuss arranged marriages. Some countries still practice arranged marriage today. What would you do if you were forced into marriage?

10. Discuss the relationship between Daniel and his mother. Maggie seems like a loving person, yet she sent her younger son away when he was seven because her husband thought it best. Taking into consideration the era, what might have gone through her mind at that time? What might have gone through Daniel's mind? Do you feel Daniel has forgiven his mother? Why or why not?

11. Lily mentions that she and Rose suffered advances by Lord Ludley when they were young, yet they never told anyone. Why do you think they stayed silent? Do you think they are scarred by these encounters? Why or why not?

12. Do you think Lily and Daniel's marriage will be successful? Why or why not?

13. How are Lily and her mother alike? How are they different? What kind of relationship do you think Lily and her mother had while Lily was growing up?

14. This book is full of colorful supporting characters: Lord Evan Xavier, Thomas Jameson, Cameron Price, Lady Ashford, and Lady Amelia Gregory, to name a few. Discuss the roles of these characters. What is their purpose in the story?

15. Rose and Cameron have a story coming next. What do you foresee in their future? What do you think will happen to Lord Evan?

ACKNOWLEDGEMENTS

I wrote *Lily and the Duke* in 2007. When I completed it, I went to the internet for resources and was blessed to find the Colorado Romance Writers. I attended their conference in May 2007, and I haven't looked back since.

Lily and Daniel were my guinea pigs—the hero and heroine in my very first romance novel. I entered the story in a few contests and received valuable feedback. My critique partners at the time, whom I met through CRW, also offered great advice. I revised the story once, and then again. And then again. In the meantime, I worked on my craft and published twenty-plus other stories. But Lily and Daniel always lurked in the back of my mind, waiting for their day in the sun.

After the last of many revisions, that day has finally come, thanks to my good friend Meredith Wild, who introduced me and my work to the men and women at Waterhouse Press. Thank you to David Grishman, Jonathan McInerney, Shayla Fereshetian, Kurt Vachon, and of course, the one and only Meredith Wild. I appreciate your confidence in me!

Thank you to my amazing editor, Michele Hamner Moore, for your diligent work and research.

Thank you to the many contest judges who pointed out places to make the story stronger.

Thank you to my former critique partners—Monica Kaye, Tricia Leigh Wood, Viola Estrella, and Cari Quinn—for all your help with this story and others.

Thank you to the wonderful members of Colorado Romance Writers and Heart of Denver Romance Writers who have inspired me over the years.

Thank you to my family and friends who have believed in me.

And thank you to my readers for helping me get this far. I hope you love Lily and Daniel as much as I do.

ABOUT THE AUTHOR

New York Times and *USA Today* Bestselling author Helen Hardt's passion for the written word began with the books her mother read to her at bedtime. She wrote her first story at age six and hasn't stopped since. In addition to being an award winning author of contemporary and historical romance and erotica, she's a mother, a black belt in Taekwondo, a grammar geek, an appreciator of fine red wine, and a lover of Ben and Jerry's ice cream. She writes from her home in Colorado, where she lives with her family. Helen loves to hear from readers.

Visit her here:
www.facebook.com/HelenHardt

After being left at the altar, Jade Roberts seeks solace at her best friend's ranch on the Colorado western slope. Her humiliation still ripe, she doesn't expect to be attracted to her friend's reticent brother, but when the gorgeous cowboy kisses her, all bets are off.

Talon Steel is broken. Having never fully healed from a horrific childhood trauma, he simply exists, taking from women what is offered and giving nothing in return...until Jade Roberts catapults into his life. She is beautiful, sweet, and giving, and his desire for her becomes a craving he fears he'll never be able to satisfy.

Passion sizzles between the two lovers...but long-buried secrets haunt them both and may eventually tear them apart.

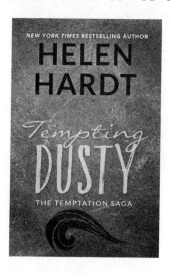
El Diablo strikes no fear in the heart of Dusty O'Donovan. The accomplished rider knows life holds much greater fears than a feisty stud bull. Diablo's owner, Zach McCray, is offering half a million dollars to anyone who can stay on him for a full eight seconds. That purse would go a long way helping rebuild Dusty and her brother's nearly bankrupt ranch.

Let a woman ride his bull? Not likely. Still, the headstrong Dusty intrigues Zach. Her father worked on the McCray ranch years ago, and Zach remembers her as a little girl when he was a cocky teen. Times change, and now she's a beautiful and desirable young woman. A few passionate kisses leave Zach wanting more, but will Dusty's secrets tear them apart?